THE SERPENT LORD

THE CROWN OF OLMALIS

WREN MURPHY

Cover design by Miblart
Map & Coats of Arms design by E.R. Donaldson at Mythic North Press
Editing by Eve Arroyo Editing
Proofreading by Virginia Tesi Carey
Formatting by Champagne Book Design

Paperback ISBN: 978-1-7374868-1-7

To Jace,
my dear friend & gentleman star traveler,
who bitchily assisted and only complained about it a little:

This one's for you.
After all the years of random, caffeine induced writing ideas
left in your inbox during the most absurd hours of the night,
you still agreed to let me write our stories into books. Thank
you for a lot of things, but especially for trusting me with
Ares and allowing me to share him with the world.

To Jeanine,
my mother & my very first best friend,
who has believed in me with her whole heart from the
minute I entered this world:

This one's for you too.
You are the strongest person I have ever known, and I can't
tell you how lucky I am to have a mom as special as you. You
are my hero, and I love you so much. I'll always be your girl.

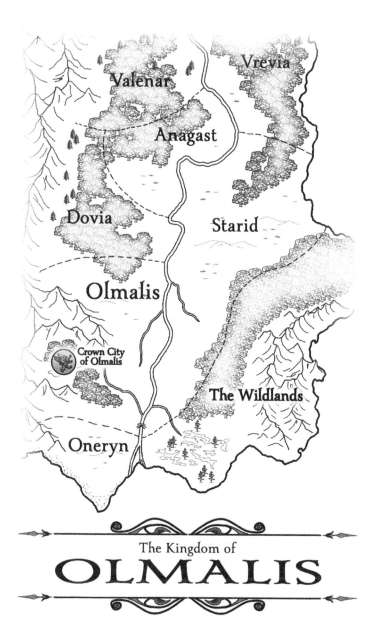

Vrevia

Valenar

Anagast

Dovia

Starid

Olmalis

Crown City
of Olmalis

The Wildlands

Oneryn

The Kingdom of

OLMALIS

House

VIAS

House
TEVELL

THE
SERPENT
LORD

THE CROWN OF OLMALIS

CHAPTER 1

BECOMING A SPINSTER WAS NOT HER INTENDED choice, but as she observed the obnoxiously dressed lords standing in a group on the opposite side of the great hall, Princess Sarra knew it was the correct one.

She watched as the men gradually moved closer, assaulting her with confident smiles over the shoulders of their friends and winking at her so much she wondered if dirt stung their eyes. Half of them looked as if they had not groomed themselves in days, with disheveled hair and lingering grime under their fingernails, though their tunics and trousers were well-pressed and clean. The unmarried ladies in their lavish dresses of various bright, eye-burning colors that fluttered around them begged to steal their attention. However, from Sarra's position atop a raised dais, she saw the women failing miserably to capture a new beau's gaze.

As much as Sarra hated being gawked at, she took some joy from the inconvenience her presence brought to those in the court. Most of them were too haughty and self-centered to talk about anything but themselves. And frankly, she had far more important things to concern herself with.

The kingdom was celebrating, and for good reason. The northernmost provinces of Anagast and Valenar had resolved their disputes, ceasing the violence along the borders of their regions. Sarra knew only of straining civil war between the two portions of the kingdom, the fighting beginning decades before she was born. Not even her father knew the true reason for the initial disagreement, perhaps even centuries ago, but it had continued with petty land disputes, which remained unresolved. However, after King Jarin's many veiled threats to dissolve their lordships drew little result, it was a recent, well-chosen love match between two wealthy, influential families that finally brought unity to the provinces, and the kingdom, Olmalis, settled into peace. Sarra supposed nuptials were sometimes a blessing.

Still, as she looked around at the stunning great hall, with its twinkling crystal chandeliers and tables covered with overflowing trays of delicacies from all across the kingdom, Sarra asked herself why her father wanted to celebrate *today*, of all days.

A brave man stepped out of the circle of lords, intent on approaching her, his smile blinding from beneath a mop of chestnut hair. His eyes, colored like bark and every bit as intriguing, crinkled with warmth. Sarra scowled, retreating further into her seat. The movement shifted the small golden crown on her head, a rogue, ashy blond strand of hair falling over her brow. She tucked it back into place with a quick brush of her hand and rolled her eyes as soon as he approached.

"Your Majesty," the man greeted her father, bowing first to him, then toward her. "Your Highness."

He sank so low in his gesture that his nose nearly rubbed

the floor, and Sarra shook her head as she leveled her gaze upon him. With his head tilted forward, she saw he had started to bald, a bare spot on the top of his head shining under the flickering light above. At twenty-three years old, Sarra knew he could not be more than five years her senior, and with a quick glance behind him, she locked eyes with the devastated young woman who fancied him. The poor girl's lower lip quivered, and she tried to hide it by lowering her chin into the ruffles around the neck of her yellow dress. The lord climbed to his feet, blocking her from Sarra's view.

"My name is Reve Virdell, Duke of Oneryn. It is an honor to make your acquaintance. I apologize for not doing so earlier in the evening." The lord smiled before he looked over his shoulder, waving nonchalantly to the other men intently watching him. Sarra crossed her arms over her chest, lips pursed.

"I was conversing with the others and wondered if you would be interested in hearing more of my province. I know my father was not much of a conversationalist when he was alive, and as the newest lord of your court, I thought it might be entertaining to tell you of my latest expedition toward the mountains. I tracked the most handsome stag—"

Sarra turned toward her father, dismissing the duke. "Why must they try so hard?"

The king sat beside her, an image of regal fashion, with his neatly trimmed beard, a jeweled crown nestled in his thick, salt and pepper colored hair, and a blue mantle threaded with gold on his shoulders. His cheeks were flushed from the goblets of red wine he had consumed, and upon first look, not even Sarra could see the irritation behind his fern-colored eyes.

"You are too critical of them," he replied, straightening his back. His gaze narrowed as he followed the retreating lord, who now resembled a wounded animal slinking back to the group of gawking men. Sarra smirked at the rejected tribute, rubbing at her face with the black lace sleeve of her dress so her father did not see. Her momentary joy fell short when she noticed the king's grip on his golden throne tightened. Sarra arched a thin brow, her smile falling.

"Too critical? Perhaps if they talked about something other than themselves, I would show more of an interest. There are far more important matters to discuss anyway. The failing crops to the east in Starid, for one." She furrowed her brow, thinking of the poor growing season. The farmers attributed it to a lack of rain over the warm months, and while it was a natural phenomenon, Sarra worried much about the people who would suffer because of it. Not a single lord offered a solution to the matter, and those whose people went hungry indulged in the luxuries of the castle instead of negotiating trade deals or asking for assistance, conveniently ignoring the disaster in their midst. Sarra pressed a hand to her forehead for a brief moment, rubbing away a dull throb in her temple. "No, Father, if these are the men I must choose from, I would rather marry a toad."

The king ignored her declaration, locking his eyes on the gathered courtiers.

"You wear black to a celebration in honor of the kingdom." His voice shook as he glanced at her out of the corner of his eye. "You rarely smile. You insult every man that approaches you, regardless of his intentions, and you have everything a girl could ever want—gold, jewels, and wealth. Still, you sulk around this castle as if marrying one of those fine young men would be the end of your entire existence."

The king sighed and pressed his thumb and forefinger to the bridge of his nose. "I do not understand you. Could you at least *try* to look pleasant?"

"I am pleasant, Father. Why do you insist that I marry one

of *them*? I have survived this long without a husband. I am confident I can continue to survive without one." Sarra lifted her nose. "Mother would not force me to marry. In fact, she would let me live as I see fit."

She gestured toward the duke, who scowled at her from across the room. Sarra narrowed her eyes at him, nose wrinkling as she returned his look with the annoyance she felt. Every lord remained the same, including Reve Virdell, concerned with their elaborate attire or the coin in their purses more than they cared for the health and prosperity of their people. *Do any of them remember my actual name, or do they only know me as "Princess"? Do they care enough to learn the things I enjoy, or will they inquire of those things before they beg my father for my hand? Will they ask me to marry them, or will they bypass my opinion in hopes the king will agree to a union without my consent? Is my social status the only thing they worry about?*

Despite the look directed at the spurned duke, the gaggle of lords talked among themselves with their heads closely pressed together, glancing over their shoulders to look at her from a distance. No other from their group dared to speak to her, but she saw the sparks of their interest, even if their stares seemed nervous. "They are afraid. How do you expect them to approach you to request my hand in marriage? I love Olmalis more than I will ever love any man. I doubt their egos can handle the competition for my affections."

"That is enough, Sarra," the king said in a harsh whisper, eyes narrowing with a frown. She widened her eyes at the sternness of his expression, a piece of her surprised at her father's response. Despite their disagreements regarding her marital status, the king had never reprimanded her for being firm in her decision, content with the explanation that she searched for the one man best to rule Olmalis by her side. Sarra had noticed his demeanor had changed in recent months, as he pushed her out of meetings and pawned her lessons off on his advisers instead of providing her instruction on kingdom matters directly. It made her wonder if perhaps she had disappointed him somehow.

"Do rein in your distaste. Elias arrives tomorrow, and regardless of what you think is best, I have decided that you and he will become husband and wife. I gave you ample opportunity to select a man you find suitable, but since you were unsuccessful, it is time I do it for you."

"Elias, Elias, Elias. You always talk about Elias, Father. I have heard enough stories about the man to last a lifetime." Sarra slumped in her seat. "How many orcs has he killed this season? Three? Five? A thousand? Are displays of violence the pinnacle of what men can aspire to?"

The king dismissed her once more, turning to take a drink from his goblet. He placed it upon the table in front of him as he finished, smacking his lips and sighing. "I expected him to join us tonight, but a messenger reported a group of violent peasants slowed his caravan outside of the province. The filthy beggars said they were hungry despite the shipment of supplies we gave them a month past."

"Perhaps the beggars *were* hungry. The failing crops to the east should not be ignored," Sarra muttered, scowling at her father. "Maybe Elias will understand that more than the duke, although my hopes are about as high as the dais. Are you certain a toad is not a suitable candidate for a husband? At least then, he would be seen and not heard, and I could carry him in my pocket."

Her father's nostrils flared, the muscles in his face tightening. "Vrevia is a wealthy province and Elias is a strong warrior. He will do well as your consort, and his family has brought honor to Olmalis many times over. You will marry Lord Berley's son."

"I do not care if Elias is a god among men. I will not marry him. *I refuse.*"

"Refuse? You refuse? It is an order. A royal decree. Princess or not, I am still the king."

"But you do not own me. I am not an animal or an object. I am a person, and I get to choose who—"

"I said *enough!*" the king thundered. The music and laughter stopped with the commotion, the great hall falling silent around them. All eyes turned to look at her, and it seemed as if the entire kingdom listened to their conversation. Her father climbed to his feet and pointed his finger toward the large door on the opposite side of the room, voice trembling as he addressed her. "You are dismissed. Until you understand that your wants are to come second to your duty to this kingdom, you will remain in your chambers unless I advise you otherwise."

Sarra turned her face away from him. The heat of embarrassment crawled up her neck, no doubt flushing her pale cheeks. She refused to meet with the gaze of anyone who watched her, but she obeyed her father's command. Sarra hastily pulled herself to her feet, beginning her descent from the dais. Before she took more than two steps, the king's voice reached her.

"Your mother would be ashamed of you."

Slicing straight through to her heart, her father's words wounded her. Sarra's shoulders slumped forward, her head hung low. She looked down at the floor as she quickly pushed herself around the table. Whispers engulfed her, and the stares of the guests etched into her skin. Her father's words burned themselves into every corner of her mind, tightening Sarra's chest, forcing her breath to catch. Without a second thought, she grabbed her skirts and rushed toward the door. The guards held it open, allowing her to pass through, but it slammed shut once she escaped.

The muted celebration continued behind her, and the sounds of music and laughter echoed into the empty corridor. Sarra could not decide if the way the celebration continued in her absence soothed her embarrassment or exacerbated the betrayal. The void swelling in her breast hinted that it might be the latter.

It angered Sarra to know that her father had tossed her aside so easily. Undoubtedly, he had already spoken with his old acquaintance, Lord Berley, about his proposition for marriage, ignoring the desires of his daughter. She was his heir, but it seemed to Sarra that fact no longer mattered. The only thing her father wanted, in her opinion, was to make her another man's problem.

She attempted a few steadying breaths, but her emotional wounds and the bodice of her gown would not allow her chest to expand. Fists clenched, she roughly rubbed away the moisture on her cheeks. Unable to hold back her hot tears, they spilled from her eyes.

She turned to face the great hall.

Your mother would be ashamed of you.

"No, she would not be!" Sarra shouted at the closed door. "The only one ashamed of me is you!"

Her father was wrong. Her mother would have been proud.

Even with the thoughts of her mother, the seed of doubt bloomed full force inside of her. The laughter now drifting from the great hall and the silence she had received during her mad dash away from the celebration made Sarra question the validity of her statement. No one stood up for her. *Do they even care? More importantly, did I make Olmalis proud? If marriage to Elias is truly what the kingdom needs from me, will I follow through with it? Will I give them what they want?* Sarra forced those questions away, begging them never to return. Her people were not cruel monsters, they would not corner her into a marriage she did not want. She had already resigned herself to the fact that she would never know love, at least not from a man of the court. She demanded respect and genuine kindness from any potential husband. Thus far, all she saw were men looking to make a leap up the social and political ladders of Olmalis.

Some old paintings hung upon the walls and a few empty suits of armor kept watch nearby. Not a single living soul heard her anguish in the empty corridor. Guards patrolled the castle grounds, but other than those tasked with that duty, everyone else celebrated inside the great hall.

Sarra was all alone.

Dim torchlight trickled down from sconces upon the walls, their light laying out a path for her as she made her way through the castle and into the eastern wing. Her thoughts continued to keep her occupied, and by the time Sarra reached her chambers, she had asked herself many questions with no clear answers. One seemed to linger the most, the same one she had asked before the duke had approached her.

How could Father celebrate today?

Eighteen years ago, to the day, when the summer turned into harvesttime, her mother, the queen, had succumbed to illness and died a most unexpected death. The cool air of the season brought with it a reminder of the late queen, and for Sarra, it also brought grief. Considering her father, a man who had supposedly loved her mother more than any other woman, Sarra felt he showed it sparingly. He wore bright colors on the monumental anniversary instead of following tradition and donning black, and he had frowned upon Sarra for attending his celebration dressed in a gown of mourning. He enjoyed wine and spirits with his men, rosy cheeks and laughter abounded. He did not mention the queen, except only to use her memory as a weapon against Sarra.

Where is his honor? Does he not wish to remember? Is my mother some nightmare he needs to forget?

Sarra pushed against a heavy oak door, and it creaked loudly as it opened. She entered her bedroom, which stayed as still and quiet as the corridors she had just traveled. Typically, the fireplace on the far side of the room kept it lit and especially warm, but despite the fire, Sarra shivered inexplicably when she walked through the door. An uneasy feeling settled in her stomach, and she looked over her shoulders to see if one of her handmaidens followed behind her. The silence greeting her confirmed her solitude. Fearful, she rushed farther inside. She ultimately blamed her discomfort on her roaming negative thoughts and the cool, breezy draft coming through an open window. Holding her arms close to her chest, she moved to close the glass panes.

The night sky greeted her, and before she shut the window, Sarra took a moment to admire the beauty of the evening. The velvety, indigo canvas of the sky was brightened by a crescent moon. The innocent sparkles from the smattering of radiant stars twinkled, unhindered by clouds. The leaves of the trees had started to turn color weeks ago, and now they fluttered in the cool breeze as it brushed past them and on toward Sarra. The fragrance of cooked meats drifted from the kitchens, and the stray scent of campfires lingered just a bit from where the guests' caravans awaited them.

It all reminded Sarra of a time when her mother had stood next to her in that very spot. Together, they had looked out over the capital city as the moon glowed high in the sky. Her mother imparted pieces of wisdom to Sarra, and the queen's words echoed in her thoughts as the princess watched out over the city.

One day, you will rule this kingdom, and I will no longer be here to help guide you. Always remember that you just need to look to the stars when you feel lost. They will never let you falter.

They had wished upon shooting stars that night. Sarra never knew what her mother had wished for, but the princess had wished for the queen's health. The signs of illness plagued the queen, and Sarra's only hope had been that she would recover. Unfortunately, she did not. The queen had deteriorated rapidly over the course of several weeks, and she had grown weaker and weaker until she was bed bound. Sarra remembered laying her head against her mother's blankets, and even clutching the material in her hands as her father and the guards dragged her away.

There had been no explanation for her mother's illness. No healer in the entire kingdom had been able to find a cure. The king had not risked himself nor Sarra's health, and out of necessity, the queen had died alone in the southern wing of the castle. Her chambers still stood as a place no one but Sarra dared to visit anymore, the king even forbidding the servants to disturb the peace of the place where his wife had died.

After her mother's death, the princess lost faith in the stories her mother had told her, the ones about magic and shooting stars. However, standing there, almost twenty years later, Sarra wondered about those tales, something inside her telling her to watch the glittering orbs intently.

Maybe just one wish?

With the stars twinkling in the sky like they were old friends, they tempted the princess to linger.

No, Sarra admonished herself, quickly shutting the

windows. She pulled the drapes closed and turned so that her back pressed against the cool wall beside her.

Magic is not real. The stars do not grant wishes. Fate is a fairy tale. Mother did not tell the truth.

She squeezed her eyes shut and took a few deep breaths. The uneasy feeling she had grappled with since entering her room unfurled wildly again in her stomach.

Something was not right. She felt it.

The clearing of someone's throat was evidence of that. Her eyes scoured the room for an intruder. It took Sarra a moment to find the source. A large dark shadow filled the open doorway, the sight of it startling her. Sarra held her breath.

"Father, is that you?"

Silence greeted her question. She concentrated hard to keep her voice from shaking, and with a deep breath, the princess took a step to the side. She hoped to grab a small letter opener from the nightstand next to her bed.

"Father, please say something," she stammered, but again, there was no response from the shadow. Sarra leaned forward, edging closer to the table. The sudden sound of booted footsteps forced her into action, and she dove forward to grasp the handle of the drawer. It fell to the floor with a loud crash just as she opened her mouth to scream. A firm hand muffled the sound, grasping her from behind, and another tugged her body backward.

Sarra flailed against the assault, but two more hands joined in the fray to hold her still. Her gown caged her legs, and a thick rope tied her wrists. Despite her struggles, fear-filled tears slipped down her cheeks.

"Put it over her head! Hurry!" a man's voice whispered in the darkness.

"If I let go of her face, she will cry out and then into the dungeons they will toss us," another male voice replied.

The first scoffed, drawing a sharp blade from his belt. He stepped forward and held the knife against her throat. "So much as a peep, kitten, and it will be the last sound you ever make. Do we have an accord?"

Sarra trembled, but she nodded in agreement without so much as a whimper.

The shadow finally moved in the doorway and caught her attention. A third man approached her, his scarred face highlighted by the flickering fireplace as he came close. He leaned forward, his warm breath scorching her skin.

"You are going to make me a wealthy man, Princess," he said with a wicked smile. The scarred man lifted his hand and caressed her cheek. He wiped away a trail of her tears before he gripped her shoulder, pulling her toward him. A damp cloth covered her nose and mouth, Sarra's cries muffled behind the material. "I hope you enjoy traveling. An acquaintance of mine requests your presence. We call him the Serpent Lord. He is eager to meet you."

Her world turned black.

CHAPTER 2

ALARGE STONE IN THE ROAD BOUNCED OFF THE RIGID spokes of a carriage wheel, the impact jostling Sarra from her sleep. The grim remembrance of her abduction and the racket inside the stagecoach made her stir quickly. Her hands remained bound with rope. A thick burlap bag covered her head, muting the faint sunlight from the windows, and with every wobble of the carriage, she bounced at least several inches into the air before she slammed awkwardly back into her seat.

Sarra instantly longed for the comforts of the castle's soft linen and the warmth of the fireplace in her bedroom. Her neck was stiff from her slouched, restless slumber, and she was cold, nearly chilled to the bone. Several days and nights had passed in a blurry, dark haze with little peace and much discomfort. Her exhaustion made her sluggish. Her stomach rumbled with hunger.

Just how much farther will this hellish journey take me?

Her captors avoided revealing any information to her, and

just how far from the castle they actually were remained a mystery. Low tree branches whipped across the cloth roof, drowning out the other sounds she heard. Sometimes, the rumbling voices of her abductors broke through the roar in her ears as they conversed with each other.

They spoke about her, but also of some dark fate that awaited her. They talked of a man and a fabled city, of ghosts and stone walls, and a giant palace closed off to the rest of the world. Sarra had never heard of such a place. Yet, as she listened to the ruffians as they prattled near her, she did not doubt it was real.

Their reward would be great, her captors bragged. More gold than they had ever thought possible.

"And he will have his way with ya too, I reckon," one of them said, poking her in the side with something sharp. Behind the burlap, Sarra winced with distaste.

"The Serpent Lord. Supposedly, he has all of his meals delivered to him like this. I doubt you are the first, Princess, or that you will be the last."

The "Serpent Lord" was an unknown figure to Sarra, never appearing as a guest of any court that she remembered. His "supposed" city was not located upon any map she recalled, and her abductors called his home by the name Ro'al, an exotic mouthful easily remembered had she heard it before. At first, on some minute level, the ideas her captors presented of the mysterious lord and his city fascinated her, but as the scattered days wore on with the ruffians only whispering his name, Sarra's unease intensified into something akin to terror. Perhaps marrying Elias was not the worst that could happen to her, and although it made her sick to her stomach to consider the idea of unwanted nuptials, becoming someone's meal did not sit well with her either.

The carriage stopped with a rough jolt, and despite her efforts to evade them, someone grasped her arm. Sarra yelped, falling to her knees after being shoved outside. The ground was firm and wet, but that was all she could decipher from behind her burlap mask.

"Now, I would stay quiet while we cross the boneyard, Your Grace. The only things that will run to your aid out here are the greenskins, and well, you could say that you are better off with us than with them."

Even Sarra admitted that was a valid point.

Despite not knowing where or what the boneyard actually was, Sarra did know of the greenskins, a more derogatory term for orcs because of their unique coloring, ranging from dark green to a greenish-brown. They lacked kindness, especially toward humans, and were troublesome creatures so torn by war, prejudice, and devastation they were blinded by it. Calling for help did her no favors if they were her only potential saviors. Her father was not a popular man among them, and they would not hesitate to take out their frustrations against her because of it. Sarra assumed she was unwelcome in these lands, so she kept her head bowed and her mouth shut tightly.

They released her hands from her bindings, but a firm nudge against her rear by a boot pushed her forward. She fell farther into the mud, palms outstretched, as she attempted to catch herself before hitting the ground. A chorus of laughter assaulted her, reddening Sarra's cheeks with anger and embarrassment. No one had ever treated her so poorly.

"You only have to reach Ro'al alive. We are not getting paid more if you are in good condition. Keep your hood in place and thank us later."

The sounds of footsteps in the mud surrounded her, and the men hoisted Sarra to her feet. They rushed her forward without giving her an opportunity to protest, and she barely steadied herself before they demanded she move. The whispered chatter died to complete silence within moments. Not even the ruffians took the chance to speak aloud in this place. That realization alone made her hold her breath. *Where are we exactly? How close are the orcs?*

Through a small hole newly punctured in the burlap, Sarra saw colorless shapes. A gray sheen covered each of them, taking the vibrancy of color away. It made it impossible for her to distinguish one object from another. The trees and the grass under her feet appeared to be dead or dying. A cool chill rushed over her skin as the wind picked up and whistled around her. Wherever she was, it was a far cry from home.

Her province, named after the kingdom itself, was lush and vibrant. Gardens of exotic flowers grew rampantly throughout the entire capital of Olmalis, and the castle stood tall and proud in the middle of them. Life was abundant, flourishing between the alabaster statues and the marble walls. Life danced along the banks of the rivers and through the trickle of the clear, blue streams. It even swayed in the breeze that brushed through the tall grasses of the plains to the east.

There were always pieces of life within the borders of the province Sarra knew and loved, and it extended into the rest of the kingdom, each of the other six provinces containing its own distinct beauty.

But within Ro'al, there was nothing.

Her captors pushed her onward through colorless forests and wasting bogs. She trudged along warily until her feet blistered and ached. As much as she wished to, Sarra refused to fight the ruffians or their orders. Instead, she kept her ears open, attempting to stay calm. Her thoughts kept her company, her memories the only lingering warmth.

Sarra knew her father would send an army. It would take some time for his men to discover her disappearance, but she felt confident they would eventually find her. Despite their recent disagreements, Sarra remained too valuable for her father to ignore her abduction. No other heirs existed to lay claim to his throne. Someone would atone for this betrayal against the king.

Perhaps Elias would ride with them, intent on saving her himself if the stories surrounding him were true. Sarra did not hold onto the thought, allowing it to drift away nearly as fast as it came. No lord of her court would mount his horse and voluntarily combat the orc horde, risking his life in the process, for a woman he did not know nor love. Elias would not be the exception to that rule. Sarra knew that with confidence, not even a single doubt begging her to think otherwise.

Whispers and small talk returned after Sarra and the men exited a tunnel. When she could do so, she stood tall with a poised grace, holding her chin high. They bound her hands behind her back again, but despite that inconvenience, Sarra refused to let the daughter of the king look feeble. Her body ached from the arduous travel, but a renewed sense of hope invigorated her as the thoughts of knights coming to her rescue provided her with some reassurance. That changed when a bucket of cold water doused her only moments later.

Sarra lost her composure, gasping aloud with shock. She thrashed about as the bag on her head threatened to suffocate her. Her fear crushed her under its weight, choking her panicked cries. She tugged against her bindings to free herself, but the burlap continued to stick to her lips and nose. Her frightful tears returned, emerging from the corners of her eyes.

"You idiot!" one man shouted.

Sarra heard a loud thud next to her, followed by chaotic movements.

"You were not supposed to pour it over her head! The dirt is on her legs! You are going to kill her and then he will kill us.

Did you forget the terms of the agreement? Get another bag. Quickly."

Someone uncovered her face, and a breeze touched her skin. Sarra inhaled deeply, desperate to fill her lungs with air. Her watering eyes blinked fast against the dim, early morning light. It only took her a moment to see what stood in front of her.

A city in ruin.

Even the citizens watching her appeared just as worn and weathered as the buildings they inhabited. She noted their blanched, sickly skin, and the way their bones protruded distinctly from malnourishment. Disease and dirt marked them. Stone towers stood in nothing but piles of sharp rocks. Houses draped like tents, hardly livable. Even the sun was suffocated by a thick, depressing drizzle of endless rain. Only two pieces of the city remained strong and completely intact, the large wall surrounding them and a palace of a remarkable size resting just as hauntingly as the city it sat in.

"Welcome to Ro'al, Princess," the scarred ruffian whispered darkly in her ear, making Sarra yelp with surprise. His dreadful laugh was the last thing she heard before her sight fell once more into darkness.

The men led her farther into the city and eventually out of the rain. She speculated about the Serpent Lord and the ruined city. The crumbling buildings saddened her. The feeble populace angered her. *What had befouled them? What had driven the city to failure? How could he let this happen? Why had aid not been sought?*

Unless the ruffians had discovered some unknown land, Sarra knew Ro'al was within her father's realm. Every inch of land the sun touched belonged to the king, his claim only negated by the rocky base of the mountains or the crashing waves of the sea surrounding Olmalis. Her father would not sit idle if he knew his people lived in shambles, and the only explanation for the state of the city became negligence. The Serpent Lord had a responsibility for the well-being of his people. Sarra vowed to ensure he answered for their suffering.

Echoes of shuffling feet melted into the sounds of doors opening. The rough hands of her captors eased.

"This place gives me the creeps," one of them muttered, a few grunts echoing the sentiment. Although the burlap covering her face prevented her from seeing, Sarra agreed with them. Wherever she was, it felt cold and unwelcoming, reminding her of a dungeon. The flicker of the torches on the walls projected warmth, but the light only played shadows through her hood.

"What is this?"

The question echoed in the corridor, a deep, masculine voice she never heard before shouting it. Sarra shivered, her head turning in search of the man questioning her captors. The covering over her eyes continued to hinder her view of nearly everything, reminding her of her disadvantage.

"We were asked to bring the princess. Well, here she is!"

"What did you do to her? Drag her through a pit?"

"Would you prefer her to be clean with a spear through her chest? The greenskins could oblige."

"Arrogant bastards," the voice growled. "Get her in that room. I will pay you, and then you can leave."

"Gladly," one man sneered audibly.

The noisy protest of a large wooden door creaked in front of her, and Sarra moved forward as they cut the restraints from her wrists. They shoved her the last few steps, and the door immediately closed behind her with a click.

For the first time since she was taken from her castle, Sarra stood all alone.

Forgotten was the bag covering her face as it slid to the floor. Her hands brushed what dirt she could from her ruined black gown. She peeled the short, clipped strands of blond hair that had fallen loose away from her cheeks. Relieved at finally being able to look around her, Sarra took a moment to peer at her surroundings, quickly concluding the room she stood in was not at all what she expected given the state of the city outside.

It was a large, stately bedroom with shimmering white marble floors and black marble trim. There was a comfortable-looking bed and several other furnishings made of fine wood, and a fountain with running water built into the far wall. A basin with clean cloth rags sat in front of it. Wicks burned atop wax candles with silver bases, and a warm fire roared in the hearth across from her. It was obvious from the first glance that whoever lived here was wealthy, but the room had gone unused for what had to be ages. Someone had hastily wiped dust from every surface, leaving streaks behind as evidence. Cobwebs still hung in hard to reach places. Drapes covered the windows, preventing what dim sunlight there was from entering the room. The water, at least, was clean.

"Take it all," Sarra heard the deep voice growl through the door as she turned around to face it. She expected it to open any second. Her muddy hands clutched at the part of her lace dress that covered her chest, and as the voice grew louder, she took a few steps back. Her hips bumped into a desk, rattling the contents inside, and Sarra placed one of her hands on top to help it settle from the collision.

"Leave this place. I do not wish to see any of you again."

She heard several sets of footsteps retreat, followed by a loud sigh and a pause. A gentle, almost hesitant knock rapped upon the door, disrupting the momentary peace.

"I have food," the voice reported. "You must be hungry."

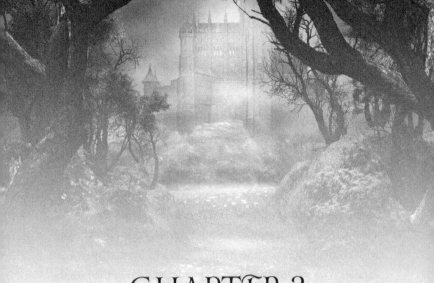

CHAPTER 3

S ARRA STOOD STILL AS STONE, HER EYES NEVER LEAVING
the door. She refused to welcome the menacing lord with
wide open arms and a smile. Dying from starvation fared
her better than offering an olive branch to a criminal, and death
awaited him as his destiny, regardless of how often he tried to
deny it or how many attempts he made to convince her to beg
her father differently.

Her nose wrinkled as she scowled. *Why should I answer
him?* Sarra owed the man nothing but a firm slap and a string of
unladylike curses. She turned her head away, ignoring him, and
her chin lifted defiantly. Her father showed no mercy to those
that wronged him. Sarra refused to show any either. She was
the princess, the daughter of the king, and despite their current
differences, Sarra's father had taught her everything she knew.

"I am coming in," the man said through the door. "Please
do not be frightened."

With his words, her curiosity piqued, a wave of unease
washing over her.

Why is he called the Serpent Lord? How ferocious can he really be?

She crafted an image of him inside of her head. Perhaps he was wicked-looking with fangs for teeth and scales for skin. Maybe his tongue forked, and he hissed when he was angry. *Does he eat his prey whole? Are his eyes thin slits and colored like bile?* With each outlandish attribute she gave the man, the more she trembled. A desire to open the door and face him lingered, but the gravity of her predicament was not lost on her. *Is he dangerous? Would he eat me as the ruffians said he would?*

Still, Sarra steeled herself, acknowledging that his trap was well placed. She saw through it with a trained eye, her father having warned her that something like this might happen one day. Falling victim to the Serpent Lord earned her no favors. Letting her guard down was a mistake.

She narrowed her eyes with determination.

The door creaked loudly before she could protest, and it shifted inward, alerting her to his entrance. The man hesitated for several seconds before he drew the door open further. He slowly came into view, and Sarra sated her curiosity with a glance. Her back remained against the wall with her green eyed gaze leveling upon him. His feet shuffled forward, directing him closer to her.

Sarra tilted her head to the side, regarding him. He appeared handsome and strong, his body solid and well-toned. One article of clothing caught her attention, holding her eyes longer than the rest. A black strip of cloth wrapped around his eyes. It appeared worn and silken as it sat across his temple and was tied loosely behind his head.

Is it possible he is blind?

Overall, the man seemed in good health, contrasting with the rest of the unfortunate people she observed earlier. His beard sat on his face in a somewhat unruly condition, but it held a noble bearing, obscuring most of his lower jaw. A single dirty-blond wave cascaded back from his temple, and although a dark, deep gray cloak kept much of him hidden, she saw he was tall and broad of shoulder. He wore a hunter-green tunic etched in gold trim, the material worn and threadbare in some places. Cracked black leather gauntlets covered his hands, and on his feet were equally tired boots. No scales replaced skin. No large fangs decorated his mouth. He looked just like her. *Human.*

Immediately, Sarra recognized him as only a servant, his shoddy garb a telling sign. She frowned with disappointment, although a large part of her was also relieved. *Where was the Serpent Lord that struck fear into the hearts of ruffians?*

Sarra's thoughts fueled a newly found annoyance once the man journeyed further into the room. Her eyes never left him, following each of his movements like a hawk. His hands held a small plate with meager offerings she blatantly ignored. When he spoke to her, Sarra clenched her teeth hard, biting back several demanding questions and insults directed at his lord. The action nearly pained her, but keeping her composure, Sarra stood silent.

"Please, eat," the man said softly, placing the tray upon an end table. The door shut behind him with a heavy thud, and he neither flinched nor altered his course. His covered eyes remained forward as he walked, and not once did they roam, searching for her. The man posed her little to no threat, or so Sarra assumed, and she considered rushing toward the door in an attempt to escape. He spoke again before she moved.

"I am deeply sorry for the way you have been treated. I will fetch you some clean clothes and warm blankets."

The man retreated toward the door after his offer, a quick indication of his discomfort at either her presence or her continued silence. The response befuddled her. *Did his lord teach him to be anxious around those of higher station?* Despite her distaste for interacting with men, cruelty toward servants disgusted her, and Sarra wondered if the blind man experienced much of it at the hands of his lord. Not even a retainer of the Serpent Lord deserved such a fate. Sarra clenched her teeth harder.

A clean gown and the comforts of warm blankets enticed her though, and she softened her posture for a moment, looking down at her dress. A thick layer of damp mud coated the black material, disappointing her. However, her disappointment faded fast. Memories of the king and the grief-stealing celebration pushed her vanity far from the forefront of her mind. A ruined black dress was the least of her concerns now, and a small tinge of regret overpowered all other feelings for a fleeting moment. *Was I too stubborn with the lords of the court? Would I have been abducted if I had agreed to my father's plans for me?*

Sarra reasoned with herself, eventually accepting that a clean dress posed little harm to her perseverance. Wearing something warm and dry would not change anything. Worse handouts existed in the world, and falling ill from a cold, damp gown loomed as a very real possibility given the state of the city and the disease of those residing within it. Visions of the sick and hungry reignited her itch to meet the true wretch of the palace, forcing her to break her vow of silence and pause her reflection on the past.

"Is your master too cowardly to look upon me himself?" Sarra took several steps forward, extending a hand to catch the door before it slammed shut behind the blind man. "I am not frightened of you, nor am I frightened of *him*, but I want to know why the man responsible for uprooting my life will not offer me the courtesy of an introduction? I think that the comfort of one's prisoner would hold less importance than that, but here you stand, proving me wrong."

Her voice projected crisp and clear confidence, unwavering as she spoke her thoughts aloud. The servant furrowed his brow, looking confused at her outburst. He halted his exit from the room and stood aside from the door, leaving it open and momentarily unguarded. Sarra saw the hallways darkened around him. A blind man needed no light to guide his way, but knowing he lacked even a candle made her somewhat uneasy.

"I am sorry that circumstances necessitated your stay here, but I assure you that your suffering is of no benefit to anyone," he said, his empathy apparent in his tone. Her gaze snapped to him, and Sarra mimicked his frown, deepening the crease between her brows as she noticed her questions remained unanswered. Maybe she would never meet the Serpent Lord. At least the blind man seemed to treat her with kindness and respect.

Still, Sarra turned her nose up. "There is more than one solution to every problem. I hope whatever prompted my capture is worth the consequences."

She made it a point to rarely speak a lie, even now as she stood in a foreign, uncomfortable place after being forcibly removed from her home. Truth unlocked happiness, and falsehoods only existed to ruin prosperity. Her words held an understood bite to them as Sarra delivered them, implying honest undertones of the repercussions even a servant knew awaited his master. The blind man bit his lip in contemplation, and without realizing it, she again repeated his mannerisms unintentionally herself. The air shifted as she watched him, drawing light to how sad and weary he looked. Sarra found herself pitying him, despite not knowing him at all.

It must be so unfair to be ruled by such a cruel lord.

"I apologize," she muttered, recognizing her sharpness with him. "You do not deserve my ire. That belongs to someone else."

The blind man shifted his face away from her. "Our resources are meager here, but I will do my best to provide for you during this time. You need only let me know what you require, and I shall oblige if I am able."

Sarra nodded her understanding, then realizing he couldn't see her, gave him her thanks. She wrapped her arms around herself as a chill settled on her skin. Her teeth chattered, and she shivered. They stood together in silence until he cleared his throat.

"If it is any comfort, I am confident you will be free soon."

"Soon? What do you mean by soon? By definition, time is relative, so what you might assume is soon could very well be ages to me. I—"

"When I say soon, it is dependent on the love of your father," he interrupted. "He knows exactly where you are. The ruffians intentionally did not hide their tracks, and a ransom was demanded. I trust he will come for you quickly. Even in these remote lands, it is well known to us that you are the most precious jewel in his eyes."

The blind man's tone turned sour. "We must hope that his love for you outweighs his love for his people."

Stunned, Sarra stilled. The conversation stopped as the weight of his words remained. He kept his face away from her, moving forward after several tense moments to walk into the lightless corridor.

"Wait!" She took one look around the empty room and grabbed her skirts. The thought of waiting alone filled her with dread, pushing her to move closer to him in an effort to follow. "My father is a smart man. He will not be easily tricked into any trap set for him. I do not know what game is being played, but perhaps this warning should be considered."

Her voice echoed in the corridor. The blind man lowered his head. The blond curl at his temple fell forward to graze the top of the silk blindfold, and he slouched his shoulders, shrinking in stature before her very eyes. Sarra attempted to remain poised, but it became painfully obvious that her abrasiveness dispirited him. He looked defeated.

"I trust you are right," he replied grimly, making Sarra swallow hard around her guilt. Her poise crumbled, and she lowered her chin from its raised position.

The servant remained silent, his broad form nearly blocking the empty hall from her view. Sarra wondered if he remembered she stood there after his quietness stretched for far longer than she thought appropriate. She lifted her hand, reaching toward his shoulder to grasp him, but a slight movement from him surprised her before she touched him.

"I meant what I said," he stated, straightening his stance. Sarra stepped cautiously backward. "I can hear you shivering. I will fetch you something else to wear."

Sarra spoke up quickly, still desperate not to be left alone. "Does one make noise when one shivers? Perhaps I am hard of hearing or maybe you are good at telling tales."

The blind man seemed to listen. He hesitated to move further.

"Have you forgotten that you do not know what I look like? Are all men as presumptuous as you?" She cleared her throat and reclaimed one of the steps she had lost previously.

"I will manage," he replied. "I can make inferences from the sound of your voice and the weight of your footfalls. If you prefer, I can bring you a selection of varied sizes, and you may choose any that meet your needs."

Sarra frowned at him. "What if you assume incorrectly? What if I am taller than you suspect? Or wider? Shorter? Smaller? Even if you provide me with a variety, how can you guarantee that one will fit?"

She found her footing, pressing the conversation onward. She knew the more information discovered of her prison, the easier leaving it became. Knowledge was power, and Sarra desperately wanted an advantage. "Please do not entomb me in a parade of gowns."

Her words seemed to introduce a touch of doubt in the blind man's mind. He raised his head with parted lips, words sticking in his throat. They croaked out as he gently smiled once her point settled. "Well, I will admit, sizing a woman for a gown is not something I am well versed in."

"I will accompany you then," Sarra said as she tugged at the dark material that clung to her legs. "As long as it will not get you into trouble with your lord. I am cold. My gown is damp, and I promise I will behave."

The blind man shook his head with a sigh, his gloved hand falling between them. "You will not be able to see. The palace is dark. The halls are not kept lit."

Sarra looked from his hand to her own. Hesitantly, she reached for him. "Very well. You will lead the way."

Her fingers laced around his, and the gesture startled him. His back straightened and his arm stiffened, but he did not withdraw from her touch. They stood there, frozen in time, before he finally agreed.

"Fine," he muttered, drawing her forward with their joined hands. "Mind your step."

Into the darkness, Sarra walked. The blind man's gloved hand felt cool to the touch as if no warm body filled the leather gauntlet. Her hand was dwarfed inside his, and he grasped her fingers back with reassurance every time her pace slowed beside him. She realized quickly that the blind man spoke the truth of the darkness within the palace. It unsettled her greatly, and fear dried her throat. No lights guided them. No torches flickered along the halls. She lacked any bit of sight. The princess put her trust into the blind man, hoping he led her safely. As their journey through the palace lengthened, she felt her curiosity overwhelm the fear that still rumbled inside of her. Her anxieties seemed to ease, if only slightly.

She wondered how the blind man had lost his sight. *Is he alone in the palace with his lord? Does he ever leave it? What is his name?* She had half a mind to ask him all of these things, but she decided not to, opting to keep her silence instead. Too many questions might lead him to abandon her in annoyance. He was her only guiding light through the palace.

"I trust you will not allow me to fall," Sarra said quietly after stumbling over a crevice in the flooring. She remained apprehensive about speaking too loudly in the darkness, and a wave of irrational fear suddenly began to cage her. The blind man held her fingers tightly to comfort her. He led her through long corridors and around corners. Her eyes adjusted a little, allowing her to see vague outlines of shapes and doorframes in the dark. They passed several rooms before they reached the end of their travel.

"Does your master appreciate art?" she asked. Sarra blinked as a stream of soft light from an open window illuminated the room in front of her. Her question made the blind man's brow furrow as he opened a door, escorting her inside.

"Art? It does not hold much meaning to—"

"Hmm. It is an odd interest for a Serpent Lord to have, but I am convinced there are statues all over these halls."

The blind man lifted her hand to help ease her through the

doorway and over a small step. The room was similar to the one he had found her in before, but instead of lavish, ornate decor, the furniture was simpler and the dust less noticeable. She spotted a large cedar chest under a window. A dresser half the size of her own stood beside it. A thick, red blanket embroidered with a design of gold rested atop a small bed. The personal items warmed the room more than the sconces upon the walls. Sarra felt her chill ease slightly.

"You will find clothing in the wardrobe," the blind man said, and Sarra tilted her head to look at him. His brows rose over the silk that covered his eyes, lips smiling softly. "If my assumptions are correct, they are approximately your size."

Sarra dropped her grip of his hand and wandered toward the wardrobe. She opened the doors by the handles, and inside hung the articles of clothing he said were there. Gowns of many colors stared back at her, and she selected a soft blue one from them. The princess held it against her waist.

"It should fit," she stated with a quick look at the blind man over her shoulder. Her hands dropped the dress to her side as she bent to pick up a leather shoe from the bottom of the wardrobe. "The shoes seem a bit small. I will continue to use my own."

Sarra straightened, her nosiness besting her. "Who does this dress belong to? These shoes? This room?"

She gestured around her with a free hand but dropped it back in place as she awaited his response. She wished not to take from someone else.

"A handmaiden," the blind man replied. "One that we cherished and adored. You may use her things. She has no need for them now."

His voice became somber. Sarra crafted a story in her head, just like the one she had created for his lord and decided that the poor girl perished in some tragic, sorrowful event. Sarra's heart hurt with a sense of overwhelming loss.

"I am sorry," she whispered, lowering her eyes, and moving toward the small bed. She placed the dress on the red blanket and stared at it. "Thank you for this small, yet kind, gesture. I am grateful, for whatever that is worth."

The blind man stayed silent. He nodded at her before he turned to exit the room. She assumed he intended to allow her some privacy. Sarra reached behind her to the strings that bound her dress to her. The jarring reminder of her laces made her turn swiftly, calling out to him to stay.

"Your cloth," she asked. "How were you blinded?"

The man hesitated, then stopped, silent.

"You cannot see me? Not even a little?" Sarra continued to question, not giving him much time to reply. Of course he could not see her. He required no light to walk the palace halls, and he rarely looked directly at her when he spoke.

"I am . . . I need your help. Before you leave, that is," Sarra needlessly motioned to the laces behind her back. "My dress is dirty, but it is still elaborate. Quite the opposite in every regard to the one I am borrowing. There are laces."

Sarra's face heated. Modesty concerned her least in her current predicament, but still, the idea of asking a man to assist her undressing made her conscious of how improper her request of him was.

"They need to be loosened, and while asking you to help me with such matters is something I would rather not do, I am afraid there is not much choice." Sarra moved so that her back faced him. "If you do not mind, would you help me? I can help you find them with your hands."

She waited with bated breath, half expecting the blind man to leave her to deal with her gown on her own. A heavy sigh from his direction said otherwise, and Sarra breathed easier with his unspoken agreement. His cloak rustled behind her as he moved, and just as Sarra opened her mouth to speak to him again, the heavy material fell upon her shoulders. Her hands reached up to grasp it between her fingers, and she turned her head to peer at him. He seemed to understand her confusion because his words caressed reassuringly against her ear.

"For your modesty. I can understand how uncomfortable you must be in situations like this."

Sarra shivered, and not from the dampness of her gown.

The servant went about his task once she placed his hands on the laces of her dress, and in silence, his fingers moved along the ties of her gown expeditiously. Sarra focused on the cloak that covered her, ignoring the subtle strain against the material at her back. It held an earthy, masculine scent. She cuddled into it, enjoying the way it made her feel. Her body gave the cool fabric warmth, and she found it curious that the cloak initially felt frigid to the touch. She struggled with pinpointing what it was exactly, but something seemed unusual about the Serpent Lord's attendant.

Sarra lacked the time to ponder his oddities. Her dress fell slack after a strong tug, and the blind man removed his hands from under the cloak with enough speed that Sarra nearly let her gown slip through her fingers. Fortunately, she caught it before it exposed her. He left her quickly and stood by the door when she turned around. He held his hands, clutching them together as if his skin burned painfully through his gloves. Sarra tensed, her chest tightening even without the laces keeping her dress in place.

"Are you all right?" She shuffled toward him, but not even her question made him pause. He reached for the door handle, easing the heavy slab open.

"You may use the cloak to dry off and clean yourself. There is nothing you can do to it that has not been done before," he blurted. "I can take you to the baths as well if you would like. I may be able to run the bellows to keep the water warm for you."

Concern gripped her, but Sarra stopped her movement when he pushed himself halfway into the hall. "A warm bath sounds pleasant," she called. "Thank you for the offer, I suppose."

The blind man nodded, his back toward her, and in another moment, he left Sarra in the handmaiden's room.

CHAPTER 4

ONCE SHE HAD REMOVED THE DIRT COVERED BLACK gown and replaced it with the blue dress, Sarra took time to explore her surroundings. She found a rag that she used to clean her bare legs of grime, opting to save the cloak the blind man gave her for a different fate. A comb of bone sat upon a small table, and she took the liberty of removing the tangles in her hair with the help of a small hand mirror. Each retrieved hair pin rested in a pile on the table, and when she finished smoothing out her hair, the strands fell only to her shoulders. Her eyes widened at the sight of it in the mirror.

In the mad journey to Ro'al, she had forgotten her rebellion. The morning prior to her father's celebration, her patience with him had grown terribly thin and she severed the length of her long, flowing hair with a sharp knife. Her handmaidens begged her to keep her disobedience to tradition secret, convinced that debuting her new, shortened hair style would serve only to irritate the king more than she already had. He believed in conservatism, even if he rarely followed it himself, and the discovery that Sarra's hair no longer draped down her back in luxurious waves begged for trouble. So, she had concealed the shorter strands and twisted them into a tight chignon, then decorated it with a gleaming crown. No one noticed, or at the very least, they kept quiet about it.

After running her hands through her hair and watching it shimmer in the light, Sarra decided to leave it down for the very first time.

The comb snagged through the frayed, dirtied ends, but she eventually finished her task and straightened herself to exit the room. Sarra remained mystified by the blind man just enough to want to rejoin him quickly.

The door clicked open and Sarra glided across the stone floor to stand before him. She felt refreshed. The color of her new gown contrasted nicely against her fair skin, making her feel beautiful despite the overall simplicity of the dress's design. The cotton material hugged her bust and curved hips just a touch more than she preferred, revealing her womanly assets, although still in what she considered a modest manner. Her confidence flowed from her person in thick, undeniable waves, and although she had only been able to see herself in a small mirror, Sarra thought she looked ravishing, even in rags.

Her hands picked at the skirt of her dress and lifted it so that the material did not drag on the stone. The soft sounds of her feet scuffed across the floor, but she stumbled on a crack in the smooth surface. The blind man acted quickly, even before she cried out in alarm, and caught her with his firm, cool hands. He made a small sound in the back of his throat which forced her to look at him, and Sarra shivered involuntarily when she did so. His blindfolded eyes stared directly at her, almost as if he watched her from behind the silk, but Sarra quickly dismissed that thought with a soft curse at her ungraceful trip.

"Did I startle you?" Sarra asked as heat ignited her cheeks, and she pulled away.

He slowly shook his head. "No, you did not."

"Good." Sarra reached for his hand and shoved the material of the cloak into it. "I could not, in good conscience, use your cloak as a rag. It would be rude to do so."

His fingers curled around the fabric and brought it toward his chest. "It is not much of a cloak anymore but thank you for returning it."

Sarra tucked her hair behind her ear and shuffled her feet. "I would still enjoy a warm bath. Is it far?"

Without waiting for permission, she gently nudged him and grasped his arm. Her fingers cupped his forearm and she waited patiently for him to lead her through the darkened halls again.

"No, not far," he answered, and they both fell quiet as they moved together back into the pitch-black corridor. Sarra's eyes adjusted to the darkness better than previously, and this time, as they walked by them, she focused on the shapes that peeked from the shadows.

Objects that reminded her of statues stood near the walls. They appeared faintly humanoid with a physique not unlike that of herself or the blind man. Too still to be alive, they also shimmered with a faint white glow, but in the darkness of the halls, Sarra struggled to see any features other than their limbs and torsos. The clusters of what seemed like porcelain-crafted sculptures piqued her imagination, and Sarra wondered what the palace looked like without the darkness shrouding it from sight.

Her thoughts constructed an image of a rich, detailed history, where people laughed, lived, and loved with sunlight and joy. Brilliant tapestries covered the halls. Thick, satin drapes hung from the windows. Intricate paintings and carpets with golden trim accented various rooms. She nearly felt the truth of her invention with the whispers that reached out to her through the walls. *What would the court look like here? Would visitors flood the halls like the statues did? Did bards sing songs and was the lord brave enough to dance with a princess?*

Her arm brushed against a statue, and Sarra yelped with surprise. The man pulled her closer, and she wrapped her arms tighter through his.

"Watch your step," he reminded her kindly. Sarra swallowed hard in response.

"Wh-what are your lord's intentions with me? Am I to be locked in a room until my father arrives?" Her voice shook as she huddled close, and Sarra's questions echoed along the dark space. She attempted to distract herself from the unsettling statues by carrying on a conversation instead, and with her asks, the blind man remained steady without pushing her away.

"There are no intentions for you." His free hand moved toward their locked arms, and his large palm pressed against the back of hers reassuringly.

"Are there others here?"

"I believe you have met the downtrodden outside the castle walls. They are the last remnants of Ro'al. You will be most comfortable inside the palace, though you may walk the grounds of the keep if you wish."

His gloved fingers twitched against her arm. "The people may receive you kindly if you revile the Serpent Lord as loudly as they do."

Sarra's face twisted in confusion. "I am not to be held captive in a dungeon? Or restricted to a small area of the palace? I will not even be forbidden from talking with others that might be willing to set me free from this place?"

"No," the blind man said with a trace of a smile. "You are as free as the rest of us."

He then fell silent, continuing to direct her through the palace. They rounded yet another corner, and he stopped her with a press against the back of her hand.

"You see, you are bound by the same forces that we are now." He untangled her arm from his, and stepped away from her, not far, but enough so she only saw his outline from where he left her. "We are trapped here."

The door clanged as it opened, and the blind man rejoined her within moments. Light poured into the darkness, illuminating a large, tiled room.

"An army of greenskins has surrounded the city. They have besieged us for over thirteen years," he continued. Sarra blinked rapidly and used one of her hands to cover her eyes. The blind man reclaimed her arm, encouraging her forward. He only dropped it once they stood inside.

"An army of greenskins has besieged this city? For thirteen years? I did not know this place even existed until—"

Sarra gaped at the impressive baths that appeared before her.

Meant to cascade from fonts high in the walls, water pooled in shallow basins at the bottom of several stalls. Of them, only two enclosures retained running water—one merely a trickle, and the other flowing well. The tile appeared to be teal in color with hints of bronze in the pattern, although a lack of use in several sections made the squares look filthy. She had expected something less elaborate, given the dusty state of every other room she had seen, but beautiful accents flourished brightly in each corner. The subtle details of the room came to life before her eyes. Still, a chill in the air remained haunting, and Sarra shivered before wrapping her arms around herself as she glanced around the large room.

"How is that possible?" Sarra whispered, turning to look at the blind man as he moved toward one of the stalls. An opening to a small room stood ajar next to it. He ignored her question, continuing forward without her.

A pair of small gongs hung near the bath, and after he approached, he chimed the first. It made a high pitched, pleasant sound. "Ring this if you wish the water to be warmer."

He chimed the second, sparking a far lower rumbling tone. "This one if you want the water to be cooler. It will take several minutes to adjust the temperature, so please be patient."

"And where are you going? I have more questions!" She clutched her skirts, lifting the bottom of her dress from the ground. Sarra started to follow after him until he raised his hand for her to stop.

"Ask your questions. I will answer as I am able, but if you would like a warm bath, I will need to heat the water for you. I can still hear you once I am inside, but please, use the bath while you can."

Sarra opened her mouth to speak, but closed it, nodding to him in reply instead, forgetting his blindness momentarily. Without waiting for her answer, he entered the connecting smaller room through an open doorway. Sarra watched him disappear inside before she walked toward a shelf and picked at the linens that rested upon it, thinking, wondering. *What did orcs want with a city as devastated as this one?*

Her fingers pressed together after replacing the soft cotton to rub the dust from them. Soon, steam rose from the water streaming from the wall and the basin beneath. Sarra removed her blue dress and began to clean the muck from her skin.

"Tell me more of why the greenskins have barricaded this

city," she shouted loudly. A small sound of movement followed a grunt, and the blind man answered her.

"I was a young man when it started. I am afraid the details of why are not entirely clear, even to me." He took a heavy breath, making Sarra frown with concern, but he continued without seeming winded at all. "They are organized, ruthless, and hell-bent on extinguishing every life within our walls. They come for us, from time to time, with sword and ax, bow and spear, claws and teeth. We cannot break their blockades, and we have too many sick and weak to mount an attack and free ourselves. Even when it began, we were outnumbered ten to one. It was quite a challenge to find someone willing to take the risk of bringing you here."

"How did your lord do it then? What made those awful men agree to abduct me?"

"Coin, mostly. Everyone can be bought, regardless of the danger. It seems to have worked well enough, considering you are here."

Sarra stepped further into the bath. The chill eased in her muscles instantly, and the comforts of the warmth on her skin made her yawn. Her exhaustion returned with a vengeance, but she persisted in her desire for knowledge.

"And what of my father? You say there are no intentions for me, yet you mention his love instead."

"The king left us to our fates," he answered grimly. "We held out for thirteen long years, imploring for rescue with any messenger able to slip past the beasts at night. We received only silence."

Sarra struggled to accept his words, nervously licking her lips to keep them moistened, but her throat felt like fire. *The man is implying my father not only knows of Ro'al's existence, but has wronged the city and the people that live within it. How can that be?*

The king fought proudly for his people, delivered justice when it was due, and yet, as she allowed her mind to wander back to the conversation at the feast where he spouted about "filthy beggars," Sarra began to question her beliefs. Perhaps the cold, cruelty of her father's expectations for her signaled something more than just familial tension.

"The people hate your father. He owed this province defense per the old treaties, and never came to our aid. The mountains behind the city protect it. Our walls are thick too, and we are not without teeth of our own."

Abhorrence of the king? Sarra swallowed the thought, nearly retching at its bitterness. Hard truths always tasted that way, but she was not accustomed to such negativity toward her father. He was loved by the people of her kingdom. No one dared to speak ill of him on any matter. He was celebrated, revered even. He had taught her everything she knew.

But, he failed the city of Ro'al? Sarra heard the conviction in the servant's voice, unable to ignore it.

"If my father was unwilling to help, why did your lord not seek aid elsewhere? There are others with wealth and armies and resources." Sarra felt small, and despite the warmth of the water cascading over her shoulders, her skin prickled with each newly learned bit of knowledge.

He answered her question with a string of grunts and heavy breaths, concerning Sarra.

"Hello?" Her voice echoed around the large room, but still, no answer came. She stepped out of the water, rubbing her eyes. Grabbing a clean cloth, Sarra dried her skin and hair. Her dress sat in a clump on the floor, and quickly, she tugged it back on before searching for her steward. She called out to him again, nearing the door. "I am finished bathing, so we can—"

Sarra hesitated. Inside the room, she found the blind man,

chest heaving and brow slicked with sweat, as he worked large bellows that were big enough to be manned by two or three people. Tangles of intricate pipework wove into a large boiler powered by the fans, and water flowed through the pipes, likely sourced from the mountains she had learned stood nearby. The liquid warmed from the heat and traveled to the bath. She had enjoyed it only moments ago.

Somehow, the servant managed his task of heating the water on his own. The room felt fiery and much too hot, and his skin glistened with a golden shimmer in the firelight as she watched him work. His chest was bare and chiseled, almost like a piece of art himself, and his muscled arms worked the bellows with a strength she had never seen before. The concentration on his face surprised her the most. His jaw locked with exertion, but he never stopped.

Did he do all of this for me? Did he heat my bath so I could find some comfort, even if it was small?

"You can stop now," she shouted just loud enough for him to hear. "I am finished."

The sound of her strained voice seemed to startle him, and he reached for his gambeson to quickly shield himself from her view. Sarra lowered her eyes, a little trickle of guilt seeping into her consciousness as she recognized that she watched him without inhibition. "Thank you for the bath."

"Of course." He turned away. "I am glad it helped."

Sarra retreated back into the baths to allow him privacy as he recovered from the strenuous work. She remained awed until he reappeared, carrying a lit metal torch with him.

"I assume you would like some proper rest now that you have bathed. I can escort you back to your room if you would like." He extended his arm for her to take, like a true gentleman, which Sarra thought about wryly. Leave it to a servant to treat her less fearfully than the men of her court. Not a single one of them dared to extend their arm to her as he did.

"Yes, I am tired." She spoke the truth with a slight yawn indicating her fatigue. Her entire life had changed over the last several days, and Sarra had yet to have time to adjust. A nice rest would do her wonders, but fear lingered inside of her. The blind man would leave her, and she would be all alone again. Sarra wished not for solitude, enjoying his company as if an inexplicable pull tugged her to him. It was likely just his kindness, which he certainly charmed her with. However, being alone in an unfamiliar place was just as unsettling as being dragged through a colorless bog, and she could not deny the possibility of that causing her anxiety as well.

"Very well." He held the torch in front of him as he directed her out of the tiled room. One of her hands held her skirt, the other holding onto him. As they walked through the halls, the statues became clearer. Several stood within the corridors, just as she originally guessed, in various humanoid shapes and sizes, but the man never strayed too close. Their features remained difficult to see as Sarra and her escort kept to the shadows.

"The lock on your door does not work." He broke through the silence, and Sarra turned her face to look up at him. The torchlight played along the angles of his jaw. "If you would like to explore the palace, you may do so. I will leave the torch for you to use."

"Thank you. Given the circumstances, you have been far too kind to me. I will not forget it." She dropped her eyes to look down at her feet, a soft smile tugging at her lips as she held onto him tighter, reflecting upon his treatment of her.

They continued in a comfortable silence for a while longer, turning and walking through a door and several hallways. With the added illumination, Sarra noticed the statues began to increase in number the farther they journeyed through the palace. Her brow furrowed questioningly, and she attempted to peer around one of the lightly colored stone pieces only to be tugged away by the blind man's lead.

"If I do meet your master, I hope he can solve this mystery for me. I think my eyes are starting to adjust to the darkness, and I see there are more statues than I originally thought."

"Yes, there are many."

Again, she tried to peek around a statue, but he shifted the torch into his opposite hand, using the newly unhindered one to hold onto her tightly. He rushed her forward, Sarra yelping with surprise at the sudden shift of pace.

"Excuse me, but do watch yourself. You are hurting me," she said with offense. He loosened his grip on her arm, and she pulled herself free with a huff.

"Apologies," he said, but a pitch of urgency touched his voice, making her frown deepen. "Please, we must continue to your room—"

"No." An uneasy, distrustful feeling made her heartbeat quicken. The air thickened with unspoken secrets. "I am not moving."

"Please," he implored, voice ragged as he sounded more anxious than he conveyed before. His unshakable demeanor throughout her visit morphed before her very eyes, emphasizing his considerable amount of stress as he spoke. He fiddled with his gambeson, his fingers clutching the material through his gloves. "I will be glad to see to any wishes you have when we have returned you—"

"I will not take another step forward until you explain yourself." Her resolve solidified. "Why are you rushing me? Is there something wrong?"

He held his tongue, though she felt him fidgeting in the darkness.

"Is it the statues? Are they poorly made?" Sarra asked, her voice harsh in the silent hall.

"I will entertain any inquiry you have, I swear it. Just—"

Sarra lifted her dress from the ground and shuffled her feet toward one of the stone figures, paying little attention to the blind man as she approached. His torchlight barely touched the shadow shrouding the statue. Her hand hesitantly reached out, and she used a nervous laugh to help ease the tension that built rapidly around her.

Peering over her shoulder, a forced smile spread her lips. "Shoddy work is nothing to be ashamed of. Children can draw better than I—"

Her fingers curled into soft cloth, not hard marble as she expected. Her words fell silent, replaced with a sharp shriek, and Sarra recoiled back. She turned to look at the statue, narrowing her eyes to see what she had touched. She moved in closer, picking at the faint outline of what appeared to be a long tunic covering its torso.

"Clothing? Why are the statues dressed?"

The blind man cleared his throat. "Your room is only just a little farther. If you would allow it, I will escort you the rest of the way."

"Statues do not need clothing," Sarra said firmly, glancing over her shoulder at him. "Come closer. Did you notice this?"

Her touch became bolder, and she trailed her hand over the shoulder of the figure. Sarra moved with her fingers, angling around to look at its face. She lost her breath the moment she stood before it.

Just as she predicted, the statue was shaped like a human. A large man, actually, and he stood a little taller than she. He might have been handsome, except it was difficult to tell because the expression on his face was one twisted in terror. Behind hands that shielded his face, his wide eyes sat frozen with fear and his mouth opened, agape with an unspoken scream. Sarra quickly removed her hand from his shoulder, placing it upon her chest to slow her racing heart.

"I do not like this one." She took a step back, then another. Something rubbed against her shoulder, startling her more, and Sarra whirled around quickly. She pulled back instantly as her eyes peered into a pair of terrified stone ones owned by another statue. This time, it was a woman, with a teardrop cemented below her lower lid, stuck forever in the same spot. The cogs of Sarra's brain stood still, the sight of fear once more etching into her memories. A small sound escaped her, and Sarra stumbled back again, flailing with careless movements.

Her gaze moved around her wildly, searching for the blind man but not seeing anything clearly. Her feet caught the ends of her dress, and she slipped along the stone floor. Her hair snagged as she jerked toward the wall, and when she moved her arm to untangle it, the feeling of a stone hand wrapped in the shoulder length strands sent her spiraling. Sarra fell to her knees, freeing herself, only to glance up into the face of another woman suspended in fright. Her rocklike hand clutched at her throat, seeming to plead for help, but none came.

Sarra turned her head, using her arm to shield her eyes from more horrors as she realized that every statue appeared the same. Terror. Fear. It leaped from their eyes and bled into their stances. *What are these monstrosities? Why did the Serpent Lord have them created?*

The small light from the torch sizzled and the hall fell into darkness.

"Please, leave them alone," the blind man's voice rang out.

47

Sarra lowered her hand and blinked, attempting to adjust to the lack of light. She wiped her cheeks, feeling dampness on them as tears rolled down and over her chin. She crawled on her hands and knees to the wall, where she used the firm structure to support her as she sat against it. Sarra huddled herself close, pulling her legs into her chest while she shook with fear.

"What are they? What happened here?" Her voice cracked with her questions, and she lowered her face onto her knees. The dress fabric muffled the sound of a small sob, and Sarra made herself smaller.

It took him several moments to respond to her question, and when he did, his voice sounded further away. "A curse was brought down upon my house, and I am the reason it is here."

Her head snapped up, eyes widening as she peered toward the sound of his voice. "A curse? Your house?"

Sarra licked her lips, her throat dry and burning once more. She pushed herself up the wall, standing to her feet. "Who are you?"

A stream of light broke through the darkness, and the shuffle of heavy drapes moving along the stone floor echoed. She shielded her eyes as they fought to adjust, and slowly, a large room came into view in front of her. Several, likely hundreds, of statues stared horror-struck, facing toward the center, and from an incline leading to the large, Palladian window, the blind man descended.

"I am Ares, son of Aremar, lord of the dying city of Ro'al."

Sarra's hand shook as she brought it to her mouth, covering it.

"And these are not statues. They are my people."

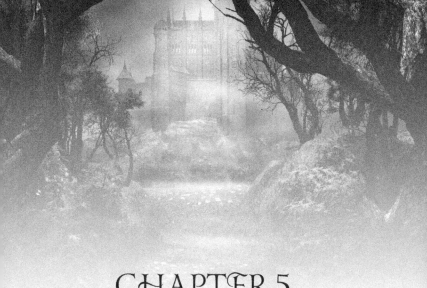

CHAPTER 5

THE SERPENT LORD.

Perhaps she was the blind one. He stood, plain as day, in a ray of sunlight from the large window. The eyes of his petrified people stared at him while his shoulders slumped, and his head hung low.

Sarra clutched the material of her dress, tugging it from her throat. *How did I miss it?*

The room was larger than she had originally thought. Easily the same size as the great hall in her own castle, the dozens of statues stood inside it comfortably.

Two grand pillars framed an expansive entryway, and Sarra placed the room as the entrance to the palace. No other room would hold as much beauty as the foyer did. It was a symbol of wealth for any reputable lord and his province, and perhaps, a memory of what Ro'al used to be.

The beautiful marble floor shimmered with emerald accents. A plush carpet ran down the center of the room, and although it had seen its prime years ago, it still remained luxurious.

The walls glittered with rare metals—gold, silver, and bronze—as deeply carved lines in zig-zag patterns played across them like canvases.

Her gaze returned to the center of the room, lingering on the Serpent Lord. Despite the grisly air about the foyer, something about him bewitched her. He should have been vile and wicked, but the way his hair fell over his temple, and he cast his face downward, he appeared more distraught and devastated than cruel. In fact, the more she considered him, the more she remembered how kindly he treated her before her fear took hold.

It was a trick. It had to be.

Her own eyes turned toward the pearly floor, lost in her thoughts.

Trusting the Serpent Lord is a mistake.

Sarra gently reminded herself of his misdeeds but looking at him once more made her conviction shift. She took slow, easy steps toward a nearby statue, remaining silent as she investigated the humanoid stone intently.

"Please do not be frightened," her captor said, making her recoil.

She quickly withdrew her hand from the statue and watched him over her shoulder.

"These people cannot harm you," he continued.

She licked her lips nervously. One look back at the statue told her that he did not lie. Life had left the fear-stricken faces of the fallen people of Ro'al long before she arrived. However, there was no guarantee the cause of their deaths had left these halls. In fact, it could be alive and well inside the palace with her, perhaps even standing only a few feet away, telling her not to be afraid. She was wise to be wary. Appearances could be deceiving.

The frozen, fearful screams told her to run. Their expressions chilled her until her skin pebbled with gooseflesh, warning her away. Still, she lingered, slowly growing braver as she walked through the sea of them along the edge of the room. "You tell me I should not be frightened, yet they tell me that is not the truth."

"I asked you not to be frightened. I never said you should not be."

Sarra quieted, angling her body to ensure a clear path remained toward the dark hall if she felt the need to try and escape. Gingerly stepping over some rubble, the remnants of a toppled figure scattered under her feet. She stumbled on the ends of her dress, catching herself with her hand on the arm of another statue. Sarra pulled back at the sensation of soft cloth against her fingertips, irrationally fearful for just a moment that the stone person would reach out to grab her.

"I hope you believe me when I say I do not mean to hurt you," Ares said, making Sarra still with uncertainty. *Why should I believe him?*

She felt as if the blind man's eyes followed her, despite the silk that covered them. Sarra tossed another glance in his direction, noting his face turned to track her movement.

"I did not mean to harm any of these people."

"You would not try to save them if you meant to harm them," she replied, voice trembling. "If your words are genuine, sending messengers to my father is proof enough of that."

Sarra stopped moving, and she cleared her throat, the fear clutching it subsiding. She stood tall, her back straightening in an attempt to restore her confidence. The expressions on the statues around her would haunt her dreams if she slept, but Sarra refused to reveal her unease to the man in the center of the room.

"There is no saving these people," he muttered, his voice sounding distant. "They are ghosts left to haunt me for my mistakes. But there are some who still live, who should live on, in the city outside the palace."

Her spirit darkened with the grim indication of his words, a sense of sorrow and mourning filling her chest as she thought of the statues before they had turned to stone. However, the more she thought, the more Sarra desired to learn of the Serpent Lord and his tale. "You give me more questions than answers, Ares, Lord of Ro'al."

"I will answer your questions. It is not my intent to keep secrets from you." The tone of his voice shifted, returning to its previous rumble, and Sarra saw his hand clench into a fist before it released and rested at his side.

"How did you do it?" she asked him quickly, not allowing him any time to recover as her barrage of questions began. "How could you possibly be the cause of your people turning to stone? Do you work magic? Are you a great, evil mage that went rogue? I did not know Ro'al existed until I arrived with those awful men."

Ares sighed, the sound barely audible in the open foyer. He looked pained at her questions, but he answered her. "When I was sixteen and the siege preventing our escape was young, I thought to reason with the leader of the orc horde. At the time, it was an elder orc—a warlock. He toyed with me during the negotiations. I was neither old nor wise enough to budge him, and I had nothing to offer that they could not take when we were starved."

He shook his head. "It was a bold misstep, the folly of youth, made against the advice of my elders. The orcs murdered my escorts and held me prisoner for three months, torturing me daily, feeding me nothing but scraps and the rats in my cage. The warlock came to me in time. He offered to release me, but for a price."

His lips pressed into a thin line. "I was too young and weak to ask what price he could possibly ask of a child left in prison to rot for months. I accepted without thought."

Ares sighed and rubbed his jaw. His cloak shifted along his shoulders.

"He did *something* to me, changed me, and then sent me on my way. When I returned to Ro'al, one look into my eyes caused . . ." He paused briefly, turning toward a statue nearby, and looked into the face of a screaming woman. "All of this."

Sarra's heart leaped into her throat, her breath catching before he continued.

She eyed the silk cloth over his eyes, unable to look away as her imagination unraveled into reality. Magic turned the people of Ro'al to stone, but the vessel that brought their doom blamed himself. He had been a boy, *a child*, and he had attempted to push the enemy away from his people. Her empathy swelled, nearly overflowing, as she recognized that if put in his situation, she would have done the exact same.

I love Olmalis more than I will ever love any man.

Her own words played like a melody in her head.

Ares lowered his shoulders, and Sarra cleared her thoughts to listen.

"I could not understand it at first. I ran from house to house, room to room throughout the castle looking for some-one who could help me."

He winced, as if reliving his memories in front of her. "Exactly as the warlock expected of me, I suppose. The price I paid was that I became a weapon. His weapon. Nearly two hundred turned to stone that day before I came to my wits and sealed myself in the castle. I did not open my eyes for a month. When my mind finally cleared, I began to try and make sense of it all. Our library is small, but we, fortunately, held old accounts of curses in a few reference books. I had been afflicted with the

Curse of the Basilisk, which, among other things, causes petrification of any living thing that looks into my eyes."

He gestured toward the dark material shrouding his vision.

"That cloth," she said pointedly. "Have you blinded yourself then? Or can you see me?"

"I have tried to blind myself." Ares shivered and the cracked leather of his gloves creaked as his fists clenched. "Multiple times in multiple ways. My eyes return or heal completely by daybreak."

His hands released slightly, but he angled his head away from her. "I can see you through it," he said softly. "It is for your protection, but it does not obscure my sight."

Sarra stepped back, uncertainty plaguing her as she gathered the skirt of her dress close. The firm smack of a statue against her shoulder made her pause, and Sarra hid a yelp by biting her lip hard.

From the beginning, the blind man had seen her. Clear as day, she had stood before him, questioning his competence in selecting a gown for her. He even assisted her with disrobing in the handmaid's room!

Her teeth pressed down harder on her bottom lip, remembering the graze of his words against her ear.

How stupid am I?

"You are too forthcoming with your tragedy. I am not certain that one should divulge so many answers to their captive, but I am grateful you are willing to entertain my inquiries." Sarra regarded him with a slight tilt of her head. Light streamed from the window behind him, and he glistened like a diamond, specks of dust floating in the air around him. The darkness suited the picture she painted. The brightness made him look too regal to fit her previous perceptions.

"Do you find it easier to feed me lies when I ask for them?

Or have I simply captivated you already?" She attempted a small, uncertain smile, her tease falling somewhat flat in the seriousness of her predicament. Her suspicions remained too great to let a jovial tone trickle into her voice, and what sounded casual in her thoughts was ushered into the space between them laced with subtle venom instead. "My charms astound even me if that is the case. I would have thought I would at least need a day or two to convince you that I am a good listener."

Something akin to a weary smile grew on his face, a faint upturn of the lip almost too minor to be noticed. "You may associate my willingness to share with you is because of your charms if you so choose. But as I have said, I bear no ill will to you, and I would not have imposed upon you had my need not been dire. I hope my openness is evidence of this."

Sarra wondered if he was just a madman. A man driven insane by the poverty that befell his people. That the statues were just pieces of art left behind when his people fled from the greenskins that assaulted them over the course of all these years. It explained his sadness. *What is a lord without people?* She felt his morosity, even as he stood so far from her, and perhaps it was his sadness that truly made her wonder. Still, her theory did not explain much else. The statues frozen in fear looked too real to be rocks chipped from stone.

Sarra lifted her chin. Ares lived a sad life, but she was not naive enough to think he would not try to play with her heart. She knew his words were an attempt to sway her, as if she were some dainty princess that could change her father's mind and convince him to spare the Serpent Lord.

However, something nagged at her, telling her to believe him.

"When my father does come, he will claim your head as penance for what you have done," she spat, but the venom laced in her words only aimed to sting him a little. "Still, I do not understand why you dragged me into this. Are you seeking revenge? Do you wish to kill my father and rule instead? How do you know that he received any of your messages?"

"I wish for neither of those things," Ares said as he lowered his blindfolded gaze back toward his feet. "And I know he received them because some of the messengers returned. Escaping Ro'al is difficult, but it is not impossible. My people are sick, and they are weak. They would not fare well if pushed into the wild without aid, and while I have kept the orc battalion at bay, I feel time is running out. I am desperate."

Sarra scowled, anger heating her body as it rushed through her. "So, you plan to lure my father here? To help you? If there is a horde of greenskins waiting along the edges of your city, he would need an army to infiltrate them and—"

"Exactly," Ares hissed. "I did not set the trap. I merely brought you into it, and now your father must trigger it to free you. *With his army.*"

Sarra had underestimated him. It became obvious as she sputtered, unable to coherently retort as she wished. His plan became clear to her like a bright beacon, shining light on the truths she had chosen to ignore. Ares, the Serpent Lord, *this very man* had sought help for his people in a manner that she respected. When traditional methods had failed him, he resorted to creativity, but most importantly, he thought not of himself.

She gaped, searching for words until she found them with a nod of her head. "For the lives of the people within your charge, if your own is what sacrifice must be made, it is an honorable one. It is also not a decision that most would come to easily, as most men, in my experience, are selfish."

They stood together in silence, a new connection forming between them. Two leaders who reigned responsibly over their charges, one destined to make the ultimate sacrifice. Sarra sobered with understanding, yet she struggled to keep her emotions controlled.

"It is an unfortunate direction," she said, returning to the conversation between them.

"May it speak to my sincerity," Ares muttered. "I will likely be dead within a week. You may retell the events which led to your capture through whatever lens you choose."

Ares did not seem to fear death, nor did he shy away from the subject. He knew the cost of his misdeed, just as well as Sarra did. The fact that he remained dedicated to his decisions proved enough to sway her opinion of him, more so than his story of woe.

She brushed her hair out of her face with her hand, securely tucking the strands behind her ear. "I choose not to wear glasses in the retelling of any story. My eyesight is not hindered in any way, not even by a cloth." Her brow arched. "Lenses do skew perception though. Are you certain you are not looking through a colored one yourself?"

Even as she chided him for his acceptance, she could not help looking around at the statues one last time. Each face stood out to her, the image of a living person that once loved and lost as she did. They had families who mourned them, lovers who remained brokenhearted in their absence, friends who missed their ideas and conversations. *Did they deserve their fate? Did the actions of their lord justify their ultimate sacrifice?*

Sarra inhaled deeply. "I need some air. A change of scenery might do me well."

"As I said, you are free to walk the grounds as you wish, although I am afraid I cannot accompany you," Ares said, drawing Sarra's gaze back to him.

"Why? Do you fear your people?"

"No, but I am a danger to them. They have no love for me. They will treat you less unkindly if they do not associate you with me."

Sarra drew her shoulders back, stiffening her spine. "Every human being deserves civility, even if they have wronged someone else, intentionally or otherwise, and as Lord of Ro'al, you only earn the respect that you command. I have not been beaten, bruised badly, or even starved. You have merely taken me on a journey far away from my home. However, that does not mean that I have enjoyed any of it," Sarra said with a huff. "Painting you in a different light does nothing for me."

He remained the enemy, the man who stole her from her home and tossed her into a world of uncertainty and fear. However, his actions did not warrant alterations in her tale. The truth spoke louder than lies, and when she returned home to her castle, the missing pieces would come to light.

Still, she questioned Ares and his resourcefulness. If only he had reached out to someone else, his life could have been spared. "If my father was unwilling to help, why did you not seek aid elsewhere?"

Ares sighed, resignation written on his face. "My father died trying to break the blockade when it first arrived. He was among the first, along with his court, who rode into battle. Not one of them returned. Our neighboring states were called to answer. Some brought the wrath of the orc horde down on themselves for recompense, and many of their villages were washed away in the green tide that followed. There was no one else. We waited as long as we could for assistance, but it never came. What else could we have done?"

How could he settle? How could he not fight harder? How could he not keep asking for help? Sarra clenched her fists, a feeling of helplessness inside her pushing her toward anger. "Ask again! *Demand it!*"

Her shouted words rang through the open room, echoing up into the ceiling. Sarra forcefully clenched her teeth when silence returned. Her desperation seeped into the air around her, her fists balled into her dress. Ares had remained calm as he told his story, only the hint of his sadness and guilt sparking on his face. He had resorted to betrayal and treason. His desperation clouded his judgment.

Why had no one else come to help him?

Sarra forced herself to relax, softening her posture, although her brows still knitted tightly together. With her eyes closed, she rubbed up and down the bridge of her nose as if the movement would ease some of her tension. "The decisions you made should never have been yours to make. Your people are as much to blame as you for how this played out. Why they allowed a child to direct them is beyond me."

Ares began to approach her, the sound of his footsteps stopping her hand and forcing her eyes open. He slowed after a few steps, leaving space between them. Though he appeared a gentle giant, it was clear he was not cowed by her regality. However, at the same time, Sarra saw the cracks in his shell begin to form.

"You were taken from your home, endangered, and dragged through the mud," he stated firmly. His jaw set as he paused, his lips thinning as he watched her. "They lost family members —loved ones, husbands, wives, children. All at my hand."

A creeping guilt lurked in the base of his tone, under a veneer of restrained calmness in his voice. "They have toiled in poisoned earth, working fingers to the bone, bled and suffered sickness, plague and famine, under my rule, because I could not set them free. Call me a villain or a noble, or even a human being if you want. I have no use for titles. But I have earned their hatred of me, and you may not pass judgment on them for it."

Ares turned away from her, and Sarra saw him clearer than she had ever seen anything before. Swallowed in his guilt, he would suffocate from it, and for a moment, she pitied him. That was the unfortunate thing about war. Sometimes, there were unnecessary casualties, and perhaps in a way, his eventual death would be one of those. Still, it did not give him the right to speak to her in such a manner.

Sarra snarled at Ares as he moved back into the room. "I may not?" she shouted. "Do you not know to whom you speak?"

She grasped the skirt of the dress and marched after him. "You are just a sad man wallowing in the sorrows of the actions you chose to take. You allow your people to hate you because you hate yourself, and what kind of leader would permit his people to see such weakness?"

Sarra grasped his arm, allowing her nails to grip harder in an attempt to dig into his skin with the force of her reach. Ares faced her, a hint of a green shimmer peeking from beneath his silk blindfold. "Do not give them grace because grace has not been earned by them. Despite the horrible experiences they've had in their lives, it was their duty to help you, and they just leave you to rot in this wretched place. You are not a god! You do not control fate, fortune, or good luck, and you are only as strong as the people who support you. Your unfortunate circumstances were caused by a combination of shortcomings, and yes, while you are the absolute worst lord I have ever met, it is not only your burden to bear.

"And now you will die because of them. Or for them, whichever allows you to sleep easier at night, I suppose." She dropped her hand again and took a step back. "You have kidnapped a princess, committed treason against a king, and at the end of the day, who is to say my father will not just punish them all? Who is to even say that my father will come for me?"

Sarra backed away a few more steps. "How would it feel to discover that your last attempt failed? Would you continue to give up on your people?"

Ares bared his teeth for a mere second, and had Sarra not watched him, she would have missed it. His tone deepened, frustration laced every word he spoke. "I have only two things I can give them—grace and death. Would you have me abandon them, as your father has, for their faults? Write them off and leave them to their fate because of past mistakes? I can survive beyond the walls. I could be gone within an hour. I would be no less monstrous for doing so than the king, for I have surely given enough of myself to them." Ares shook his head. "I have never given up on them. I may be a terrible lord, but these people need me whether they revile me or not. And, unlike your father, I could not live with myself if I consigned them to the reaper.

"And your father will come for you," he continued, turning his head away from her. "He must secure his bloodline, and it is well known how he cherishes you." His expression grew thin, some level of optimism returning to his tone. "He could not be so merciless as to punish those who knew nothing about your capture, and I would hope you could not be so merciless as to allow him to do so."

The flames of anger licked at her own self-control. One moment, Sarra stood as the image of pristine royalty, the next she threatened to devolve into pointing fingers of blame.

She did not trust Ares. He had ripped her from her safe pedestal without remorse. The Serpent Lord had not only placed her into a precariously dangerous situation, but he had completely ruined the vision she had built for herself. No one would ever see her as a strong leader. Instead, she would remain Princess Sarra, the girl that was kidnapped and had to be saved by her father because she couldn't save herself.

"You sound so certain. I will remind you that my father is not an idiot, and there is a reason he has not sought to help you. I would not hold my breath if I were you." She crossed her arms, turning her head away. "As far as I am concerned, I would also not count on my personal assistance to help you achieve any of your goals. You are, effectively, my enemy, regardless of how you like to see yourself. You have not given one thought about what this means for me or for all of us when I step into my father's role."

Sarra brushed yet another stray strand of hair out of her face and once more attempted to tuck it behind her ear. "You are the lord of your people, and by default, you represent them. Your actions speak for them, especially on a grand level such as this. You might think that what you have done will not paint them guilty, but I beg to differ. Innocents do not deserve to die, but you have written their fates in blood. You have abandoned them and left their lives in the hands of others, a risky gesture if you were to ask me. Perhaps they will be spared, perhaps they will not. It is not my decision to make in this matter."

She tried to pass herself off as cold and heartless, but deep down, Sarra knew she could not watch these people suffer. The only one that deserved to die was the man standing before her, and that was the fate he chose for himself when he decided treason was the only way of earning attention. "Regardless, I am afraid that we shall likely always disagree on, well, most things, and as much as I am entertained by this story of self-pity you have expertly woven for me, I would much prefer to get some fresh air."

Ares rubbed the back of his neck, avoiding her eyes. "You

are entitled to your hatred of me, Princess, and I will nonetheless pray to the gods for you to never find yourself in a situation that makes you understand why I had to do what I have done."

Sarra collected her skirts and lifted her chin. She brushed past Ares, heading toward the large doors that led outside. "Leave a torch lit for me by the doors. I will find my own way back to my room when I am ready."

When she finally stepped into the cool air outside the palace, it did little to dampen her anger.

CHAPTER 6

THE WIND SWEPT LOOSE TANGLES OF DAMP HAIR INTO her eyes. Sarra fought to push them out of the way. She stood on a worn, broken road made of stone, sharp edges jutting from the ground when she stepped away from the palace. Looking across the expanse of land in front of her, ambient despair amplified her anger.

The gray city of Ro'al.

Sarra would never forget the way it haunted her.

Nothing about the dismal beauty of the city escaped her, and despite its colorless sheen, it had obviously prospered once upon a time. Its past successes shone in the sparkle of the partially standing buildings. Strong, sturdy foundations rose from the mud and grime of the weathered streets, and what remained of the structures proved Ro'al held mineral wealth. Perhaps it had once functioned as an epicenter of trade.

Behind the palace, mountains stood guard. They protected the city like strong warriors, their peaks weapons that scared the orc invaders away. A large wall surrounded the city.

Made of stone, piles of rubble from fallen buildings reinforced its weaknesses, and Sarra felt immensely grateful it had held on for so long.

The tired, sickly people lived in shanties with tarps of animal hide draped over rotten slabs of wood in an effort to keep the elements at bay. The ground appeared dull and sickly, and small farm plots were scattered throughout the city on whatever land was available. Sarra weaved around them as she descended from the palace, noting deformities in the crops that grew. Root vegetables were covered with knots and dark, bruised spots. Withered grapes grew from pale vines. Nothing appeared hearty, crisp, or healthy.

The citizens looked oddly at her as she wandered past them. Sarra marveled at the destitution, lost in the various trinkets and contraptions assisting the people with their daily tasks. She spotted objects of immense value functioning more like commodities than luxuries. A beautiful golden chain belt morphed into a repurposed bucket handle. Crude, dirty cloth patched silk gowns and trousers. Metal goblets became tools, and books fueled small fires. Her face twisted in wonder. Sarra had never seen poverty to this degree before.

Olmalis flaunted wealth. In the center of a caldera, the mineral enriched land of her home province produced vast crops, and fresh water came to them in plentiful amounts from a lake that was rumored to have no bottom. Streams trickled from the tops of the snowy mountains that protected her castle. The dormant volcanoes sleeping in the caldera seldom rumbled a threat. No foe dared test their luck with the natural fortifications of Olmalis.

Until the Serpent Lord.

Her nose wrinkled. It had been so easy for his ruffians to steal her.

Sarra pushed toward the giant wall, reflecting on the poverty and suffering within Ro'al. She had never witnessed either to such a degree before, and as she muttered to herself, she argued against the desire to forgive Ares for the state of his city. Every twist and turn through the streets fueled her fury, overriding the impact his tragic tale had on her and fueling her outrage. It was no wonder her father had never mentioned Ro'al. The city ruined every image of prosperity the king strived for. It was a disgraceful blemish upon the entire kingdom!

Sarra refused to believe her father had ignored requests for aid. She rejected the idea that no other province could offer the level of assistance needed to quell the orc horde. It remained a mystery to her why the greenskins targeted Ro'al. Perhaps the greenskins did not even exist to begin with!

The closer Sarra stomped toward the wall, the more her frustration grew. Her fingers dug into the material of her dress, tugging it from under her feet with a muttered curse. More citizens watched her, their brows furrowed as she scowled unintentionally toward them. Sarra approached a set of stone steps that led toward the flat top of the wall, and without thinking, she opted to climb them to prove her newest theories correct.

Ares is a liar. Surely, he only wants to steal Father's crown.

Finding her way up the first set of stairs, she heard shouts behind her, but she ignored them. Her theories circled in her head, wrapping Sarra in a thousand different distractions as she continued to take the steps nearly two at a time. Under her breath, she spat more curses toward the Serpent Lord.

I could walk out of this city without consequence. There is no real danger here. I have yet to see an orc!

She reached the top of the staircase with her eyes cast down at her feet. The last step crumbled under the pressure of her weight. Sarra yelped, jumping onto the flat platform before she fell. As she collected herself, she smoothed out her dress and turned to look out over the open expanse before her.

Sarra abruptly stopped. A loud cry tore from her lips.

Gray swampland removed any resemblance to her own province. Trees stood in the distance, nearly ten to twenty furlongs away, the only sign of a normal, less barren landscape as they swayed along with the wind wafting through their leaves. Everything between them and the wall lacked intensity, and she almost overlooked the hulking shapes driven into the mud beneath her. Sarra pressed against the stone wall, taking a closer look over the edge.

There was no mistaking it. The aftermath of Ares's curse was before her.

Her eyes widened, and Sarra stepped back. Within the palace, the statues of petrified humans totaled many, but what rested in the sinking wasteland outside of Ro'al was inconceivable. Snarling orc faces with tusks and bone piercings froze in various directions, forever petrified and lifeless. Sarra reconsidered. Perhaps the greenskins did exist after all.

A heavy hand pulled her farther back from the ledge.

"You shouldn't stand so close," a gruff voice said. Sarra's gaze snapped up from the statues in the bog. A young man stood beside her, and an older woman next to him nodded her agreement. He moved forward, looking then pointing down toward a barrier a few feet from the wall. Arrows and spears jutted from the mortar. Sarra swallowed hard.

"Never know what will come your way if they catch sight of you. You are a bit hard to miss in that color." The man motioned toward a group of people standing at the base of the stairs. "The lot of us assumed you were not from around here."

Sarra shook her head.

He extended his hand to her, which she grasped firmly as

he escorted her down the wall to the ground below. He smiled warmly, and his brown hair rustled in the wind. Kindness shone in his amber colored eyes, and just like the others in Ro'al, he looked unhealthy and malnourished.

"I am Erol." He gestured to the woman that followed behind them. "And this is Rowena. She does not say much these days, but she is the closest thing to a mother I have anymore."

Erol turned toward the palace. "My ma is in there, nothing but a stone statue, no thanks to the monster that lives there."

Sarra sucked a sharp breath between her teeth. "Yes. I know of him. Unfortunately."

She glanced behind her, looking at the wall. "I am terribly sorry about your mother. It is a worse death than, well . . ."

Sarra shivered, the meaning of her unspoken words clear.

"Where are you from?" Erol asked. "You do not sound like the rest of us. Your accent is a bit proper for being from Ro'al, especially now that there really is not a Ro'al."

He shrugged and gestured toward her with his hand. "I am surprised that someone such as yourself has made it through the barricade intact. I have only heard of one man making it through alive, and no offense, love, but you don't look like you are capable of taking on one orc, let alone hundreds."

Sarra's cheeks burned, but she raised her chin proudly. "You have yet to see me with a sword, Erol."

"You know how to hold a sword?" Erol grinned at her and gave her a short bow. "Well then, lady, perhaps we shall find you one and you can be our savior."

She returned his smile, and Erol motioned for her to follow him, walking toward the crowd.

"That lord of yours. Is he always so . . ."

"So much of a bastard?" Erol interjected. "Yes, and worse too."

"He kidnapped me, you know. Took me away from my home and somehow smuggled me in here."

"Is that right?" Erol grasped her hand, giving it a reassuring squeeze. "Well, you have a place to sleep and food to eat should you need it. We might not look like much, but you are entertaining and rather pretty, I must admit." He gave her a toothy grin. "For a proper foreigner."

With a scratch to his head, Erol regarded her for a long moment. "But I do not know why he would want you. Unless it was to marry you, I suppose, but that seems like a far reach considering he does not leave the palace."

Sarra frowned. "It is not me that he wanted, but my father instead. Olmalis is so far that I do not suspect your lord will get what he wants, at least not for some time."

"Olmalis? From the king's land?" Erol squinted, sizing her up. Rowena jabbed him with her elbow, pointing at Sarra with a scowl.

Sarra gave the woman a perplexed look before shaking her head. "Yes, from Olmalis. I suppose your lord thought it was the best idea to antagonize my father causing him to bring his armies. You would think if one were intelligent enough, one would not want to face the wrath of the king."

Her eyes lifted. The looks on all of the faces around her spoke volumes louder than the hushed whispers passing between them.

The king.

Sarra had made a mistake.

Erol's expression fell. His brow creased, and a slight lift curled his twitching upper lip. He ripped his hand from hers, staggering back a few steps as disdain etched into his weathered face. Murmurs burned through the crowd like wildfire.

"You," he growled. "You are the king's daughter?"

A fresh cry of derision rose from the crowd, the people moving closer toward her.

Erol snarled, hate in his eyes unlike any that Sarra had ever seen. "He left us for dead! He ignored our treaties and left us for dead!"

Everything changed in a second.

Slowly more of the denizens of Ro'al emerged from their meager shelters, scowling, and quickly joining the new confrontation. They gave her no mercy and jeered at her with vigor.

Erol's hand grabbed her again, but this time by the shoulder. He squeezed her tightly, pressing his fingers into her until Sarra whimpered and attempted to pull away.

"I lost my ma because your family left us here to rot," he cried. "My father! My brothers! I cannot even remember a time I was not trapped in these walls because of you people!"

The chanting grew louder around her.

"We have all lost family!"

"We have all suffered!"

"Toss her over the wall!"

"Kill her!"

A dull roar erupted, the mob thirsting for violence.

Unexpectedly, Erol's free hand whipped across her face. The loud slap momentarily stunned the crowd before the assembly erupted in cheers. Sarra clutched her cheek, bending at the waist as the sting burned along her skin.

"Stop! Please!" she pleaded, fear rushing through her, but Erol spat on her instead.

"I wonder how your father will feel when he loses someone!"

Hands from all directions grabbed at Sarra. Several held onto the fabric of her dress, tearing at it with dirty fingernails and scratching her skin. Two different men grabbed her by the hair, dragging her roughly to her knees. Even Rowena, sweet looking and kind before, kicked Sarra's legs roughly.

Between the pain from the hands holding her and the fingers threatening to rip her hair from the roots and her cries drowned in the chaos, the princess fell to the ground without grace. Resisting her attackers became impossible, with their mob mentality and their hatred of the king driving them to react in such a horrifying way. Weakly, Sarra accepted her fate. Perhaps she was meant to die at their hands as repayment for the actions of her father.

"Enough!"

A loud voice boomed, ringing like a shock wave. It carried a weight that halted the angry mob, sending those assaulting her scuttling backward with looks of fright. All hands released Sarra, and the people fled from her, moving several steps away.

The crowd parted as she looked up, revealing Ares in their midst. He approached her with his hand resting in warning on the cloth covering his eyes. His cloak, draped over his shoulders, rippled in the wind.

"Back," he growled to his people, moving closer to her. Sarra watched him intently, still trembling with fear as the ground dirtied her knees. "Stay your hands. This woman has done nothing to harm you."

"The king! The king is her father and he—" Erol started.

"She is not her father!" Ares thundered, kneeling beside Sarra, pulling her under his cloak. He moved his arm slowly around her waist, hoisting her up into his arms. Her body shook as he touched her. She avoided meeting his gaze.

I am a princess! I must show strength!

Even if she felt none of it inside of her, showing resilience was her duty, but tears rose beneath her swollen eyelids. She hid her face with her hands, refusing to allow anyone to see her cry.

With the touch of her fingertips along her cheek, she noticed it tingled to the bone with her injury, and she bit back a sob as she imagined what she must look like. Her reception by the people of Ro'al was a nightmare. Forgetting it was out of the question.

"You nobles are all the same!" someone in the crowd screamed. A stone hit the back of Ares's shoulder.

"Burn them both!"

"Throw them over the wall!"

"Kill him too!"

More rocks pelted his cloak, falling all around them like a barrage of arrows. Sarra cried out in pain as one hit her above the eye.

"I said back!" Ares roared, tearing the blindfold from his eyes. The people wailed in horror, frantically turning away from them. Sarra glanced up, hesitantly tracing along Ares's face to see he kept his eyes clenched firmly shut. However, he had made his threat, and the people recoiled toward their hovels.

Ares coaxed her further into his cloak, his touch gentler than the ones she had endured from his people. Sarra huddled in close. Stones and rotten vegetables continued to assault them as he carried her back toward the palace.

He never opened his eyes, not even when a brick caught the side of his face. The people grew bolder, tossing small tools and whatever else they found as the palace loomed nearer. Ares never retaliated. He only stumbled with a soft hiss from the impact, and he kept his hold on her secure.

When the heavy door closed, and they stood in the large foyer of the palace, Sarra understood her ability to wander freely outside the palace had disappeared. Ares and the statues of his people were to become her only company because Ro'al was unsafe now that the citizens knew her identity. However, after her experience outside the thick walls of the palace, she preferred it this way. Being attacked for who her father was deterred Sarra from wishing to explore Ro'al personally.

Ares lowered her to the ground, carefully placing her on the worn, luxurious carpet. Her body continued to shake, eyes squeezing shut as the roar in her ears grew louder now that the screams of the people had faded. She heard the beating of her heart thrum over and over as she sank to her knees, defeated.

"Are you hurt?" her savior asked. A soft touch found her shoulder, and Sarra opened her eyes. Ares replaced his blindfold, and he looked her over, ensuring she was in good health and not seriously harmed. A steady trickle of a dark, blueish green liquid dripped from a gash in his forehead over the cloth.

Sarra could not answer his question. She had barely processed what happened.

Am I hurt?

Physically, she ached, but the damage looked worse than it truly was. Bruises would heal in a few days. Perhaps she would retain a scar or two from the deep gash the rock had given her above her eye. Her limbs still functioned normally. No broken bones. Only her muscles remained stiff and battered.

Emotionally, Sarra crumbled.

The sting of the tears she hid burned to the brink of falling. Her bottom lip quivered. She turned her back to Ares in an effort to preserve her dignity.

"Can you stand?" The gentleness from him broke the dam. Fear, sadness, and rage trickled down her cheeks in large droplets.

"Do not look at me!" she shouted, ignoring his question. Sarra used her dirty, tattered dress to wipe her tears away. She sobbed into the cloth ends, pressing the cotton to her face to hide her reddened eyes.

Her entire life had been turned upside down in only a

WREN MURPHY

matter of days. She took an unexpected beating at the hands of her subjects in a city she never knew existed. She thought herself kind, just, and well loved, but in Ro'al, she was seen as awful and rotten to the people as the hated man next to her.

"One slip of my tongue and I am treated like a monster. Like I am no better than an animal. As if I am just as horrible as an orc." The sounds of her despair echoed in the room, witnessed only by the statues and Ares. Sarra's shoulders shook, each anguished cry ripping from her harder than the last.

She turned her face to the side. "You sacrificed your life for miscreants such as those? Do they even deserve it?"

Ares unhooked his cloak, and with his head turned aside, he placed the heavy cloth over her shoulders.

"It was wrong of them to treat you so," he said calmly. "They have been caged far too long, and it has made them like animals in many ways. There is good in them, but they are distrustful and quick to anger. They are like a pack of wolves, more than they are men at times."

Sarra gripped the edges of the cloak, wrapping it around herself like a blanket. She shifted, drawing her knees into her chest. Her sobs continued, although they quieted into small, wounded sounds.

Sarra knew she was sheltered and withdrawn from the harmful ways of men, certainly a ploy by her father to protect her from the cruelty of the world. Her castle had always been her safe place, and she had never experienced negativity in such a demeaning way before. Ro'al began to change her views of the world, its darkness infiltrating and dampening the pristine image of herself in her mind. In the lightless halls of the palace, Sarra slowly sank into the realization that her vision of life was naive, that perhaps she was not as loved by all of her people as she had always thought.

74

"I am sorry," Ares whispered.

"You are sorry?" Sarra choked. She lifted her head up slightly, just enough so her words were not muffled behind the cloak. "Sorry for what? Ruining everything?"

Turning herself around, she wiped her wet nose with the sleeve of her gown, and her green eyes winced with pain, burning from her tears. Her cheekbone ached as she ran her fingers over it. A few odd scratches and scrapes marred various places on her body, making her lips quiver as she noted them while looking over her arms and legs.

"I have done nothing to deserve this. Nothing! After this display, how could I even begin to hope that your people get the assistance they need? They are heartless, selfish fiends that would dare to hit a lady. Perhaps this is just fate's way of giving them the rewards they deserve. Good people would not harm the daughter of their king."

Sarra turned away, curling back into herself. Her harsh words felt foreign and cruel. As soon as she said them, she knew they were unlike her. In Olmalis, Sarra was the champion for the poor and downtrodden, always standing up for equality and fairness when the opportunity presented itself. Damning the men and women of Ro'al because of their mistreatment of her was wrong, even though her blood boiled from their assault. With a deep breath, Sarra reminded herself of their suffering, and although their actions were harsh, she knew she spoke more out of fear than indignation.

Ares remained on his knees next to her.

She wanted comfort, yearned for it, but received nothing. She missed home.

After a long moment of reflection, Sarra tried to climb to her feet, but her legs and her hands trembled so much she was not steady enough to do so. The lingering effects of adrenaline coursed through her, and she reluctantly sat back on her rear.

Her attempt to stand did not go unnoticed. Ares extended his arms to catch her if she fell, but he withdrew once she settled again.

"Your head," Sarra said as she fidgeted with the edges of the cloak. "You have something on it, above your brow."

She furrowed her brow. "You turn people to stone with a look. Your people are disrespectful and rude, and yet, you readily give up your life to save them without hesitation. You abduct a princess, and now, there is something upon your face that looks as thick as blood but is the wrong color."

She wrinkled her nose, peering at him. "Are you part troll? Or are you just that unfortunate of a man?"

At her prompting, Ares lifted a hand to his head, his fingers grazing the gash. He winced then chuckled at her questions. With a quick swipe, he rubbed the blue ooze off his fingers onto the cloth of his shirt.

"Another manifestation of my curse," he replied. "My body is about the only thing I kept from my past life. Very nearly everything else is different. It will heal quickly. Basilisks, I ascertain, are very sturdy creatures, though I would say that is the most generous of their traits. They seem like miserable beasts otherwise."

"So, unfortunate it is," Sarra said with a sudden tiredness in her voice. Her eyes drooped with fatigue. Her injured cheek felt tender with every word she spoke. She pressed her hands against her face with a sigh. The Serpent Lord would not hurt her. He even seemed amused by her. "I learn something new about you every minute. You do not have red blood and you are sturdy, but miserable."

Ares smirked. "There is very much to learn, and almost all

76

of it worthless. You would be forgiven for having glossed over your lessons on nearly extinct magical fauna were it not for this exact situation."

Sarra's lips lifted into a smile. She attempted to hide herself a little more, unwilling to allow him to see the shift in her mood with their shared humor.

I am too tired to care.

"It has been a long few days," she muttered, lowering farther onto the carpet, and curling into a bundle of material on the floor. The warmth of Ares's cloak kept her comfortable, even on the chilled floor beneath her. "I am not confident that I can walk."

Her eyes drooped despite her efforts to keep them open, and Sarra rubbed at them with her hand.

"My head throbs where those beggars pulled my hair, and if there was anything to smile about, I know it would hurt," she muttered. With a yawn, she tugged the makeshift blanket tighter. "I shall just stay here. Right here, wrapped in this tattered cloak and surrounded by terrifying, stony figures until I can move again."

"What kind of host would I be to let you fall asleep on the floor of the foyer, milady?" Ares asked, an airy, regal tone infiltrating his voice. "I may be a loathsome, sturdy, kidnapping monstrosity, but I am not without my civility."

He shifted toward her, one hand finding its way below her knees beneath the cloak, the other moving to support her shoulders.

"There is no need for you to lie on stone," he said gently, rising to his feet. Ares lifted her off the floor, carrying her into the darkened halls of the palace.

CHAPTER 7

"**Y**OU ARE A FASCINATING ENIGMA FOR A KIDNAPPER,"
Sarra said with her arms looped around his neck
as he carried her through a blackened corridor.
Slowly, she began to relax, finding comfort in the firmness of his
chest. She curled a little farther into him with each step he took,
closing her eyes with a soft sigh. "Loathsome, sturdy, unfortunate,
miserable. I am still not entirely convinced you are not part troll.
Now you say that you are a civil man. These are not qualities I
often find placed together."

Her lips lifted into a small smile, her words whispered gently as she spoke. "Dare I venture the thought of adding more to
your characteristics?"

Chivalrous. Honorable.

The words swam in her mind, over and over, as she considered Ares. It would be easy for him to manhandle her in any
way he chose. Her vulnerability amplified with her fatigue, and
the glimpse she had stolen of him in the boiler room spoke of
the power he commanded. He carried her as if she were as light

as a feather. Her weight hindered him not in any way. She wondered if he would attempt to touch her in an untoward manner.

"You do not behave the way a kidnapper is meant to," Sarra said softly.

Ares looked straight ahead, his lips forming an easy grin. "Oh? And how many kidnappers have you met?"

No, Sarra decided. He would keep his hands to himself. "Only one," she laughed, then grimaced at the pain it caused.

They continued in warm silence, winding through the corridors as Ares carried her to her makeshift bedroom. The statues of his people stood as grim reminders, but Sarra did not focus on them. Instead, she wondered about Ares and the path that led him to his decisions. She blamed her father. *How could my father be so cruel as to torture this poor lord and his unfortunate people?* It went against all of her teachings. Everything Sarra knew shattered with falsehoods and lies. The throbbing of her scalp worsened.

"Ouch," she hissed, pressing a hand to her forehead. Ares lowered his head, the scruff of his beard rubbing slightly against her hair.

"Are you all right?" His grip tightened, holding her more securely.

"My head is sore. That is all."

"Rest will help. You will feel better after you sleep."

Sarra believed him. Her cheek pressed into the soft cloak.

Light flickered under the door as they approached. Ares pushed it open with the toe of his boot, making it creak into the quietness of the palace. He carried her toward the ornate bed and placed her on the plush bedding among several pillows. As he reached for a blanket, he seemed to reconsider. His fingers paused above the cloth, and he withdrew.

"If it pleases you, I will fetch you more clothes now that I know what will fit you," he said. Sarra shifted, drawing up to her elbows. Her hand yearned to reach for him, the word "wait" on the tip of her tongue as feelings of panic and fear sped up her heart.

Ares took a step back, but hesitated to retreat further. "Unless you are afraid to be alone."

"I am not afraid," Sarra said adamantly, attempting to convince herself of the lie. Her eyes exposed her anxiety, and they darted from him to the door. "But you never answered my question, Lord of Ro'al. Do you not have enough manners to finish a conversation with a lady? Did no one teach you proper etiquette? I want to know."

He arched a brow, the thin shape lifting over his blindfold as he pursed his lips thoughtfully. "What do you want to know? If I have manners? Or does something else bother you?"

Ares slowly walked toward a vanity next to the bed. A small, plush chair perched in front of it.

"What other qualities should I add to your growing list? I said you are a fascinating enigma for a kidnapper. I could not care less if you have manners." Sarra grimaced, easing herself into the cloak and pillows behind her.

"I fear there is little of any import beyond what you already know." He grabbed the chair and moved it toward the edge of the bed. He took his seat, facing the door directly, never turning his head to meet hers.

"My blood runs cold," he said, removing his gloves from his hands. He placed them over his thighs and clasped his fingers together. Sarra watched him, even as her eyelids grew heavy.

"Your blood is not warm?"

"No," he said with a shake of his head. "I also cannot eat." Ares winced. "Well, that is not entirely true. Any food that passes my lips turns to ash. Most of my nourishment comes from the sun. So, as my people wither and fade, I remain healthy. Though, if I am honest, my hunger can never be sated."

Sarra gnawed her lip, her curiosity ruling her thoughts. "What of your sight? You were able to walk through your city with your eyes closed the entire time. You did not even stumble."

He gestured toward his blindfold. "I can see without my eyes, in a manner. I can feel the space around me, sense heat and bodies, heartbeats."

Sarra lifted her head in surprise, a red tint shading her cheeks. If he knew of her embarrassment, he stayed quiet. "But I can also see through the cloth, though not well."

He shifted uncomfortably in his seat. "Was this what you intended? Or did you not mean to hear more about my curse?"

"Hearing about your curse is fine, although I was more curious about you. Who you are, how you have lived all of these years in solitude. Do you not grow lonely here?" Sarra scooted toward the edge of the bed and extended her hand toward him. "I want to feel for myself. Do you have scales too or is that not part of it?"

As if by reflex, Ares drew his hands away, though he quickly stopped and held one out toward her. Sarra watched his face carefully, searching for signs of discomfort as her warm skin caressed his cool palm. He was not icy or slimy or waxy like a dead thing, just cool, perhaps even soothing. Her soft fingers traced over his rough skin. His hands felt calloused and worn, but his grip remained strong. She wondered what they were capable of. *Would he be a different man if he had never been cursed?*

"No scales, to speak of," he answered. His cheeks darkened with color, and Sarra quickly withdrew. Her own face mimicked his, flushing as she settled back into the bed.

"It does grow lonely here," Ares said after he cleared his throat. He replaced his hand on his lap, far out of her reach.

"There's not much to be done for it, though. I am a danger to anyone I am around, including you. It is better this way."

"A danger? Ha!" Sarra confidently laughed. "You only say that because your advantage is far greater than mine. Turning people into statues with just a glance is almost cheating."

"I certainly wasn't trying to compete with you. You can be the deadlier of the two of us; I relinquish the title."

After a brief chuckle, they fell into an awkward silence, and Sarra looked down at the cloak, her fingers playing with the tattered edge. She opened her mouth to speak again, but Ares acted first, clearing his throat.

"If you think turning people to stone is an advantage, perhaps I should not tell you that I have read through most of our library as well. There is not much to do during the day other than read, so I have learned a lot through literature. I have also taught myself to play two instruments in my spare time. I do not know any songs to speak of, though, so I would not call that much of a skill."

His voice warmed when he spoke, drawing Sarra's interest. His claim of being well read surprised her. Reading an entire library, perhaps even more than once, how divine that must be! Sarra desired to know everything—what he had learned, how educated he was, his thoughts and feelings on the greatest publications of their time. Once reality settled in again, she stamped down those thoughts. She did not need to know him all that well. His death loomed near, only days away.

"I have never seen a basilisk before," Sarra admitted softly. "And I did not understand your statement about hunger. Perhaps you require a delicacy from another land or even something that lives in the sea?"

"Perhaps. I have not found any food yet that does not turn to ash on my tongue, and I have tried many things, but after a time I just gave up." He made a moue of disgust. "One can only choke on ash so many times before the hunger pangs just seem simpler to deal with."

Sarra frowned. "I like to believe that I have many answers. It is unfortunate that we had to meet under such dark circumstances."

"What of you?" Ares asked quickly, changing the topic of conversation, directing it away from himself. "I have heard stories about the Princess of Olmalis. That she is wise and just and lovely. That is how others speak of you. What characteristics do you use to define yourself?"

Sarra closed her eyes, her lips upturned, despite the quick spear of pain that shot down her cheekbone. "Wise, just, and lovely are merely terms used for flattery. I am not cruel. I am not horrid, and I find myself more of a humanitarian than most heirs to any title of importance. My people matter to me, but I have lived a most sheltered life that keeps me from truly understanding them."

She wrinkled her nose. *How much can I trust him?* Peeking at Ares, Sarra watched him carefully for a moment. If anyone could understand her, it was the man who risked his life for his people. Deciding to honestly answer his question, she sighed, lowering her gaze to stare at her hands. "If I were to describe myself, I would say I am, well, boring. Prim and proper, always following my father's rules, and rarely do I ever step out of line. Some would say I am well suited to be royal, but they do not know that I cut my hair despite my father's wishes. He would have it long and luxurious so that I stepped on it every time I walked, but I took a knife to it not long before your ruffians stole me from the castle. Being confined to such a mold becomes suffocating."

Sometimes, she wished for a different life, mainly on the days where shooting stars and dreams made more sense than the requirements given to her day to day, season to season. Her destiny had been thrust upon her, written by someone else on the day of her birth. She grew to accept that fate and the fact that she could not change her life regardless of how much she wanted to. Reality was cruel when she got to the bottom of it, but surprisingly, it did not sadden Sarra as it once had. She resigned herself to the pre-marked path. She settled. She grew complacent. Something sparked rebellion inside of her, though, and her father's demands of her pushed her to act out. No man would want her with hair like hers.

"Short hair suits you."

Surprised, Sarra stilled, feeling Ares's gaze upon her. Despite the thin fabric tied at his temple, she dared not look at him, fearful of turning into a statue like his unfortunate people. She did wonder about his eyes though. What color were they? If eyes were windows into one's soul, perhaps just one look would give her a glimpse into his.

Consciously, Sarra reached up to tug on the shorter strands of her hair. "If at least one person has those thoughts, then I suppose I will keep it. I have not grown comfortable with the drastic change, despite it still remaining about my shoulders. It is not usual to see my hair loose anyway."

She shivered, curling tighter into the cloak. A reassuring scent within the fabric wafted up. It smelled of cinnamon with the smooth touch of sandalwood and a hint of rose. Sarra found comfort in it, making her feel less afraid. The blanket sat untouched at the end of the bed, her body too exhausted to reach for it.

"Do you sleep, Ares? Do you dream and wonder to yourself if the life you are living is just that, a dream? That one day, you will wake up and it will all be over, as if it were just a nightmare?" Sarra tried her best to listen for his answer, but in moments, her own dreams overwrote the answers to her questions.

CHAPTER 8

H ER DREAMS HAD BEEN FILLED WITH VISIONS OF
Ares, and as Sarra woke, she swore he was nothing
but a figment. She knew when she opened her eyes,
she would see the familiar landscape of her royal chambers. Her
handmaidens would have her breakfast waiting. If she focused
enough, she could even taste the strong tartness of her morning
tea. The wind would caress her skin once her ladies opened the
window, and Sarra sighed with an easy smile at the potential
her day would bring.

Except when she opened her eyes, Sarra experienced none
of those things.

She rubbed at her face, still tired, and straightened herself.
Blankets fell into a pile around her waist, as her stomach rumbled loudly with hunger.

Blankets? She remembered a cloak, the same one the blind
man had put over her shoulders in the streets of the city.

No, not the blind man. His name is Ares.

Still, she did not remember covering herself with blankets.

Sarra brushed her hair out of her eyes, wincing when she touched a sore spot on her forehead. Then she saw him, sitting in the same spot, slouched in that uncomfortable looking chair as if he were a statue himself.

"You stayed," she said, her lips parted. Perhaps it was a ploy, some game he played in an attempt to convince her she should negotiate for his life when her father came. As if standing watch, protecting her from the dark halls and the horrid urchins who had accosted her was enough to get back into her good graces.

It was the smart thing to do. The wise thing to do.

However, her heart told her he did not act with such devious intent.

Ares smiled. "I did not want you to wake alone. I hope you have slept well. How do you feel?"

"Ravenous," she muttered, turning to look at the plate that still sat atop the end table. Sarra shifted, grabbing a small green apple. She looked it over before testing it with a small bite, the sour taste making her lips pucker. "But, yes, I did sleep well, thank you."

She kept the fact that she had dreamed of him to herself.

"Good. I am glad."

Sarra crunched the apple between her teeth, continuing to rub sleep from her eyes in silence as Ares moved from his seat.

"I can get you more fruit or meat or vegetables, if you prefer them," he offered, but Sarra shook her head, satisfied with what she held in her hand. He nodded.

Sarra paused, facing him with her lips lifted and her nose wrinkled. "Is it nighttime? I am afraid being your captive has my sense of time thrown off-balance."

"Yes, the sun disappeared hours ago. I stayed here. With you." Ares ran a hand through his hair, ruffling the golden strands with his fingers. "No villager has entered the palace in

86

over a decade, but it does not hurt to be cautious. I suppose we both must have dozed off. It is late."

An awkwardness fell between them, the only sound in the room was that of Sarra eating her apple. Ares cleared his throat, relieving an unspoken tension between them. "Do you wish to go back to sleep?"

Sarra shook her head. "I do not think I can sleep more. I am wide awake."

"I can take you deeper into the palace if you would like," Ares offered. "Or you can explore alone if you would prefer. I think you may find the library especially comfortable."

A quick spark of fear at wandering alone made her anxious, especially at the rogue thought of the citizens of Ro'al storming the castle in search of her. Sarra pressed a hand to her chest, feeling the rapid beating of her heart beneath her palm.

"Yes, the library. I can occupy my time with a book." She attempted to hide her fear behind her steady voice, grabbing a piece of bread from the plate. She looked at it, feigning interest when all she wanted was to hide under the blankets instead. Sarra took a deep, steadying breath and lifted her eyes to peer at him. "Are you positive it will be safe?"

His lip curled up gently, with a soft, somewhat rueful chuckle. "The people fear me far more than they despise you. They will not set foot within these walls. You have my word. It will be safe."

Sarra mulled over his words, at first questioning their validity. *He is the Serpent Lord, but has he done anything to harm me?* Besides stealing her from her castle, he had not lifted a hand against her. He had not attempted to advance upon her, or embarrass her, or manipulate her in any way. Sarra scrunched her nose, accepting that he told her the truth. The palace would be safe if she chose to explore with or without him. *After all, I am free to roam the grounds as I wish, am I not?*

Sarra returned the piece of bread to the plate. "You have read the whole library. Perhaps you can provide me with a recommendation."

"I can make several," Ares said, his smile warming as it stretched wide on his face. "We have volumes on the history of the surrounding regions, which are a bit of a dry read I am afraid. There are several works of fiction by local authors who never reached widespread renown. Some of them are actually quite good."

He extended his arm to her, and after a tense moment, Sarra accepted his gesture. She lifted herself out of the bed, using his arm as an anchor, and straightened her skirts once her feet found the floor.

"Then we have some books of sonnets and poetry, if that is more to your liking." Ares led her toward the door, opening it for her. "Tell me what interests you. I am confident I can supply something that you will enjoy."

"You know these books much better than I. As long as it is legible and in a language I understand, I am sure I will enjoy anything you give me."

Their conversation about his favorite volumes in the library flowed easily as Ares helped her navigate through the still dark corridors of the palace. Sarra smiled as he told her about the various books he enjoyed. He was not the man she expected when his hired mercenaries brought her within the walls of Ro'al. The picture she had painted of him in her head as she waited to meet him for the first time had been all wrong. He was not a beastly man with fangs for teeth and scales for skin. *Was Ares, Lord of Ro'al, actually a benevolent, mysterious man shrouded in devastation and darkness?*

Oddly, she thought about the what-ifs had their lives been different. Perhaps they might have been friends if he had not been cursed and she had welcomed him to her castle. She had half a mind to say as much as he led her further, but Sarra kept her thoughts to herself. They were foolish and inappropriate. Ares would forever be known as the man who abducted a princess. Girlish fantasies would never change that.

Her father would arrive soon anyway. She could only imagine what the king would say if he discovered the kindness she showed Ares. How deeply he would frown when he learned of the ideas she entertained. It was likely her genuine smiles and her slight enjoyment of the "rotten lord" would cause her to fall out of her father's good graces.

Sarra knew her reputation was at stake. Her people would perceive her as weak if she spared the life of the man that had abducted her, even if it was the right thing to do. She risked so much by showing Ares kindness, but after he saved her from his people, it could not be helped. Her thoughts sparked warm feelings, and Sarra knew she would find a way to argue for his life. Dying for kidnapping a princess was one thing but sacrificing himself for the people of Ro'al was everything. At least, to Sarra it was.

Quickly, she shoved those thoughts away, instead focusing on other questions burning on the tip of her tongue. "Do the orcs not frighten you?"

Her voice cut through a comfortable, short silence, and she clutched Ares's arm tighter. "Despite being cursed, I cannot imagine that you are invincible. Every man has a weakness, and if you can turn someone to stone with just a look, I would wager yours is significant."

His curse intrigued her, and her people whispered about magic like a taboo. She thought it nearly make believe herself, full of falsities like wishing upon stars, but Ares walked next to her, proof that it was real. No one spoke of magic openly unless it was with fear. Some respected it. Some claimed to know the secrets behind it, and Sarra wanted to know all of them. If his curse were an act of evil, she wondered what amount of good magic could create instead. Because everything in life functioned as a balance, she could not believe that magic was so one sided.

Is there no way to save him?

A light illuminated the hall in front of her as they rounded a corner, pouring from the bottom of a wooden door. Sarra looked up at Ares, eyes softening as they traced his regal outline. He directed her toward it with a gentle press of his hand.

"The orcs do not frighten me. My curse does work on them, though not with the same efficiency that it does with humans. It takes significantly longer to petrify an orc than a man. I am loath to call my sight an advantage, though it has benefited me in the past. Remember that it is the double edged sword that cuts those I loved as well as those I hate."

Ares reached for the door, opening it, and leading her inside. The brightness blinded her momentarily, but once her eyes adjusted, Sarra saw its source.

A single, beautiful point of light.

A small round stone about the size of a closed fist suspended in a freestanding metal sconce in the center of the room. The small orb effused a perfect, mute white light, creating soft shadows on everything it could not directly touch. Sarra moved toward it, her hand slowly reaching out to touch it. She glanced over her shoulder, silently asking Ares for permission to do so.

"It is a moonstone," he said with a wide grin. "Enchanted quartz. My father knew a powerful enchanter who died before I was born. My father aided him in his younger years, and this gift was given to him as the enchanter's thanks."

Sarra pulled her hand back as Ares stepped closer to the stone. He plucked the perfectly round orb from the sconce, placing it in her hands. "There are only a few in existence. It glows at night and provides a perfect reading light."

Sarra shuffled the smooth stone through her fingers, feeling as it hummed with energy at her touch. Her eyes never looked away, glued to its magnificence and rarity. It glistened better than any crown, shimmered more than any gem. It was magic, and she held it in the palm of her hand.

"My father kept it here because he loved to read late at night, undisturbed," Ares said, and Sarra looked up from the stone, blinking away her amazement at the sound of warmth in his voice. Her gaze turned toward him, and Ares's grin widened. With a broad gesture of his hands, he drew her attention around them.

"Welcome to the library."

Books covered every inch of space possible, including shelves built into the walls. Simple scrolls, leather bound manuscripts, even some clad in metal plates like armor decorated shelf after shelf. Stacks of them climbed toward the ceiling, towering like the large mountains behind the palace. The room reminded her of the bedroom she had woken in, but perhaps twice the size. While not overly large by any means, it held a comforting warmth with marble accents and a plush red rug in front of a fireplace. Atop the mantel hung a large portrait of a beautiful woman with hair the same shade as Ares's.

"Let me start a fire for you. It will keep you warm." Ares moved away from her, heading toward the fireplace. In moments, red, hot embers burned, and the wood sparked, snapping as flames licked the bark. The scent of parchment and ink mixed with smoke eased her fear as it reminded her of her own castle. Libraries always smelled the same, and Sarra breathed a heavy sigh.

She looked to Ares, but he moved, walking toward the shelves to pick through books. Sarra almost followed him, but something caught her eye as she shifted. Upon a central table-top near the sconce in the middle of the room, one especially worn tome called to her. She gnawed her lip, glancing at Ares before deciding to reach for the cover and skim the pages. A chair stood next to the desk, and Sarra pulled it back with ease, placing the moonstone beside her. She perched on the seat and leaned over the ragged book with wide eyes, tongue caught between her teeth.

"My father would lock the door to keep the servants, sometimes even my mother, from interrupting him. The lock still works, so feel free to use it. You will be quite safe in here until I return." Ares continued to scan the titles as he spoke, pulling one book from the shelf and returning it just as quickly. Sarra barely heard him, her attention glued to each page as she flipped them, one after the other, until an illustration of a large, strange serpentine beast glared at her from the parchment.

A basilisk.

Does this book hold the answers to the Serpent Lord's curse?

She traced the curves of the monster's snakelike body, pausing over the large horns protruding from its head and dipping down to the emerald eyes that gleamed in the bright light from the moonstone. Sarra tilted her head, drawing nearer as she attempted to get a better look at the picture. Her nose almost touched the page when its eyes narrowed and the serpent struck at her, forcing a strangled shout from her throat, and sending her backward in a loud crash toward the floor.

The chair clattered against the marble, but Sarra remained upright, practically floating in the air. Her breath came in short gasps, Ares gripping her under her arms. She pressed a hand to her chest, allowing herself a few moments to recover before she moved to stand. Once her feet returned to solid ground, a giggle bubbled out of her lips.

"Are you all right?" Ares asked, alarmed.

Sarra nodded, laughing harder.

"Yes. I am sleep deprived. I thought the book was going to eat me!" She covered her eyes with the sleeve of her dress, doing her best to wipe away the embarrassed burn in her cheeks. "The ruffians claimed you would have me for dinner, not the rabid books hidden away in the library."

Ares loosened his grip, arching his brow. He bent to retrieve the chair from the floor, leaving Sarra to grab for the book. She flipped it shut then tucked it under her arm.

"I think I will read this one," she said as Ares replaced the moonstone back into the sconce. "If you do not mind."

"You may," he replied softly, though the mood between them shifted, dampening. Sarra narrowed her eyes, noting that although his own remained covered by silk, Ares's face lowered pointedly toward the book. "Though I would not ask you to waste your time educating yourself on such obscure trivia. There is only one person I have ever heard of with the curse, and it will not be my burden for long."

The note hung sourly in the air between them. Ares turned away from her, moving toward the door.

"You may lock this behind me." Ares pointed to a key in the lock. "I will be away for several hours. There is a bedroll in the corner of the room if you wish to sleep."

"Where are you going? You do not seem to have many stately affairs to address."

"To hunt."

Sarra squeezed the book tighter to her side. The mysterious

basilisk remained a beast shrouded in the unknown, and she wondered just what similarities Ares shared with it. *Is it a fierce hunter? What prey does it seek? Ares mentioned food turned to ash on his tongue, but does he search for something to satiate his never-ending hunger anyway?*

"What are you hunting? More princesses to abduct?" She lifted her lips into a smirk, stepping forward to lean her hip against the desk as she gently teased him.

"No, I assure you, one princess is handful enough for my collection. I am hunting for meat. Deer mostly. A wild boar or two on occasion, although those do not stray so close to the city walls anymore. I also forage for berries and other useful plants." He turned to face her, rubbing the side of his face as if he already knew her next question.

"Why?"

He looked at her, thoughtful, with a slight crease in his brow. Sarra stood patiently, but her curiosity nearly suffocated her. Ares intrigued her. *What other details can I uncover about the ferocious man before me?*

"To provide for my people. They need nourishment, and there is not much growing inside the walls of the city." He sighed and dropped his hand to his side. "Originally, I tried to give them supplies directly after making it through the orc patrols. They threw it over the walls every time, thinking it was tainted in some way by me. I leave it on a small shrine these days. They have made up a god—Pateus, I believe—who provides them with sustenance and is responsible for the gifts I bring them."

A strange, warm feeling swelled inside of Sarra. She lowered her eyes, staring hard at the top of the desk in front of her, tracing the lines in the wood as if it could hold the emotion back. She peered up at Ares after a long moment, noting he watched her from the doorway.

"You do all of this for people that hate you?"

Ares nodded. "I do. Their circumstances are not the result of their misdeeds. They should not be forced to suffer any more than they have." He turned on his heel to face the thick door. "I will be back soon."

Before closing the door, Ares hesitated. "Please do not open the door for anyone but me. I do not anticipate that you will have company, but, still, it would be for the best."

"Yes," Sarra said softly, lost in her thoughts as he turned. "Thank you."

He left her alone in the library then, standing, booked tucked under her arm. Her thoughts began to spin a new, unexpected image of the Serpent Lord inside her head.

CHAPTER 9

FTER LOCKING THE DOOR AND REMOVING THE KEY, Sarra pressed her back against the wooden frame. Blowing a tuft of hair out of her eyes with a heavy sigh, she looked over the numerous shelves of books. Quietness enveloped the room. Ares's footsteps faded with each second that passed, but as fearful as Sarra was of being alone, the library invited her. No statues loomed in the sea of dusty tomes, and the furniture offered luxurious comfort. An odd familiarity made Sarra's shoulders relax. The warm glow from the moonstone highlighted the path to the dusty book on the desk. With purposeful footsteps, she carried herself back, settled in the chair, and reached for the book.

The book itself was a compendium of sorts, a bestiary of the creatures of yore that were thought to once roam the land. Sarra remembered stories of them from her childhood, noting that most of the creatures she skimmed over existed on purely speculative records or were hunted to extinction many moons ago. She returned to the basilisk, once again running her fingers over the serpentine drawing.

A heavy thump overhead drew her attention away from the thick pages. Sarra paused, listening intently for any other sounds indicating the cause of the jarring noise. The clatter echoed, again and again, as someone stomped across the ceiling. Blood rushed in her ears, and thoughts of the villagers overrode her rationality. The sound of a window opening moved her to stand. Instinctively, she ran to open the drapes on the far side of the room, opposite the door, and tugged the heavy cloth open. Moonlight cascaded through the glass panes of the tall window, stars twinkling brightly in the sky. The sudden appearance of a dark form zipping through the air made her breath hitch.

On a line made of rope, Ares took flight.

His cloak fluttered behind him as he descended from the palace toward the outer edge of the city. He hit the ground feet first, never losing his balance. Sarra watched as Ares made his way toward the wall, unable to draw herself away from the window. He paused at the top, looking out over the land beyond before he dropped over the edge. Sarra squinted, losing sight of him. She pulled back, searching for something to help enhance her vision. Finding a telescope placed nearby, she moved behind it to dial it into focus. She waited for several breaths, looking along the mire for signs of him to no avail.

He was gone.

However, as suddenly as he disappeared, bright flashes of green blinked in the darkness. Sarra gasped, using the telescope to watch the scene unfold before her.

A trio of orc scouts, although she suspected there had been a fourth, lumbered outside the city's stone wall. They stood an extra two heads taller than Ares himself, gruesome with limbs thick and broad like tree stumps sinking deep into the mud with each step they took. The hair on Sarra's arms stood at attention, the skin pebbling as unease ravaged her while she watched them trudge along.

Ares held an unsheathed dagger in his hand as he stalked closely behind the tailing scout. His foot slipped in the mud, and the massive creature whirled on him with a torch, a look of shock on its face as it cried out to the others. Sarra screamed aloud with alarm, grabbing the telescope firmly between her hands and pushing her eye against it hard enough to hurt.

Ares dove forward, knocking the torch from the orc's hand. He leaped up and drove the dagger deep into its neck. Sarra gasped as the wound spurted thick, tar-like blood, glistening black in the moonlight. Ares used the leverage from the dagger to pull himself up, planting a foot onto the orc's knee and throwing himself onto its monstrous body. He extracted the dagger and jammed it into the monster's skull. Its jaw slackened, eyes rolling back as it toppled over backward. Ares rode it straight down as it slammed to the ground, the body sinking immediately into the muck.

Sarra could not look away.

The remaining orcs turned, and Ares reached for a longsword nestled against his back. The closest orc swung his blade, which was nothing more than a sharpened sheet of metal. Ares parried it to the side and deflected it into the mud, burying it. As the orc struggled to retrieve the blade, Ares tugged on his blindfold, catching the scout's eyes in his own.

A strangled cry left Sarra's lips as the beast's face morphed with terror and stone crept over the horror-struck expression, turning the orc to solid rock. Sarra thought of his earlier words. *If orcs took longer to turn to stone, just how quickly did a human?*

Ares replaced the blindfold over his eyes as the final orc fled from him. He sheathed his sword, pulling a bow from his shoulder and nocking an arrow fluidly. The string pulled back, aimed carefully at the orc, and the arrow flew through the air into its shoulder. The orc never stopped running, disappearing into the night. Ares paused, appearing to catch his breath. He looked around before he, too, dashed off toward the tree line.

Sarra's breath shuddered in her chest as she stepped back from the telescope. Her mind swirled, fighting to understand the scene she had just watched. Ares had turned an orc to stone. Several of them, actually, because the numerous orc statues outside of the city walls stood as proof.

His curse was not his only weapon. His prowess with a blade surpassed her expectations. Ares appeared demure, unassuming, and reserved. Yet the sight of him driving a knife into the neck of an enemy made Sarra reconsider who she thought she dealt with.

Perhaps ruffians were right to speak of him in whispers.

Sarra shivered and wrapped her arms around herself as she moved toward the desk. His kindness toward her had masked the danger he posed. Sarra thought herself naive for assuming she was safe. Leaving the drapes open behind her, the princess allowed moonlight to mark the library as she returned to the book.

She found herself lost in thought as she flipped the thick pages. Her perception of her predicament had been all wrong. A new, fearful feeling directed at Ares flooded her, and Sarra narrowed her focus, turning the pages of the book with a new purpose instead of meandering in mere curiosity. Knowledge remained her greatest defense. She needed to know if there was anything she could do to protect herself.

As she read, Sarra discovered the bestiary held not only details of basilisks, but of curses like Ares's as well. The text focused on the basilisk's propensity to petrify any who looked into their eyes, adding in detail that those afflicted with serpentine curses often had the same ability. The book mentioned a handful of enchanted or powerful species that would not turn to stone when locking eyes with a basilisk, although other outcomes varied by creature. Some became blind, others mad, and even a few were completely unaffected. However, Sarra learned that humans and other humanoids remained the most susceptible to this magic.

She read a passage about phoenixes, a natural enemy of the basilisk, several times before she took a short break. The mythical birds were immune to petrification, but from her history lessons, she knew they had not been seen in Olmalis for an exceptionally long time. Even those documented records still in existence were based on speculation, and, as she recalled, the feathered beasts lived in enchanted forests alongside elves. As far as she knew, no magical forests or elves existed inside the borders of the kingdom, leading Sarra to believe the information penned inside of the book most likely came from a children's story or something of the like.

After a walk around the room to reorganize her thoughts, she returned to her task. The book continued to detail other traits of the basilisk and those with its curse. Cold blood coursed through their veins, rendering them cool to the touch, and the memory of Ares's hand proved as much. They avoided chilly habitats, the book mentioning the majority of those cursed actually died of hypothermia within their first year. Sarra began to consider the early fatality a kindness.

As with the snakelike creatures, she learned the skin of the afflicted toughened, but remained indistinguishable from human skin. The text specifically noted that cutting it with a blade became considerably difficult. Sarra also learned the afflicted person's vision was altered in a sense as well, allowing them to recognize body heat and heighten their senses to assess the physiology of prey more keenly. Ares could sense blood rushing throughout someone's body and any emotional reactions they had, much to Sarra's embarrassment.

Last, the book confirmed that the afflicted could no longer take sustenance from food, just as Ares had said. They survived on warmth and sunlight, their bodies able to turn those things into nourishment, not entirely unlike plant life. The curse granted the afflicted a long life, but the trade for this was that any food passing their lips would promptly turn to ash. To Sarra, this explained why Ares retained his good health while his people suffered and starved outside the palace.

The curse appeared to be quite detailed and unforgiving. Whoever caused Ares this level of suffering was especially ruthless.

Sarra flipped through the rest of the book, mulling over the bits she had learned. Toward the back, the pages turned more worn and well used, catching her notice. Some were ripped or bent, others faded from time. The fragile parchment softened under her fingertips, and as she neared almost the end, a drawing made her pause.

A horse stared at her, its mouth opened in an unheard neigh. It reared on its hind legs, front hooves in the air. A horn atop its head sparkled in the moonstone's light, glistening like a gem. The sight made Sarra's heart leap, and joy poured from the smile that spread her lips wide. For just a moment, she forgot about basilisks and men who turned people to stone.

A unicorn!

Just like every other little girl, Sarra had once dreamed of seeing one for herself, but as with the phoenix, the horned equine were nothing but fairy tales. Out of all the beasts said to have once roamed the land, the unicorn was supposedly the most magical. Stories spoke of their creation, some hypothesizing that they came from the very cosmos itself, alongside winged, lizardlike beasts called dragons. Vessels of the gods, unicorns gave other beings their magic, and seeing one was a sign of good fortune.

Sarra sighed dreamily, putting her chin in her hand as her elbow rested on the desk. If only they were real, she would simply find one to fix all of her problems.

With a sigh, she closed the book and stretched, her thoughts drifting back to Ares. She wondered if his hunting was successful and if he would come back soon. An inkling of concern popped into her mind, *would he come back at all?* But she shook it off quickly, reminding herself of the new addition to the stone orcs outside the wall.

As she sat back in her seat, Sarra wondered if Ares was someone to be afraid of. She leaned forward, her slender fingers quickly flipping the pages of the old tome again until the green eyes of the basilisk glared at her from the parchment.

CHAPTER 10

SHE GREW RESTLESS AFTER RETURNING TO THE BOOK, her concentration eventually ruined by her fatigue. Sarra rubbed at her eyes as she paced back and forth in front of the window, one free hand holding onto the pages of the book firmly. She read about the basilisk over and over, making her own comparisons of the mythical beast to the man residing inside the palace until she found herself thinking in circles.

Ares could turn a greenskin to stone. The memory of what she had seen made her shiver every time she paused to look out the window. The frozen, fearful face of the orc remained where he had left it, and Sarra peered through the telescope once or twice to be certain of that. Ares was powerful. Graceful. Capable.

The same questions continued to plague her, over and over. *How easy would it have been for him to use those skills against me? How quickly could he snap my neck and leave me broken, dead for my father to find? Would he eventually turn me into a voiceless or-nament?* At least then she would decorate the palace halls in-stead of some unworthy man's arm. While her circumstances still seemed grim, it was not hard for her to realize her overall good fortune with the Serpent Lord. Her father could not meddle in her personal life if she were stone.

But why is Ares so kind?

Perhaps he had only wanted to charm her, *just like a snake*.

Sarra dropped the book on a plush chair near the window. It bounced off the cushion and clapped loudly against the floor. She scowled at it, hand on her hips with a searing gaze, as if she could smite it herself. Nothing happened. The book did not even move. Tossing her hands up with frustration, she turned away from it and walked toward a nearby bookshelf. "Zero solutions, a thousand questions, and I think I have been duped again by a man who had his hands on my laces!"

She had enjoyed having him close, though. His breath had sent a shiver down her spine. His words had whispered against her ear like a delicious, inviting caress. Sarra put her palm to her forehead, wincing as she accidentally touched her battered face. Her cheekbone still ached, her head felt tender, but that did not stop her from running her hands through her hair with frustration or rubbing her face when she needed a moment of clarity to think.

Nothing made sense to her anymore.

Obviously, she was in danger. Ares could take down not one, but four orcs in a short span of time. She had to escape. She needed to leave this foul palace!

Still, she fought with herself, back and forth, because her heart reminded her logical mind, again and again, that Ares had not harmed her when there had been ample opportunity for him to do so. Easily, Sarra thought Ares the worst villain. Her father never treated prisoners with kindness. In fact, the king nearly always tossed them into dungeons or sent them off to his favorite provinces as a source of indebted labor. When the dispute between Anagast and Valenar finally reached its apex, scores of people with supposed malicious intent were taken to Vrevia, the home province of Elias, the man her father wanted her to marry. Although, Sarra always wondered where those people had come from. Rumors from castle visitors, the bards, and adventurers who traveled the land claimed they were not from the two warring provinces, but from the crowned city and its surrounding province itself. The thought had never settled as truth in her heart. At least, not until she discovered Ro'al. The more she considered this in the quietness of the library, the more Sarra recognized only one man deserved to be feared.

The king.

Sarra scowled, dropping her hands to her sides in clenched fists as she stopped her pacing. "Father would not do such horrible things."

She looked at the moonstone, gleaming brightly from the table nearby, and paused.

Would he?

Lost in her thoughts, she remembered the way the impoverished people outside had screamed. Their response had been immediate, without doubt that her father had truly betrayed them. Guilt swelled in her chest. She touched her sore cheek.

She could not curse them for responding as they had.

Sarra turned toward the door, distracted, and made her way to the table. When her fingers clutched the smooth stone, she looked down at it and then back at the wooden door in front of her. Outside the door stood people, humans just like her, petrified for the rest of eternity.

If her father were truly to blame for the devastation of

Ro'al, her abduction was still not justified. If anything, it reinforced that Ares was as much of a monster as the king. He had ruined her reputation the instant he had acted, and instead of considering the consequences on the rest of the kingdom, he abducted the heir to the throne. *What if I had died? What if he had accidentally turned me to stone?* Everyone would be up in arms until she was returned, and Sarra would never live down the fact that she would stand in history as the princess that had to be rescued by her father.

But those were selfish thoughts.

The lives of the people of Ro'al mattered more than her reputation. *How can I fault Ares for acting out of desperation?* The conditions inside his city embarrassed her more than her future designation as being helpless. Still, that did not mean Ares did not pose a dangerous threat. He could turn on her in an instant. Her father had caused him indescribable pain, and perhaps, he would want the king to feel as much in return. In a way, Sarra understood, but uncertainty clawed at her.

She needed to craft a plan to protect herself.

Swallowing a lump in her throat, she walked toward the door, moving around various pieces of furniture in her path. The moonstone lit her way, and with her breath held in her chest, Sarra unlocked the library door. She turned the iron handle, her hand trembling, and the wooden slab opened with a loud creak into the darkened corridor. Fear licked at her, pebbling the skin of her arms until she clenched her teeth from a chill. However, Sarra squared her shoulders, her decision made.

There was no point in barricading herself inside the library. He could just break down the door.

One foot fell in front of the other, and Sarra glided out into the hall. The moonstone removed the darkness surrounding her and she gasped as the palace came to life before her eyes.

Tapestries of impressive beauty proclaimed stories of Ro'al's history, hanging upon the walls like rich, inviting paintings that made Sarra crook her neck as she walked by. The glittering rare metal accents of the foyer continued throughout the shrouded corridors, boasting of a mineral wealth that she had underestimated. The city sat at the base of a mountain, and as she passed an end table decorated with a bronze figurine atop it, Sarra assumed mining once played a key role in its infrastructure. The more she learned of Ro'al, the more she did not quite understand why her father would not take the risk to save it. Its resources alone made it more valuable than Sarra could even begin to fathom.

The first statue stood only a few feet from the library doorway, and as she approached, Sarra turned her eyes away. A woman pleaded silently, a hand outstretched as if she desperately wanted to grab her. Her dress resembled the one Sarra wore herself, her face youthful and smooth too. *Was she the beloved handmaiden? The one who had left behind the items that I borrowed?*

"I am sorry," Sarra said, lowering her eyes to the floor. She stepped around the statue quickly, pushing further down the hall.

Sarra did not know if the direction she wandered was the right one, but as she continued to walk, the statues began to grow in number. She kept her gaze to the ground, tracing the carpet with her eyes instead of meeting their screaming faces. They still frightened her, and her ears strained, listening for signs that one of them had suddenly come to life. By the sheer volume of them alone, Sarra wondered how Ares could think she believed him when he said it had all been an accident. She passed by several rooms, each with their doors shut, but she did not linger to investigate.

If I barricade myself inside the palace itself, there is no way even a monster like him could destroy the foyer door to get inside.

The fear of the statues pushed her onward. Their numbers were increasing more and more the further she walked. Before too long, they stood around her in such number that Sarra hoped her destination neared.

The moonstone's light shifted along the walls, prompting Sarra to look up from the carpet, and she saw the foyer remained just as she left it. With its thick, heavy drapes closed, no light came in through the windows, not even from the stars and the moon outside.

While the statues were plentiful, they were not the only eye-catching items worth noting. Now that she could see clearly, the decor stunned her more than it had before. Beautifully carved end tables rested against the stone walls. Chairs of matching wood were scattered around the room. A large silver birdlike figure watched from a shelf across from the palace entryway, a decorative shield with various inlaid gemstones hanging beneath it. Although she looked about the foyer awestruck, her amazement only lasted a moment. Sarra straightened her shoulders, thinking of Ares.

I have to keep him away. He is dangerous, and I do not want to stay here forever as part of his petrified collection.

Determined to block Ares from reentering the palace, Sarra weaved around the stone people of Ro'al toward the heavy double doors. She considered how she would do it. A drawbar sat forgotten off to the side, resting against the wall and covered with dust. Two giant iron handles were bolted to the thick door, but Sarra dismissed the notion of lifting the heavy plank to secure it. As capable as she was of many things, heaving the slab through the brackets was not one of them. She opted instead to use a smaller, cylindrical pole that had been forgotten in a pile of rubble, likely the handle to some weapon or even a broken javelin. It slid easily through the iron handles, and Sarra dusted her hands after a job well done.

She turned around and pressed her back against the door. *It won't be enough.*

She remembered the way he had worked to warm the water of her bath, and how he had single handedly fanned the fires with bellows so large they required more than one man to function under normal circumstances. His chest had glistened with sweat, the muscles of his arms and shoulders working under the stress, rippling with each movement. It would be easy for him to snap the pole through the iron door handles with a hard shove.

Sarra also considered the orcs outside the city wall. Ares had taken them on alone, just one man to four greenskins. Not even Elias, a warrior known throughout the kingdom for swiftly killing orcs himself, could hold a torch to the Serpent Lord and his prowess. Ares was intelligent. Sarra knew she would have to be more creative to lock him out of the palace.

Laying the moonstone to one side, she spent a long while pushing every table she could find against the double doors. Chairs were stacked on top of them next, and anything else easily moved followed those as well. Soon, she had a misfit collection of furniture and decor pressed up against the palace entrance. Her chest heaved with her exertion, but Sarra triumphantly stood in front of her handiwork, and not a single statue had been disturbed, as Sarra refused to unsettle them from where they rested.

She looked around to ensure she used every possible

object in the foyer to build her blockade, and a creak echoed loudly through the room. Sarra jumped with alarm, turning to stare at the door as she took several steps away.

Had Ares returned? Is he trying to get in through the door?

The wind whistled outside, rustling something through the small space between the doors.

Sarra sighed, pausing her wild retreat. She bent to retrieve the moonstone she had deposited on the floor and something at her foot glinted with the light, catching her attention. Sarra squinted, trying to decipher it.

Is that a sword?

It rested at the base of a statue, the hilt grip black with three gold bands spaced evenly apart. At the base, a small, circular gold piece attached, an image of a bird carved into it. The blade remained safe inside of a leather scabbard, likely untouched for many years given where it rested.

Sarra frowned to herself, standing up with the moonstone in hand.

Would taking the weapon be considered stealing?

"I will just borrow it until my father arrives," she muttered to herself, walking forward, and approaching the statue. Sarra swallowed hard as she looked up into the petrified eyes of the stony man. "I promise to return it."

After untying the sword belt from the statue's waist, she bent down to retrieve the scabbard on the ground. Age had weakened the leather, but Sarra rigged the belt, pushed the scabbard through a loop and tightened it around her waist. With every step she took, it banged against her thigh, but it remained secure in the crude holster she had created.

Combat was not her forte, and her father had always refused to allow her to learn swordsmanship. However, Sarra was of the mind that defense needed to be her greatest priority. *What better way to defend oneself than with a sword?*

She gave her barricade one more moment of appraisal before she ventured away from the doors to the center of the foyer. Sarra found herself standing in the very spot Ares had during his grand reveal, prior to her adventure in the city. She looked over the heads of the frightened statues, taking in their terrified features and memorizing them. When her father came, she would honor them, ensuring they were provided with a proper burial without being broken into rubble. It was the least she could do for them.

Sarra did eventually notice something odd about the statues though.

While they numbered many, it appeared they only stood through one hallway branching from the foyer. The others remained empty, not a stone figure in sight. Sarra rubbed her eyes, blinking them rapidly to clear them. Was she overly tired or did some of the statues face away from her? Curious, Sarra weaved through the rows of petrified people, confirming those standing in the corridor faced into it as she thought. The others in the foyer turned opposite, looking toward the window and the center of the room instead.

She scratched her head with her free hand, holding onto the moonstone tightly as she moved from statue to statue, entering the hall once more.

If Ares had turned his people to stone, why were the other hallways empty? Maybe he sought them out, pinned them with his malicious gaze, green sparks erupting from his eyes until they succumbed to his curse and forever stood in stone. *Was he that cruel of a lord? Had he proven he was capable of being a monster enough already?*

Sarra stopped suddenly in the darkness, lip trembling,

and she hid her face behind her hands, her thoughts and feelings overwhelming her. She propped herself against a nearby doorframe, attempting to collect herself, but it became difficult for her to find an emotional anchor as her mind raced out of control.

What was the truth? What was the lie? She did not know.

Warm, wet tears slid down her cheeks. She fought them, using the back of her hand to rub them away. A few deep breaths calmed her, and with a quick sniffle, she raised her chin.

The smoothness of the moonstone pressed coolly against her heated skin.

Her fear poisoned her, clouding her judgment and muddling her thoughts. Her mind created unrealistic images and illogical histories. She did not have the full story laid in front of her. She needed more information. Sarra squared her shoulders as she took a deep, steadying breath, reminding herself of her strength. Her eyes closed briefly while she fought for quiet serenity, and when they opened again, she saw the corridor in a new light.

The answer she searched for was etched in the frozen faces surrounding her.

Like a map, they led away from the foyer, deeper into the palace, toward the library. Perhaps even beyond. Her feet carried her, faster and faster, down the long hall. She passed the closed rooms, the random offshoots that led elsewhere, the library, and then finally rounded a corner. Her fingers grasped her dress, holding the material from falling under her feet so she did not tumble. Sarra's breath came in soft gasps, her chest squeezing with anxiety and anticipation.

At the end, one lingering, solitary statue stood alone.

Sarra slowed her mad dash, approaching the stone figure

from behind. Just like the one outside of the library, the petrified woman's hand stretched outward, reaching for something in front of her. However, her head bent, covered by her other palm, shoulders slumped as if she sobbed instead of screamed. Her gown sparkled under the moonstone's light. Sarra moved closer, touching it gently to gain a closer look.

Diamonds.

The only diamonds she had ever seen were the ones inlaid in her mother's crown. The gems were rare, so rare the sight of them embedded into the fibers of the dress took Sarra's breath away. Her fingers rubbed the fabric longingly, but she released her hold on the dress, allowing it to fall back into place.

Who was she?

More importantly, why had she been crying?

A door stood partially ajar in front of the statue, revealing a spiraling staircase leading upward. Sarra looked over her shoulder, reassuring herself she was alone, then proceeded forward, pushing the door open completely. She eased up the steps, twisting around as it took her higher in the palace. As she neared the top, Sarra used the moonstone to look over the flat platform and into a room opening before her.

At first, the room looked similar to her temporary bedroom. Ornate wood pieces accented the walls, and a large fireplace stood at the far end. All commonalities ceased there, and Sarra's eyes widened as she took in the rest of the room.

There was a complete lack of furniture. No end tables next to the bed, and no dressers or chests to store clothing. Char and ash had been piled in the center of the room as if someone made fires on the floor instead of within the confines of the fireplace. As Sarra investigated the pile closer, she found partially burned furniture of various shapes and sizes, explaining their absence.

The drapes hung closed, just as they did in the foyer and in the library before she had opened them. A pile of straw underneath the windowsill appeared to be a makeshift bedroll. Dirt coated the marble floor, darkening cracks and crevices in the surface. The room smelled of smoke and a stale musk, as if it had been sealed away for far too long. However, it was the numerous rags coated in a dark, dried blue substance sitting discarded in a corner that pulled her understanding full circle.

Ares's blood.

Based on the quantity of soiled rags, he had been injured numerous times. Sarra could not decide if his wounds had been caused by the greenskins outside the city or the people living within it. Both posed threats to him, although for quite different reasons. One was his enemy, the monsters suffocating his city. The other was the people he had sworn to protect, and from firsthand experience, Sarra knew he would never raise his hand to strike back at them for tossing rocks and moldy crops in his direction. Perhaps Sarra was wrong about him after all.

One by one, she played through the facts she knew of Ares, each one resonating more than the last. He had abducted her. He had sent men to her castle, risking their lives through the barricade of greenskins and then again with her when they returned. He did not regret his actions, nor did he apologize for his desperation. The people of his city hated him. They saw him as vile and cruel, a monster only capable of delivering death rather than salvation. Yet, Ares would give his life for them, and a graveyard of petrified orcs decorated the land outside the city wall as proof. He could turn greenskins to stone, taking down four of the giant beasts single handedly, easily.

Still, the greenskins held his people hostage.

But, perhaps most importantly, Father had been the one to not send help.

With the swell of compassion beneath her breast, Sarra knew she could no longer describe Ares with negativity. While she had not viewed the state of every other room inside of the palace, she knew they did not look as ruined and unclean as this one. The library stood untouched, its books safe from use as fuel for warmth. The furniture in the foyer remained intact, despite being unused. Dust still covered portions of her temporary bedroom. Even the handmaiden's room seemed full of personal touches left behind by the woman that had previously inhabited the palace. Ares gave up his comforts so they, his people, did not have to lose theirs, even in death. Maybe Ares did not believe he deserved those comforts to begin with.

In her mind, she built up his story. A young man rushing through the doors in the foyer, his people gathered around to welcome him. Confused and scared, he looked from face to face, the familiar and friendly smiles greeting him like a warm embrace. Once the first few turned to stone, his people panicked, and he ran, terrified. Down the corridor he dashed, looking over his shoulder as people he loved and cared for pleaded for him to stop so they could help him. They all suffered the same fate. Not a single one was spared.

She knew he had not purposely turned so many people to stone. It was an accident, a tragedy, she was certain. Sarra hugged herself, angry that she had jumped to conclusions so quickly and irrationally and accused him of being such a cruel monster.

He was anything but a monster. He was a true, honorable example of a lord, a man who thought of his people before himself.

Slowly, she backed out of Ares's personal space, exiting the room down the winding staircase. Her journey back down the hall returned her to the library. She mindlessly wandered into the room, resuming her pacing once she picked the bestiary off the floor. Sarra attempted to read some more of the pages, but guilt racked her conscience as she mulled over her feelings.

Ares had been thrust into a situation not of his own making, and upon the death of his father, the people of Ro'al had become his responsibility. How he had survived for thirteen years under siege impressed her, but Sarra stood truly awed by the fact that his people had also survived, even if they lived in shanties in a city of ruin. Ares rose to the challenge given to him without balking or selfishly escaping the orc horde alone. Sarra decided at that moment that she had much respect for him. In another life, she had no doubt they would have been friends, and he deserved the civility she had spoken of before she had gallivanted into the city.

Sarra glanced up, looking out the window. The sky began to lighten. Oranges, yellows, and reds would soon melt with the blues, blacks, and purples of the night. Suddenly, her eyes widened.

Morning.

Sarra dropped the book in the plush chair near the window again, returning to the telescope to peer outside. She scanned along the wall, searching for the cloaked figure of Ares. She spotted him after a few long breaths, unable to miss him as he hoisted a large deer onto a platform near the edge of the city. He unloaded several additional items from under his cloak, and Sarra smiled, warmly at first, until she recalled the barricade at the foyer doors.

"Idiot," she muttered to herself, dashing away from the window.

She retrieved the moonstone from its sconce and rushed out into the hall. Weaving around the statues became less of a chore the more times she did it, and Sarra easily found her way back to the foyer. With the moonstone secured in a safe spot on the floor a few paces behind her, she began to lift furniture away from the door. Chairs clattered. Metal figurines clanged. A few wooden pieces cracked with the roughness of her placement. Sarra breathed heavily, wiping sweat from her brow. There was no way she would be able to remove the entire barricade by the time Ares returned.

A throat cleared behind her, startling Sarra. She yelped, her instincts pushing her hand to dive for the sword still dangling against her thigh. She pulled the hilt roughly, whirling around on the toes of her feet as fast as she could. Her weapon flew in her grasp, swing arcing wide as the blade sought purchase. A mighty roar ripped from her lips.

A blunt force knocked the sword from her fingers as it came in contact with a rogue end table, and Sarra opened her eyes as it hit the ground with a noisy clang. Ares stood in front of her, a smirk on his face.

She gaped for a moment, heat rising in her cheeks.

"You have never used one of those before, have you?" Ares broke the silence, a laugh catching his voice.

"I . . . I do not know what you are talking about. I am very well trained, and I—"

Ares held the leather scabbard up in the air. It must have come loose from her belt.

Sarra lowered her eyes, shuffling her feet until she

peeked up at Ares sheepishly. "I found it by a statue and thought it smart to have on hand just in case."

She moved to collect the weapon in question, picking it up and giving it a thorough inspection before she approached Ares to collect the scabbard.

"It is certainly a noble thought," Ares said, handing it to her. Sarra sheathed the sword and began affixing it back to her belt, refusing to meet his blindfolded gaze. He moved to collect the moonstone from the floor. "But if you are not trained to use a weapon, you could injure yourself more than the foe you intend to."

Sarra shrugged. "Perhaps."

Ares chuckled. "I see you have barricaded the doors. Not a bad idea, actually. It will keep my people from entering the palace in search of you."

"Yes," Sarra agreed. She bit down on her bottom lip, eyes shifting to her feet, avoiding his look to the best of her ability. "That was my intent."

"If you are finished, I can show you to the secondary entrance in the back of the castle. You may also barricade that one, although I do not know if anyone else is aware it exists."

A small, strangled sound escaped her. *A second entrance?* Sarra focused on a speck of dirt on the floor, forcing herself to breathe instead of curling into a small ball of embarrassment on the ground.

Ares cleared his throat and extended his hand for her, finally drawing her eyes up to his face. "Or perhaps back to the library instead? I apologize for my disheveled state. I will need to find clean clothes before I can continue to show you about the palace. You may wait for me in the library if you would like."

Sarra accepted his gesture, taking his hand as he offered

it. Splotches of a thick, dark substance covered his gambeson, and red flecks of blood marked his face.

Carefully, Sarra eased into step beside him, avoiding any unnecessary contact with his stained clothing. "I could live in your library," she admitted softly. "I do not mind waiting for you there."

CHAPTER 11

"**D**O YOU REQUIRE ANYTHING? I CAN BRING MORE food if you are hungry."

Ares stood at the door of the library, his hand on the wooden frame. Sarra meandered toward the chair by the telescope, settling into it with a new book she had plucked from the shelves. Her newly acquired sword sat forgotten next to her seat, and Sarra occupied herself by flipping through the pages, not giving it much thought as she focused on Ares. Her embarrassment had ebbed by the time they reached the library. He kept her distracted with idle chatter along the way.

"Food would be nice. I am a little hungry." Her stomach rumbled on cue, and Sarra quickly placed her hand against it, hoping to silence it. It only growled louder. Her memory of the journey to Ro'al remained hazy, and Sarra struggled to recall eating anything while in the company of the ruffians. *Was the sour apple the only sustenance I have had in days?*

"Very well. I will come back shortly with food then." Ares hesitated, and as Sarra looked up at him from her book, she swore she heard his internal debate. He took a deep breath, head lifting to look at her. "That is, if you will have me?"

"If I will have you?" Sarra arched a brow, smirking as she looked at him. "I do not think I have much choice unless I wish to remain behind a locked door forever and opt to never eat again."

"I suppose I could always smash your food for you and slide it beneath the door?" Ares said, leaning his shoulder into the doorframe.

"Loathsome, sturdy, unfortunate, miserable, part troll despite saying otherwise, civil, and dare I say, honorable for asking if I will allow you to enter the same room that I occupy? Your attributes are adding up nicely." Sarra glanced back down at her book. "Of course I will have you, Lord Ares. Providing you with conversation is the least I can do in return for your hospitality."

Looking up, Sarra saw Ares's lips curled into a coy smile, and when he spoke, the tone of his voice sounded lighthearted and teasing. "Perhaps your father will leave you here after all."

The princess gaped, stunned by his retort, until she giggled a few breaths later and hid a grin behind her hand. "Perhaps he will. I shall leave the door unlocked for you."

"Very well, I will return shortly," he said with a nod, closing the door as he moved into the hallway. Sarra looked up as it clicked shut, smiling warmly after their playful banter. Returning to her book, she relaxed in her chair, shoulders slouching while she tucked one leg under the other.

Time dragged by as she awaited Ares's return. Closing her eyes for a period, Sarra rested, allowing the quietness of the early morning to pull her under. She drifted off into a light sleep, but soon, a soft knock jolted her awake.

"I have returned," Ares announced, his voice deep but

gentle from behind the door. Sarra rose to her feet, rubbing sleep from her eyes as she walked to greet him.

"Thank you for your patience," Ares said as he shuffled forward, reentering the library. "I brought you some more clothes. I thought you might like to change before you eat. Your dress is torn."

Sarra lifted her head, frowning at the mention of her dress. She had never noticed, but the citizens of Ro'al had torn the garment. Various tears in the material made her look rumpled. She sighed, glancing at Ares blankly for a moment. The instant recognition hit her, her heart fluttered at the sight of him.

Gone were the frayed edges and worn material of the clothes he had previously worn. Instead, Ares had replaced them with attire better suited to his station. His dark gray suit matched well with the hunter-green embellishments on his jacket. What she assumed was his family crest decorated his shoulders. His clothing did not overwhelm like armor did, nor did it appear drab like his daily wear. Instead, he looked presentable and appropriate enough for an audience with a princess.

Sarra yearned to touch the green accents of his clothing with her fingers. However, she kept her hands close to her chest, fidgeting with the material of her blue dress instead. Odd, foreign feelings that she could not explain swirled inside of her as the light from the moonstone hit him just right. She marveled as if she saw him for the very first time. Her mind muddled with rogue thoughts of what their relationship might have looked like in another life. Despite everything she went through because of him, Ares captivated her in a way no other man had. He piqued her curiosity, making her desire to learn more about him. Even as she stood there, her lips curled upward into a brilliant smile until she recognized her boldness and hid it behind a small, fake cough.

As he neared her, sandalwood scented the air, and Sarra inhaled deeply, knowing she would always associate the smell with the ferocious Serpent Lord. Thinking about Ares in such a manner made her chuckle to herself. *Why did I ever doubt his intent?* One look at him as he kindly brought her clean clothes, and Sarra knew he would never harm her. Spotting the cloak he had used to shield her draped over his arm, she wondered if Ares would allow her to keep it. Even if it was tattered and ripped in places, Sarra enjoyed the soft, worn texture of the fabric.

"Yes, I think I would like to change. Thank you," Sarra replied, moving toward the desk in the center of the room. Ares met her there to deposit the items. He stood aside while she picked through the various outfits, eventually selecting a more elaborate gown than the one she wore. Red and gold accents hinted against an off-white base, and Sarra smiled, pleased by the vibrancy of the colors.

"How has your evening been?" Ares said, interrupting her admiration of the gown with small talk. Sarra grinned up at him, holding the garment to her body as if trying it on in a mirror.

"My evening was terribly uneventful. No one even attempted to storm the library. What do you think? Is this one suitable?" She twirled a little, letting the material fall around her legs.

"I am glad it was uneventful," he responded with a chuckle. "And no, I fear it is hopelessly too plain for you. I regret that if there is a gown to do justice by your smile, it is not in my castle. Does one even exist at all?"

Sarra warmed at his unexpected compliment, looking away from him with a soft laugh of her own as she twirled the ends of the gown again. "I am afraid plain will have to do. Do you mind allowing me a moment of privacy? I would like to change dresses before I demand you show me more of the palace." Her stomach grumbled loudly again. "Namely, the kitchen."

"Yes, of course." Ares nodded, bowing slightly before he moved to leave the library again. "I shall wait just outside the door."

In the moments after his exit, Sarra's simple blue dress fell into a pile on the floor. She tugged on the new gown with enthusiasm, eager to be back in Ares's company again. However, she encountered difficulties with her attire when she discovered a section of lacing in the back, hidden under a piece of red fabric.

"Ares? Are you there?" Ensuring her dress covered her chest, Sarra shuffled toward the door with the red material clenched between her fingers.

"I am," he replied, voice muffled by the wooden door between them.

"This dress has laces. I cannot tie them myself."

"I see. That is a problem."

"Would you be so kind as to help me?" she asked confidently. Internally, Sarra struggled with her anxiety because now she knew he could see her through his blindfold. She felt as if the library warmed nearly instantaneously with her thoughts.

"I am starting to think you are resorting to dresses with laces intentionally. Is your aim to sabotage? Do you mean to make me besmirch my honor, good woman?"

Sarra giggled again, grinning wide at Ares's light banter. "I would do no such thing. Besides, it is for the sake of men that women are forced to wear such gowns. It is only fitting that you assist me."

The door creaked open, and she shifted quickly, turning her bare back to him as he entered. Sarra attempted to hide her face, certain it would expose her inappropriate considerations. She felt Ares move behind her, and she opened her mouth to speak but before she could utter another word, his worn cloak settled over her shoulders. His hands moved under the material, and Sarra shivered when his cool fingers grazed her skin.

"Laces," he grunted, placing a palm on her back for a breath before pulling it away. "How ladies gracefully tolerate such an inconvenience is beyond my comprehension."

Sarra laughed, unable to help herself. Her body tingled with awareness, and she silently wished his touch would return. "Appearances mostly. They tend to be more flattering toward one's figure. The tighter the string, the smaller the waist. Is it not appealing to you?" She attempted to glance at him over her shoulder. "Do you prefer to look at women with no shape?"

His breath brushed her ear as he chuckled, and Sarra closed her eyes briefly with the sound. "I have always imagined myself falling for a woman of more substance than mere shapeliness. However, there are a good many women who happen to be in possession of both, and for them, I maintain that there is no need for them to resort to laces."

Is it possible I am being flattered by this villain? Except in her mind, Ares's role in her story had shifted away from antagonism a while ago. *If I am the heroine and he is not the villain, who is he then? The dashing hero meant to rescue me?*

No, Sarra thought. She did not need a hero to save her. He was someone else. Perhaps just a lonely, curious side character. Somehow, Sarra knew that was not right either. Maybe she had it all wrong. *What if I am the one meant to cure his distress?*

Is there no way to save him?

The stony barricade in front of her heart chipped a little.

"Was your hunt successful?" Sarra quickly redirected the conversation as Ares tugged the strings at her back. "I would wager that resources in the locale are quite sparse. Do you have to travel far?"

"It was successful. My people will have meat to supplement their crop for another day, and medicine for their ills a little longer. It is a bit of a journey to find plants that still bear fruit and game large enough to supplement a meal, but it is not unachievable in one night." He tugged once more on her gown, making Sarra inhale sharply, then removed his hands as he took a step back. His cloak fell down her back, settling about her hips.

"Thank you," Sarra muttered, drawing the cloak closer to her chest. She turned around, smiling kindly. With a quick tuck of her hair behind her ear, she met his gaze and uttered an embarrassed apology. "I am afraid this dress does not fit me as well as the other one did. I must be a disheveled sight, especially for a princess."

Ares shook his head and made a small gesture with his hands, directing her attention at the library around them. "Take a look around you, Princess Sarra. For you to appear disheveled among this disrepair would take considerably more effort than you have to expend at the moment."

They stood in a warm silence, regarding each other. Sarra wondered if he could hear her heart beating.

"If . . . if you should like and are not too hungry," Ares said, rekindling their conversation. "I could take you up to the parapets to watch the sunrise. It is quite beautiful this time of year, and I am sure you would like to see the sun again."

"Do you treat all of your captives so nicely?" Sarra teased as she took a step toward him. "First you compliment me like a true gentleman, now you suggest taking me to watch the sunrise. If I did not know better, Lord Ares, I would almost assume you are enjoying my company."

Sarra reached her hand toward him, touching his arm gently. "Seeing the sunrise would be lovely." She lifted her eyes to smile at him, forgetting the cloth kept their gazes from truly meeting.

"I am enjoying our time together," Ares said softly. "You have been far better company than I am deserving of."

Sarra took a moment, her eyes searching his face. *Did he weave some type of magic?* He ensnared her with his compliments, each one bringing about a new warm flattery she had never experienced before. The men in her court were tactless and vapid. Ares was giving and kind. He proffered an arm to her, which Sarra reached for, but he abruptly withdrew it. "Oh! Wait, one moment!"

Ares walked around her, moving further into the library. Sarra watched with confusion. "The parapet steps can be treacherously dark before dawn. You will need a light."

He retrieved a small, black leather pouch with a soft, silken liner from one of the shelves, and then plucked the moonstone from the sconce. Ares placed it carefully into the pouch, bringing it with him as he returned to her.

"You should take this with you," he said, presenting it to her. He took another step closer, taking her hand, pushing the bag into her palm. "In fact, you should keep it. I have little need for it. It is a thing of uncommon beauty, and such things should be among their kind, I think."

Stunned by his gesture, Sarra looked at the gift in her hand. She quickly shook her head, presenting it back to him. "Ares, I cannot accept this. It is far too valuable to be given away."

"No, it is all right. I will have no need for it soon."

"Thank you." Sarra pulled the moonstone close to her chest, peering up at him. Her eyelashes fluttered atop her cheeks, and she longed to show her appreciation, uncertain how. His hand moved to brush a rogue lock of hair out of her eye, pushing it back behind her ear gently.

"You are most welcome, Princess Sarra."

Time ceased to exist, and with that small gesture, another chip broke loose from around her heart.

Ares seemed to catch himself before Sarra did, and he lowered his arm with a nod for her to take it. Sarra swallowed a lump in her throat as she accepted his gesture, and when she slid her arm through his, she questioned what that moment meant. They walked in comfortable silence, Sarra clutching Ares's arm as he directed her through the hallways of the palace. Once they reached the far edge, he assisted her up a tall, spiral staircase resembling the one she had climbed to discover his sleeping quarters. The steps were too numerous for Sarra to even consider counting, but his arm supported her well. Ares took each tread at her pace, guaranteeing her comfort as they scaled up the spire to the top. As he had promised, darkness shrouded the staircase completely, but the moonstone proved invaluable, the crisp, white light clearly illuminating her path.

When they arrived at the top, Ares dropped her hand.

"I think you will enjoy this," he said, motioning for her to peer over the edge. Sarra tossed him an uncertain look, but she obeyed his request and approached the parapet walls.

From her vantage point, she saw the entire region Ares called home. A red-purple glow indicated the exact spot the sun would breach the horizon, but beneath that stood the stone walls of Ro'al. The people in the shanties below had begun to stir, but the early morning still rested in quietness. The wretched bog waited behind the stone wall, the sea of orc statues almost like ornaments in the muck. Behind the bog, the forest full of green trees still rustled in the cool breeze. Sarra widened her eyes once she looked beyond the tree line. The most impressive sight awaited her there. Excitedly, she turned to Ares, tugging at his sleeve, as she exclaimed, "Is that the ocean?"

Ares nodded. "It is."

The water seemed to stretch out into infinity. White birds fluttered around high in the sky, and, if she looked hard enough, Sarra could make out the waves crashing against the beach. The sea sparkled a beautiful cerulean, and there was a hint of salt in the air. She sighed longingly. Sarra had never seen the ocean before.

Before long, the sun broke the horizon. The waves of the sea reflected the sun's magnificence, extending its radiance as if the water surrounding it caught fire. As the light reflected off the waves, it passed through the gases lifting off the mire, causing them to shimmer and dance before Sarra's eyes.

"It is so beautiful. You must come here every day," she said with awe, because Sarra knew for a sight like this, she would. Ares nodded as the sun crested the horizon, its beautiful and vivid display in full bloom before them.

"Every morning," he replied.

Sarra stood quietly for a long while, watching the sky and enjoying a comfortable, companionable moment with Ares, her kidnapper, a man proving to be thoroughly good even in this sick and dying part of the world.

"Ares," Sarra said softly, still looking at the sunrise. "I am sorry for what my father has done to you and what you have had to endure because of his absence. I am grateful that you have not held his decisions against me like your people do."

Sarra shifted, looking at him next to her, and placed her hand upon his arm. "Life is sometimes simply unfair to good people that deserve more than they are given." She looked down at her hand, his arm underneath her fingers. "I wish that we might have met under different circumstances. Perhaps we could have been friends."

A heaviness settled in the silence between them, something

Sarra struggled to understand. Ares turned to look at her, the sun's rays beginning to warm her skin as it rose higher in the sky and highlighted the gold in his hair. Sarra tilted her head back, peering as hard as possible into the blindfold covering the eyes she desired to see, a piece of her desperate to make Ares understand just how apologetic she was. His fingers moved, barely brushing against her gown, and Sarra braced herself, anticipating his touch to draw up to her face. She longed for the cool sensation of his skin against hers, but it never came. Ares dropped his chin, his hand falling back to his side. Something told Sarra his eyes met hers despite the silk covering them.

"Yes, I wish that as well," Ares said with a slight nod. Sarra continued to watch him carefully, noting the way his jaw worked itself until he turned away to face the sun. She withdrew her hand from his arm quickly, uncertainty gripping her, and looked down at the stone flooring beneath her feet. *Did I make him uncomfortable?*

She caught the movement of his hands out of the corner of her eye as he lifted them toward his face. She heard the soft bristling of his stubble as his fingers rubbed along his cheek. "I wish I could have met you in any way but the way we did. I hope you know I am truly regretful that it had to come to this. Were there anything I could do to make it right, I would do so in a heartbeat. It was never my wish to subject you to such troubles."

She lifted her head. "Perhaps it is just the way things are. Maybe we will meet again in another life, where we are not bound by restrictions and rules, by life or death scenarios, or held at the mercy of a battalion of orcs." Sarra turned to face the sunrise again, her lips tilted into a playful smile. "Next time, I shall kidnap you instead."

Ares chuckled beside her. "Well, it would only be fair for you to take a turn as the captor."

"I would show you not the sunrise, but the sunset from the top of the parapets," Sarra said, her smile widening. "Because twilight is just as beautiful when it fades into the darkness as it is coming out of it. Perhaps, in this other life, you would not have to hide your eyes from me."

Her mind crafted a perfect reality. It drew Ares flawlessly. Strong and warm, his face enticed her gaze, and Sarra never wanted to look away. His smile brightened every dark corner that dared try to suffocate it, and his eyes crinkled at the edges, exuding kindness.

"I wonder what color they would be," she wondered aloud. "Blue like the sky or gray with wisdom? Perhaps green or purple or gold? I have pondered their color since we first met."

Sarra peeked at Ares, but her blond tresses obscured her view. She quickly pushed it away, tucking it behind her ear. "Perhaps neither of us would have kidnapped one another. Instead, we could have met at a grand ball. You would wear the colors and crest of your house, and I would wear the most beautiful gown."

Ares took a deep breath, and Sarra pushed forward, her lips smoothing into a lopsided grin. "Would you ask me to dance? Or would you brood in the corner like the rest of the men of the court?"

He stood silent next to her, back straight and face forward. Anxiety swelled in her chest like a heavy pressure as Sarra convinced herself that she had once again misstepped with her teasing conversation. Ares shifted again beside her, and Sarra held her breath.

"A battalion of bloodthirsty orcs could not keep me from asking you for a dance," he said in a low, gravelly voice, and the answer she heard in his tone spoke more to Sarra than the answer in his words. Her heart fluttered wildly, and she pressed a hand against her chest, rubbing against the swell of her breast as if the strange sensation inside pained her. Reality crashed around her hard. It was too much too fast, and Ares was a dying man, his life forfeit before she had even met him. *Why do his words bring such strong feelings to my heart?*

Sarra gnawed on her lips, furrowing her brow with concentration. As Lord of Ro'al, Ares was of noble blood. *Would he have entertained the idea of us in that other life? Is it possible soul mates exist in more places than fairy tales? And if they do, is it possible he is mine?*

Sarra's breath shuddered through her lips, and she quickly cleared her throat to ground herself. A sadness squeezed her heart, lingering even as she boldly lifted her hand to press once more against his arm. "Loathsome, sturdy, unfortunate, miserable, part troll despite saying otherwise, civil, honorable, and surprisingly great company. A true gentleman who would never leave a lady wanting in the middle of the ballroom."

She pulled away again, covering her mouth to stifle a laugh with one of her hands. "I think most men are intimidated by me. Do I seem unnerving to you? Perhaps it is my tongue. Too sharp for them, I suppose. They do not appreciate wit, or perhaps they have none themselves."

"You are well worth being intimidated by," he responded, his serious tone taking her off guard. However, within moments, Ares smirked. "I understand you have an interest in kidnapping men. You have mentioned it before."

A laugh bubbled out of her lips. Sarra shook her head with a smile, leaning forward to glance over the land again. "Out of all of the men, I would accept a dance with you, but only to a song that would make you smile. Maybe one that would make you laugh too."

Her eyes traced over the bog, imagining what it had looked

like before it had become so sickly. "You would enjoy the castle, I think. It is so large that even I get lost, but the gardens are full of beautiful, exotic flowers that have been brought from all over the land. This is lovely, but I could give you something even better to admire instead."

With a sigh, she continued to watch the dancing rays of the sun as it colored the sky. She pretended Ares was not doomed to die in an effort to settle the growing hunger of her imagination. *Would he be happier in that other life? Would I?*

"Could you escort me back inside?" Sarra closed her eyes, fighting back a wave of emotion unfurling inside of her. "I am suddenly very tired again and would like to rest."

"Of course," Ares said, proffering his arm again. As she took it this time, he brought his gloved palm to rest on top of her hand. "Be careful. The stairs can be unforgiving in the descent. I have you."

True to his word, Ares kept a firm hold of Sarra's hand, ensuring she did not tumble.

CHAPTER 12

AFTER A STOP IN THE KITCHEN, WHERE ARES retrieved some food from his meager stores to calm her growling stomach, the pair walked back toward Sarra's temporary bedroom with easy, lighthearted conversation. As she nibbled on another apple, Sarra noticed the route became more routine after each foray into the palace, and she began to feel comfortable navigating the halls, thanks to Ares's guidance.

Winding through the corridors with her hand upon his arm, Sarra's mind drifted as they fell into a cozy silence. The moonstone's light once more illuminated the dark path, and the more she saw of the glimmering walls of the palace, the more she thought about the image of the other life she had crafted upon the parapet with Ares. As odd a thought as it was, the alternate version of their lives made her long for it more than she had originally expected. How cruel their current reality was to bring a man that stood as a glint of perfection into her life, only to rip him away.

Devastation rose like bile in her throat, threatening to

suffocate her with its thick, putrid taste as Ares gently nudged her along. Sarra knew she would return to her castle when her father rescued her, and with that thought, her grasp on Ares tightened. Elias awaited her, as did the destiny her father had crafted for her without her input. She wondered if the king's intent was to pair her with a man who would steal her rule from under her own feet. Sarra knew little of the lord her father wished to betroth her to, but the knot forming around her stomach squeezed harder as if confirming her suspicions.

She pondered what would happen if she never returned to the crowned city. *What if I hid within this very palace and my father never found me when he arrived?*

Sarra glanced at Ares and swallowed hard over the lump in her throat. She knew the questions she asked herself could never become a reality. Her people deserved better, and after everything Ares had gone through to lure her father to Ro'al in an effort to save the frail people of this place, Sarra could not in good conscience allow that plan to fail. Still, her heart hurt at the implications of what that meant. *Why did Ares have to die?*

She closed her eyes as they rounded a turn into the palace corridor containing the door to her room. Her breaths, frenzied from her dark thoughts, steadied as she imagined what her perfect life would look like.

In her mind, Sarra stood at the top of a grand white marble staircase in the middle of a lavish ballroom decorated with gold. No one else stood before her, the entire room empty, but she felt eyes upon her as she descended step by step to the main floor. Her gown contrasted vibrantly against her pale skin as she lifted it with her hand from under her feet. The violet material looked as smooth as satin between her fingers, and it shimmered under the light of the many chandeliers hanging strategically about the room. Stepping away from the final stair, Sarra glanced upward from her feet, catching the sight of arresting blue eyes upon the most regal of faces.

There he was, Ares, stealing her breath in her imagination, capturing her with his warm, kind smile as he extended his hand for her to take. In her reality, Sarra reached up, wiping her free hand under her eyes to clear the building moisture there in a silent defeat.

The image of perfection. A man who placed his people before himself. A lord that understood the duties he had been given at birth, and a soul that knew righteousness without fear. How long would it take her to fall in love with him within that perfect, dreamy world?

Sarra opened her eyes. Her lip trembled slightly, but she bit down on it, hiding her feelings behind a false smile. She refused to show Ares her weakness, and that he had become it. He slowed as she collected herself, bringing their movements to a halt, and returning her smile with a grin of his own. He reached in front of him, tugging open the wooden door to her room with ease.

"I hope you are able to rest. I am sure it is difficult to sleep in a place as strange as this," Ares said as he encouraged her forward with his hand. The bright torches on the walls flickered into sight, and they moved into the room together to stand next to the ornate bed. Sarra released his arm, and Ares tucked the glowing moonstone he held away into its black bag, placing it on the end table when he finished.

"It is not as difficult as you might expect. I am so tired, not even the morning sun will keep me awake." Sarra yawned and sat on the bed. She began to make herself comfortable by pulling a thick blanket over her legs and tucking it about her waist. Her hands moved behind her back, loosening her dress as much as possible without asking for assistance then dropping to the cushion beneath her when the material fell slack. "It is quiet and cool here. Almost like waking up on a winter's morning when you do not want to leave the warmth of your blankets because it feels too nice beneath them."

Her eyelids felt heavy, and they drooped with her soft sigh. Ares stepped back, avoiding her gaze to look about the room. "Do you wish for me to stay with you again, Princess Sarra?"

Sarra glanced up, regarding him for a long moment. "Princess is such a formality," she finally said. "Perhaps you could just call me Sarra?"

Ares stilled, swallowing hard. He remained silent for a breath then turned from her view. "Sarra, then."

She looked away from him, focusing on the chair near the bedside, telling herself she did not want him to leave. The seat looked uncomfortable though, especially if someone were to sit in it for long periods of time. There was no cushion, no upholstery. Only firm, solid wood, held in a straight, stiff shape.

"I would not say no to your company, but I do not wish for you to spend all of your time in that uncomfortable chair." Sarra twisted her fingers into the blanket, biting down on her bottom lip again as she considered her wish for him to stay. "Perhaps you could tell me another story? Just one? You may leave once I fall asleep, if you would be willing to stay a while longer."

"Of course," Ares replied, stepping forward and taking the chair by the back before moving it closer to the bed. He sat down, scooting to close the final distance between them, and used the edge of the plush bedding as an armrest. Taking a deep breath, he relaxed for a moment, then began his tale.

"When I was a boy, Ro'al was quite wealthy, so prosperous that the city itself reached far beyond where the stone wall rests now. My father was known for many things during his time as its lord, but everyone knew that he was particular about his horses. He had a stable on the outskirts of the city where the strongest bloodlines were bred and kept. I was not allowed to bother those horses until I was old enough to handle one on my own, but I befriended many of the children throughout the city in my youth, and I allowed one of them to convince me I was capable enough."

As smooth as silk, Ares's voice relaxed her, and Sarra closed her eyes, listening to him. She smiled at the image of his mischievous youth, knowing he had not been restricted by the same discipline and structure she had as a child. Ares was of royal enough blood, thanks to his lordship, to get away with certain consequences, but he was not royal enough to be forced to endure the rigidity of the life she led. A piece of Sarra became jealous, but she did not linger upon those thoughts for too long. Instead, she focused on Ares, memorizing the sound of his voice so she remembered it forever.

"You stole one of his horses," Sarra said, her smile growing as she peeked one eye open to look at him. "Was it your father's favorite?"

"One of them, yes. He had many favorites," Ares replied with a chuckle of his own. "I wanted to go swimming at a beach nearby. The ocean is not far from the city, only a short distance on horseback and, at the time, without the threat of an orc barricade standing in the way. My father was busy, occupied with his lordly duties undoubtedly that day, so one of the other young boys and I decided to go on our own. So, I borrowed one of my father's horses."

Ares chuckled again as he ran his hand through his hair. "The horse was a good sport for most of the journey. At least, until it decided to act out once we reached the beach. Tossed us both into the ocean and soaked our clothes within moments of reaching it. I thought for sure it had run off into the forest for good after that. My friend and I walked back to Ro'al shivering to death in cold, wet clothes. I crafted the best story to tell my father when he demanded to know what happened. His horse missing would not have gone unnoticed, and I looked awfully suspicious coming home soaked to the bone and smelling like sea water. But as luck would have it, the horse was back in the stables where it belonged when we returned nearly half a day later."

Sarra smiled. "Must have known you were up to no good and wanted no part of it, or perhaps your father just had it trained extremely well."

"Both, I assume. Horses are more intelligent than I think most give them credit for. As you can imagine, my fondness for them has been lacking since that experience. I cannot remember the last time I traveled atop one, nor do I think I have desired to since."

"That is quite unfortunate. I happen to enjoy riding on horseback, although my father finds it too dangerous and refuses to allow me to travel outside of the city walls except in the back of a carriage." Sarra huffed, adjusting her blanket, clutching it to her chest. "The stable hands let me sneak off with one of the mares from time to time, usually when my father is away and there is no one around to tattle on me. She's gentle and I feed her carrots, which she appreciates."

Sarra shifted to her side, opening her eyes as she pushed herself up to her elbow and faced him, blanket still modestly covering her loosened gown. "Tell me more of the ocean. How beautiful is it in person? I have only read about it in stories and seeing it from atop the parapet was the first glimpse of it I have ever had."

Ares tilted his head, seeming to regard her for a moment behind his blindfold. "You have never seen the ocean before?"

Sarra lowered her eyes and shook her head. "The ocean is too far from my castle to travel, at least so it seems on the maps I have studied. My father would never allow me to leave the province for that long of a journey. I am afraid the only time I shall ever see the ocean is from atop your palace. Until I am queen, at least, and even then, the chance of traveling far from the castle will be slight."

Elias would keep her like a trophy, only to be seen as a glistening object of beauty to mark his rule. Sarra felt her chest tighten. Her fingers curled into the blanket, nails digging into the fabric as if she held onto it for dear life.

"Now," Ares said, his voice low and warm as it caught her attention. Sarra lifted her eyes to his blindfold, her smile long gone as she thought of her father's fury and how he would wish to lock her away in a stone cage when he came to rescue her. "That is truly unfortunate, Sarra."

Her name on his lips sent a shiver down her spine, and Sarra felt her throat dry as Ares's voice repeated itself inside her head. Her breath shuttered through her lips, seeming harsh to Sarra, and her body shifted to lie back on the bed. Her head sank into the pillow, and for a brief moment, she stared at the white ceiling above her. Ares moved also, the chair creaking, as he undoubtedly adjusted himself into a more comfortable position.

When he settled again, he obeyed her command of him. "The ocean. Well, it is blue."

Sarra giggled, clapping a hand over her mouth while her shoulder shook for just a moment. "Is that so? I thought it appeared green."

"You must relearn your colors then. It is most certainly blue, astoundingly blue, and when you look at it at night, the moonlight glistens atop the dark waves as if the water is full of diamonds. Sparkling diamonds in a sea of black."

"It sounds beautiful." Sarra closed her eyes, imagining it.

"It is. Very much so. Absolutely breathtaking." Ares fell silent for a brief moment, and Sarra nearly opened her eyes to look at him, but he gently cleared his throat and continued to speak. "The water crashes against the cliffs and the large rocks around the beach like a song. You can sit in the sand with your eyes closed, and the sound of the waves will lull you right under into a relaxing trance until morning. Sometimes, if you are truly fortunate, you can hear sea creatures sing along with the waves too."

"Sea creatures? Like sea dragons?" Sarra asked, awed with the prospect of giant scaled beasts swimming under the water. *Does the bestiary in the library contain a section on the aquatic monsters?* She almost dared to ask Ares but decided she would investigate the useful book after she woke.

"If you believe in them, perhaps." Ares shifted again, the chair creaking gently with his movements. "The beach nearest here is mostly just a place of solitude. A place of peace. A place where I feel comfortable enough to take off the cloth over my eyes and pretend my curse does not exist. There is no one else that visits the beach anymore. Not even the orcs venture that close to the ocean's edge. My favorite part is the sand. In the summer, it is warm to the touch, and it feels nice against my skin. Yes, I believe you would enjoy seeing the ocean in person. However, I am afraid my descriptions fail to do it near enough justice, and I hope you have the opportunity to see it yourself one day."

"I hope I do as well." Sarra yawned quietly, curling into the pillows surrounding her. "Thank you."

"You are welcome, Sarra."

Before long, her exhaustion caught her, and she fell into a deep slumber. She dreamed of Ares, of the dance they deserved but would never receive. They stood with one another, under the twinkling stars in the night sky as the various flowers within the royal gardens of Olmalis glowed with vibrant life around them. A sweet melody created expertly by bards and musicians playing a variety of stringed instruments caressed Sarra's ears. She hummed along with a smile, swaying slightly with the tune. The rich green and gray colors of Ares's house decorated his courtly doublet. The scruff on his face had been shaped into neat lines along his jaw, and the dark blindfold covering his eyes disappeared. He reached for her, tilting her chin up and toward him with the gentle touch of his hand. His eyes stared deeply into her own, his face morphed into a soft expression she had never seen on a man before.

Sarra sucked in a breath as Ares leaned forward with intent. Barely a breath away from her, his lips moved, and his words warmed her skin as he spoke to her.

I do not know if I will feel your absence after I am gone, but if I do, I know I will miss you terribly.

His forehead pressed against her own, his lips still seeming so far away. Sadness choked her, and Sarra closed her eyes in silence. *Why does he have to go? Why can he not stay here with me forever?* Sarra reached for Ares's hand to thread her fingers through his. She held onto him with a tight grip, unwilling to ever let him go.

"Then do not leave," she whispered. "If you stay, you will not have to miss me."

CHAPTER 13

S ARRA ROUSED HERSELF IN THE LATE AFTERNOON.
With her eyes still closed, she breathed a deep sigh
and burrowed into the blankets covering her, revisiting
the sweet dreams of the man who had abducted her just a day
and a half ago. *How did he sway my opinions of him in such a
short time?*

Her body angled itself toward one side of the bed, her
arm outstretched, and one of her hands dangled over the edge
nearest to the chair Ares had sat in before she had fallen asleep.
Sarra's eyes opened instantly, a soft sound of alarm escaping
her at the memory of their conversations earlier in the morning. She pulled her rogue limb back toward her body as if she
had touched an open flame with her bare fingertips, and her
heart thrummed fast inside her chest, expecting him to be gone.
However, she found him still in the chair beside the bed, his eyes
closed as if he slept as soundly as she had.

He had stayed, but most importantly, his blindfold had
shifted down.

The thought of Ares waking suddenly concerned her, made her heart race with anxiety. One look and she would turn to stone, but he looked peaceful in his resting state. She wondered how often he had the chance to relax, then she noted one of his hands rested beside her own. Vaguely, she remembered her fingers lacing together with his, but Sarra could not be sure, despite the evidence in front of her.

"Ares?" Sarra whispered, afraid of startling him. "Did you stay the entire time? Surely you had better things to do than to sit by my bed."

She sat up, scooting so the plethora of pillows behind her supported her back, and drew her blanket closer. Her eyes looked from Ares to search for his tattered cloak among the bedding, the unintentional gift offering the most comfort Sarra had found in the cold palace except for perhaps the lord himself. After locating it, she wrapped it around her shoulders, fastened the small latch to hold it together at the top of her breastbone, and securely clutched the material with her hands.

Sarra watched as Ares straightened himself after he woke, immediately fumbling to replace his blindfold, and he sat upright with a small smile aimed directly at her. "No, there is precious little I can do during the day besides sit in the sun." His smile grew into a teasing grin, the tone of his voice shifting into a lighthearted melody that made Sarra's heart leap. "Besides, someone needs to make sure you do not escape."

Despite reality crashing around her, Sarra struggled to brush the remnants of her dreams of him from her head. Even as he spoke and interacted with her, those moments of make believe had felt more real than him sitting next to her beside the bed. Her selfishness distorted her from the truths she knew in her heart, but with a deep breath, Sarra shined her brightness upon him in a brilliant, toothy smile, even as she asked herself how long she would have before her father's arrival took Ares from her instead. *How can I save him? How can I convince my father to spare him?*

"This is true. Allowing your prisoner to escape would make you the worst abductor in history." Sarra kept the conversation lighter than the heaviness inside of her, but she hid her grief well with her words. She had never expected life to take such a turn. In fact, she had always envisioned it to be much more boring than her present. Ares was a kink in the chain, so to speak, someone she had not quite anticipated meeting in any version of the life she dreamed of. Yet, as they conversed, she could not bear the thought of never knowing he existed. He had charmed her with his wit, impressed her with his determination, and Sarra felt a kinship with him she knew she would never find again.

He locked eyes with her, and for a moment, neither of them seemed able to breathe. Ares diverted his gaze away from her first, but Sarra also looked down to her lap as heat unfurled in her cheeks like wildfire. He spoke first, clearing his throat loudly so she turned her head to the side, watching him. "You mentioned to the serf outside your skill with the sword. Has your father allowed you to be trained? Do you spar often?"

Her jest had reached Ares's ears, and after a short pause, a string of giggles erupted from Sarra, echoing around the room. "You heard that, did you?"

Sarra shifted her body, positioning herself so her legs dangled over the edge of the bed. "My father would rather die than allow me to hold a sword. I am a princess, after all. There are others who have been tasked with protecting me. Why should I learn to protect myself?"

Her eyes narrowed as she leaned forward, closer toward him with a mischievous grin. "It is not like I expect to be abducted. Who in their right mind would do such a thing? I am but an innocent, a beautiful young woman who would hardly hurt a fly. Surely, no one would have their eyes set upon me."

Ares laughed heartily. "There are many dastardly, sinister, roguishly good looking men out there who would enthusiastically abduct such a prize, and for the sake of not allowing them to sully my accomplishment in doing so—as I consider myself to be an excellent abductor, not to be outdone by inexperienced upstarts, and yourself to be a sublime abductee—I think it is important that we train you post-haste."

"Oh? Are you changing your adjectives now?" Sarra covered her smile with her hand, her shoulders shaking with mirth. "Now you are dastardly, sinister, and roguishly good looking? I do not believe I agree with such words."

Sarra arched a brow, observing him intently for just a moment. Ares had not a single bone in his body that could ever truly be called dastardly or sinister. He was handsome. In fact, she had never seen a more physically appealing man in her entire life. However, roguish, Ares was not.

"And you want to train me to use a sword?" She shook her head with disbelief, but he reached for her, grasping her hand firmly to lift her from the bed himself.

"Yes. Come. I will take you to the armory. There is an excellent place to practice there." Ares continued to smile, while Sarra, startled by his gesture, quickly pressed her free palm against her dress, holding it in place as its loosened ties threatened indecency.

"But what if my father finds out? What if he—"

"You should be able to defend yourself," Ares said,

grasping her hand tighter. "Besides, I am in the unique position where I will not need to fear retribution from your father for the treacherous act of teaching you."

"Okay," Sarra said uncertainly. "To the armory then."

Her abductor led her away.

Inside a deep cellar within the walls of the palace, the armory awed Sarra with the wealth of weapons it contained. She had never been allowed to spend much time near the barracks of her own castle, per order of her father, but Sarra suspected the equipment stored within the armory rivaled the quality seen upon the men guarding her home. Halberds, shields, and a few maces lined the walls, intimidating her with her lack of familiarity alone, but she found herself drawn more toward the simple, less outlandish arming swords resting on the opposite side of the room. The weapon racks sat somewhat bare, a telling sign to Sarra that many warriors of Ro'al perished in war with the greenskin or perhaps fell victim to Ares's curse in the foyer. However, the craftsmanship of the weapons themselves proved whoever created them possessed an invaluable skill she instantly envied.

"These were made for the guards of the city," Ares said, catching her attention as he dropped her hand once they reached the center of the room. He moved toward a collection of blades, and picked up a wooden short sword, the decoration of the hilt resembling that of the weapon she had handled in the foyer. He rotated it in his hands, assessing it, before he seemed content enough to tuck it under his arm. He then selected a wooden dagger small enough to fit well within the palm of her own hand to accompany the sword. "When you prove that you are not overly dangerous to yourself, I will allow you to have a real sword and dagger, but these will do for now."

Sarra frowned, nose wrinkling as she huffed in distaste and folded her arms over her chest. She eyed him carefully for a moment, her lips tilting into a coy little smile as she held out a hand to accept the blades. "Prove that I am not overly dangerous to myself? I assure you, Lord Ares, I am only a danger to you."

Ares walked to her, chuckling with a shake of his head as he moved around her once he approached. He retained the weapons, not giving them to her as she expected him to, and Sarra dropped her hand with a small sound of disappointment. "As a woman, a man will be surprised to see you draw a sword," Ares said from behind her. "When you parry his first attack and then thrust with a concealed dagger, he will be blindsided, which is to your advantage. You should be comfortable using both."

He raised the cloak still wrapped around her shoulders, and his fingers deftly moved to help tighten the laces she had loosened earlier. He left them only slack enough to grant her freedom of movement, no longer forcing Sarra to hold her dress close to her chest with her hand. Something pressed underneath the remaining laces, firm but quick, once Ares finished securing her gown, and Sarra scrambled to reach behind her as the cloak fell down her back and over her searching hands. Her fingertips brushed the hilt of the wooden dagger, the blade tucked securely in the tight hold of the laces. Sarra looked at Ares, her question on the tip of her tongue, when he grasped her other hand and placed the short sword in it.

"Leave the dagger be for now. How does this feel in your hand? Are the weight and size of it comfortable?" he asked.

"It feels unusual. Foreign." Sarra tightened her grip on the short sword, bringing her other hand to join the one wrapped around the hilt. "I have never touched a weapon before I arrived here. This is only my second time holding a sword."

She maneuvered the wooden weapon in her hand, waving it wildly in front of her until she began to laugh. "Have you ever observed a lady in a gown dueling with a sword?"

Her smile widened, giggles bubbling out of her as she took a stance with her legs slightly bent at the knees and her sword thrust firmly in front of her. "I can see it now, fighting orcs with not only my deadly beauty, but also with an attractive swordsmanship that could only be taught by a dastardly, sinister, roguishly handsome man. It will be a tale written into the historical records and stashed in lavish libraries such as your own."

Ares laughed heartily, enhancing her sounds of amusement with his baritone ones.

"They say you should never judge a man's character until you've stared him in the eye. I shall remind you that you have not yet done so and teasing me about my nefariousness is something I warn you to be cautious of." He deepened his smile, and Sarra's cheeks began to ache from her own. "Perhaps my devious ways have yet to be revealed. One will never know until it is too late."

"Perhaps. However, if you were truly villainous, why would you give me a sword?" Sarra rotated the hilt in her hand, and she looked down at the wooden blade when a thought of uncertainty suddenly struck her. "Forgive me," she said with a frown. "But must I hold it a certain way?"

Ares nodded and moved to make a wide path around her to avoid the dangerous arc of the previously swinging blade. "You must," he answered her, and Sarra turned her head to glance at him over her shoulder. His hand extended next to hers, and his cool fingers coiled over her right hand. Ares drew her left one away with his free hand while his leather boot tapped at her right foot, gently nudging it forward.

"Power and agility start here in your stance. Bend your knees like they were and lower yourself just a little." Ares moved along with her, drawing her forward and backward as if their movement were subject to the ebb and flow of the tides. "Do you feel that? That steadiness?"

Sarra nodded. "I do."

"Good. Your left arm counterbalances for the right. Both hands on the blade make you front-heavy. This is a short sword. It is dangerous but lightweight, so you will be able to wield it one-handed with practice." Ares guided her hands through a full arc with the blade in a deadly semicircular pattern. Her balance remained steady. "Just like that."

"Just like that," Sarra repeated, stunned at the ease of Ares's teaching. He spoke to her as an equal, and he did not make her feel inferior for her lack of knowledge or skill. In fact, he almost seemed entertained by it, as if helping her learn something new brought him joy. Sarra found herself appreciating the opportunity to hold a blade, even if it was made of wood. The way Ares moved with her reminded her of a dance. Enthusiastically, Sarra turned in Ares's grasp, angling herself so she stared into his blindfold. "Again. I want to do it again."

Ares nodded with a laugh. "As you wish, Princess."

Sarra's face dropped quickly as her lips twisted into a frown. Her mouth opened slightly as she made a move to correct him for his fumble.

"I apologize," he said, bowing his head slightly toward her. "As you wish, *Sarra*. Habits are difficult to break. You will have to excuse me. I am not used to casually addressing a woman whose father is the king."

He nudged her to return to her previous stance, demanding her focus upon his hands. "Work in movement of your wrist to increase the speed of your arc. Your arm is a useful tool, but the trick is to use the whole of it."

Sarra practiced with Ares, over and over, trying a few additional chops and slashes at his command. She learned quickly, easily working into a rhythm and technique she felt more comfortable with. Gradually, Ares withdrew, and he watched from beside her, providing advice when she fumbled and praise when she did not.

"So, you will be fighting orcs, hmm?" he asked her after a break in the practice, allowing her arms and legs a rest from the exertion. "That is an easy thing to teach."

"Easy?" Sarra frowned, watching Ares as he moved away from her. "They are at least twice your size and could eat me whole. I do not think fighting them is 'easy.' I think you are delusional."

Ares hefted his longsword, two-handed, and hunched his back in imitation of the bestial greenskin foe. "I am not delusional when it comes to battling orcs. For all of their hideousness, they are a vain and prideful creature. They seek to end any battle with a single well-placed blow, relying on strength alone. An orc would be most tickled to crush you from head into your feet. Your strength against an orc is your speed, your precision, and his own hubris."

"Vain and prideful?" Sarra asked as Ares and his towering stance forced her to imagine the most ferocious, ugliest, green skinned creature. Her own skin pebbled like goose-flesh, and she shivered, knowing if she ever stood face-to-face with such a foe, she would be far too frightened to remember anything Ares taught her. "I find it difficult to believe, but you are more experienced with these things than I."

Ares drew close to her slowly, hoisting the flat of his wooden longsword high up over his head with both hands. The sword nearly touched his back as he approached her, and although he did not appear to be outwardly aggressive toward her, the slow, intentional movement intimidated and frightened Sarra.

"They will attempt to bring their weapon down onto your head, and they are very predictable in this way." Ares held his pose, not moving any closer once he stood only inches from her. "An orc's chest is thick. Even if you were to skewer them on the spot, it is unlikely to do enough damage to prevent their attack."

The sword began to move very slowly in an overhead arc that would eventually smash down on her. "Their necks are thick, their spines inflexible. At the top of their arc, they will not be able to see you if you duck in toward them. Step out of their path and bring your sword and dagger to bear."

He suspended his swing, placing his sword on the ground, then moving behind her to instruct her further. "It is a dance, of sorts. Follow my lead."

As their imaginary foe swung the blade down, Ares placed his hand on her own, swinging the wooden short sword upward from right to left to knock the imaginary blade clear of her. "This will take little force. He is bringing his blade down, not to the sides, and even a small impact here can help keep you free of the blade as you move."

As he spoke, Ares tugged her left leg back with his boot, whirling both himself and Sarra around. Maintaining the momentum of the short sword, he helped her pivot on her right foot before continuing a vengeful arc with the blade, smashing the tip into the imaginary beast's rib cage. "This will not kill him, but it will buy you necessary breaths to finish him off."

Ares guided her free left hand under the cloak, to her back, searching for the dagger hilt. "Tug your dagger free," Ares said, pushing Sarra's fingers around the leather of the hilt. She obeyed, ripping it free, and with a firm grasp, Ares forced her dagger to jab upward, in front of her, until she reached the imaginary orc's neck. "Very good."

Sarra breathed for the first time in several moments as Ares released her hands and stepped away. She looked at him wide eyed, feeling her blood pumping beneath her skin. *Why does this make me feel so alive?*

"Slide your dagger under your laces. Now you will try it against me. We will take it slowly."

"Try it against you?" Sarra laughed, her voice shaking with nerves. "But surely, you will win."

Ares took up his longsword again, facing her with his most intimidating, hulking stance. He lifted the sword over-head, moving slower as he began to bring it down over Sarra's head.

Sarra straightened her pose, still finding Ares's stance in-timidating, but swords were nothing more than a tool used in a dance. Ares had directed her through steps less complicated than a simple waltz, and Sarra nearly stepped into her move-ments with her eyes closed.

However, that was not how this particular dance took place.

She misstepped once, catching her dress with the heel of her foot, but caught herself before her gown dragged her down to the ground. She fell forward slightly, her hands pressing against Ares's chest to use him as an anchor.

Glancing up, Ares looked down at her, and although his eyes remained safely covered by silk, Sarra knew she stared directly into them.

"I will wear pants when I fight orcs. You might have stolen a horse, but my nefariousness led me to once steal a pair of trousers from a servant." Sarra steadied herself, pulling back from Ares to brush a lock of her hair out of her eyes. "I wonder if they are still hidden under my bed."

"I will gladly find you trousers to train in, but remember, you may not always have the luxury of knowing what you will be wearing when a battle begins. Be mindful of what you are wearing and remember the basics of your stance. It could save your life." Ares smirked. "Also, a gown that shows some leg has better mobility. You must carefully weigh your modesty versus your mobility."

Sarra took a step back, hands moving to hoist her sword in front of her. "All right then. A dress that shows skin. I will remember that. Now, do it again," she demanded with a lift of her chin, determination fueling her.

CHAPTER 14

THEY REPEATED THE MOCK BATTLE SEVERAL TIMES, Ares critiquing Sarra's footwork and deflection until she kept up at full speed. She learned to use both her heel and her toes to move nimbly and smoothly, and while her speed supposedly made her a dangerous foe to an orc enemy, her confidence truly gave her the advantage. Sarra followed the precise directions Ares had given, and gradually, her hard work began to pay off as she successfully completed the steps without stumbling.

"You are an apt learner," Ares said as Sarra wiped her forehead with the back of her empty hand to remove a small pooling of sweat. She smiled brightly, her heated cheeks tightening, and she dropped her sword to her side.

"You sound surprised. Is it because I am a princess or because I am a woman?"

Ares shook his head. "Neither. Most struggle with the finesse of using a blade, man or woman. You seem to understand better than most novices, although you still have much to learn."

"I have much to learn because the only monster you have taught me to defeat is an orc." Sarra straightened her back, fingers still firmly grasping the hilt of the short sword. "What would a human do? How do men fight? Show me."

Ares laughed again. "A man might be even more predictable. As a woman, a man will generally want to capture you, not kill you. You are worth more alive than dead in almost all circumstances. A man who attacks you is not. That is your first advantage." Ares moved closer. "Your second advantage is that he will absolutely underestimate your abilities. Remember how you held the blade when you first picked it up? Do it again."

Sarra moved the blade, holding it in front of her, and Ares's hand moved along her forearm to curl his fingers around hers again. "He sees this, and immediately believes he is dealing with a novice who will likely yield to intimidation. When he moves close to restrain you," Ares put his other hand on her waist, his feet moving beside hers, and he shifted her back with him. "You coil, like an asp."

The short sword twirled quickly to deflect an imaginary incoming blow, and then it lunged forward, aiming at the enemy's heart. "And then you strike. If he is not alone, you capitalize on their surprise." He maneuvered her hand to sweep the blade in two broad arcs, one to the left and one to the right. "You cut them down before they even realize how formidable you are."

Ares released her, stepping away. Sarra watched him, impressed by his knowledge, but also curious. *How many enemies has he battled? How long has it taken him to learn as much as he has?*

"Remember, an orc is content to smash you, and his intent is his folly. Men will want to use you, and that motive is their downfall. Success in battle is not just brute strength. It is in knowing your foe and exploiting their desires, proving you are stronger. It is wisdom and balance and knowing yourself over time." Sarra remained quiet as Ares took his longsword again and approached her differently than when he pretended to be an orc. He swaggered a little, emulating any of the hundreds of men in the kingdom who thought they could bully her or intimidate her into submitting.

"Show me," he said, raising his blade threateningly.

Sarra arched a brow at his display, her lips curling with a mischievous grin screaming. She playfully tapped her nose with her finger, bringing her sword to rest against her side. "So, men are as simple as orcs?"

The idea sparking inside her took hold, although she quickly attempted to push it away. However, Ares so willingly stood before her, inviting her to show him the things he had taught her. Sarra wondered if he understood the wiles of men were so easy for a woman such as herself to navigate. Interest caused their distraction, and Sarra mused about the men of her court, those she had turned down time and time again. *Is there something other than a sword that might prove to be a more valuable weapon?*

"All right. Just one moment," Sarra said quickly as she padded her feet over toward a table and replaced her wooden dagger with one made of iron. She looked it over, rotating the small weapon in her palm for a few moments before she bent down to her knees. A loud rip echoed in the armory as Sarra slashed through the skirt of her dress. She finished with a pile of red material pooled on the floor in front of her, her ankles exposed along with a decent amount of strong, shapely pale legs. Turning around to face Ares, her coy smile stretched wider, her movements growing bolder as she sauntered toward him with swaying hips. Her hands snuck the iron dagger behind her back.

"My first advantage," Sarra began, her voice smooth and confident. "Is that I am worth more alive than I am dead."

The dagger ripped through three of her top laces, her dress sagging lower to reveal her collarbone and the top swell of her breasts. Content with her disheveled appearance, Sarra placed the dagger securely between the still intact bottom laces. Her eyes never left Ares, and she stared at his blindfold, eyelids lowered in a sultry invitation. "My second advantage is that he will underestimate my abilities. Is that right?"

Ares watched her as she approached, lips quivering with uncertain distress. He took an uneven step backward, his hip brushing a chair and knocking it over in the process. The loud clatter startled him, and Ares looked away from her to gather it from the floor. Sarra's grin widened, pleased with the response her change in dress caused. She tugged her bottom lip between her teeth, her hand brushing at some invisible irritant near her breastbone once he looked to her again, bringing Ares's attention to her chest. "Do you underestimate me, Lord Ares?"

She invaded his personal space, attempting to use her charm against him. *Is he just like every other man I have ever known? Can I lure him into lowering his guard so I can fight as he had wanted me to?* The dagger burned through the material of her dress, begging for her to strike. One of her hands moved behind her back, grasping the handle of the dagger in preparation for her attack.

Ares turned his face toward her, and upon his lips sat a faintly sad expression. Sarra could not see his eyes, but the air between them shifted from a coy playfulness to something deeper, more resounding. She knew Ares looked into her eyes, despite the cloth between them. She felt him memorizing every detail of her face, almost as if he could see into the very depths of her soul. Sarra lost her breath, a sea of flutters awakening in the pit of her stomach, amplifying when his hands touched her arms. Sarra felt longing. She felt desire and want. She felt powerful.

"Never, Sarra," Ares whispered as his fingers drew her wrist holding the dagger forward. He moved her hand slowly, bringing the steel of the blade to his throat, swallowing roughly as he continued to stare at her. "I could never underestimate a woman such as you."

"Ares," Sarra said through her parted lips. She could not tear her eyes away from him, not even to continue the little game she had begun. Her entire plan went awry, but that did not matter. Not when the way he spoke made her feel seen for the first time in her life. His words made her lip tremble, and Sarra wondered again why fate was so cruel to her, to them, to Ares. It would not be hard to love a man like him.

Perhaps she had even begun to love him before she had ever met him.

He held the dagger in place for a long moment, his hand cool as it lingered on hers. The nature of their training escaped both of them as Sarra's eyes continued to meet his behind the blindfold. After a deep breath, Ares released her hand, and he took a step back with a slight shake of his head as if trying desperately to release whatever spell she had bewitched him with. "Now, if you are quite done fighting dirty—"

Sarra attempted to stop him with a reach of her hand, but midstep, his foot caught on one of the legs of the chair. He whirled in an attempt to regain his footing but caught his other foot instead. Ares toppled over, trying to catch himself with his hands before he impacted the floor. Before his palms hit the stone, his forehead cracked against the corner of the table, a loud, wet sound echoing through the armory. Sarra recoiled at the sound, horrified at the scene before her. Too stunned to move, she watched Ares roll onto the floor, remaining on all fours as he faced the ground. A breath later, he lost his balance, crumbling to lay on his back. Immediately, Sarra fell to her hands and knees to help him.

The gash on his forehead had torn open again from the impact, but it was far wider than it had been before. His blue blood ran down his face. "Ow," he grunted, pushing Sarra into action.

"Are you all right?" She reached behind her, grasping for a piece of discarded cloth from her dress. She caught the material with the end of her finger, bringing it back to her torso and using it to press against Ares's forehead. His lids lowered heavily, and his hands opened and closed several times at his sides as if trying to stop himself from falling even after the fact.

Worry plagued her, and to get a better angle, Sarra moved to straddle his waist, thighs holding him secure and still. The top of her gown hung precariously low in her position, but Sarra's only concern was Ares and how she had been the cause of his distraction. "I apologize for playing coy with you. I did not mean to make you lose your balance and smack your head against the table."

She pulled back the cloth, looking to see if his wound still leaked blood. When she saw it did, she reapplied pressure to his forehead. "Can you see straight? How many fingers am I holding in front of you?" She held her hand in front of his face.

It took him a moment to recognize her, but when he did, he stared up at her, mouth slack with wonder for a moment. He appeared to struggle with focus, rubbing his hand over his blindfold several times and shifting himself slightly to look in various directions. His head tilted toward her chest, a soft groan escaping his lips, before his brows lifted above the blindfold, and he quickly pressed his hands down as he attempted to push himself upright. Instead of meeting the floor, Ares slapped onto Sarra's bare thighs. His fingers curled into the plush skin, and

Sarra squeaked with the unexpected advance. His hands flew from her as fast as lightning struck, and Ares turned his head away from her quickly. Sarra still remained atop him, frowning down at him in confusion. *Why is he trying so hard to escape?*

"Sarra," Ares whispered, a flush apparent even on his dark face. "You are not entirely decent."

Sarra sat back, her rear just above his groin, and she removed the pressure of her hand against his forehead. Her lips turned downward with a slight pout. "Decent? What does that have anything to do with—" Her eyes widened with understanding, mortification stunning her for just a moment.

Then a giggle bubbled between her lips followed by song-like laughter.

"Are you concerned about my modesty? You silly man! No one would believe you even if you were to tell them that you had me in a compromising position. I am the princess. If anything, the people consider me too much of a prude for my own good." Sarra reached for Ares's face with both of her hands and moved it back into position. "Now hold still until I can get this bleeding under control."

She pressed the cloth back to the wound on his forehead, nibbling on her lower lip with concern over his bleeding, and after waiting quietly for a bit longer, Sarra lifted the material once again to see if the cobalt colored liquid had stopped seeping from his wound.

"You will survive," Sarra said, running a finger over the newly clotted gash to ensure it remained dry.

"Must I?" Ares asked ruefully, stifling a small chuckle. "I daresay you shall add ungraceful to the ever growing list of my qualities."

One of her hands cupped the side of his face as she shook her head with a smile, and as she finished addressing his wound,

Sarra's eyes dipped down to look Ares over carefully. Her hand trailed along the stubble of his cheeks. She felt his skin, tough and more weathered than her own, and at her leisure, she began to burn the image of him into her memory. "How do you feel?"

"I am . . ." he began, but paused, lost in thought. Sarra's hands continued their exploration, her fingers trailing over every rough edge of his face. "I feel good."

Sarra nodded. "Can you see me clearly?"

Her breath came a little faster, heart rate picking up as adrenaline and desire pulsed like a hot flame through her. Her body pressed closer to him. Her eyes involuntarily dipped down to his lips. He pulled her unconsciously into him, and one of Sarra's hands moved to the collar of his shirt, fingers curling into the material as she prepared herself for what came next.

"As clear as crystal," Ares said, just as breathless. He shifted under her, hands moving to either side to press himself upward off the floor.

A shaky, shuddering breath escaped her lips, forcing Sarra to fall from her trance and blink a few times in quick succession before she pushed herself away from him gently. "I apologize. I thought I saw another wound on your face. It was just a speck of dirt instead."

Her cheeks heated, her body desperate to stay in his grasp, but Sarra eased herself off Ares and pulled herself to her feet. She stood next to him, fingers clenched as she questioned herself relentlessly. Taking advantage of a man with a head injury was not her most shining moment.

"Please, there is no need to apologize," Ares quickly replied. He rose to his elbows, gradually pushing himself upward until he sat on the stone floor, facing her.

"You are nothing like I ever could have imagined." His voice, gravelly and low, rolled over her like a wave in the ocean.

It pulled her under until she stared at him, awestruck. There was nothing special about her. She was a princess who followed the same mold as every other had before her for centuries. Yet, Ares praised her as if she were somehow a rarity among them. "You have shown me more grace and kindness in these few days than I have experienced since—"

He fell quiet, and Sarra knew it had been far longer than he could remember. It pained her to accept that truth. His own people had shunned him. He had suffered alone for too long. *How could they not see the heart that beat in his chest? It was made of solid gold. It had to be.*

Ares leaned forward, gradually shifting onto his knees and standing. "Let me show you the ocean," he said. "It is beautiful, a remarkable sight to see in person, especially at night. I want to show you my gratitude for all of your courtesy."

"The ocean? To thank me for being kind to you, you want to take me to the ocean?" Her face twisted into a look of uncertainty. "Are you mad? What of the orcs? What if we get caught? They will eat us alive before they let us return. Are you certain you can get us there safely?"

Remembering her own words, Sarra hesitated. *Will I live the rest of my life with regret, knowing I could have seen the ocean but denied myself the chance because it was too risky?* That word, risk, burned itself into her, and Sarra realized in that very moment that her father had not saved Ro'al because he refused to take the risk. He would let his people die rather than gamble on his success, and Sarra bit back the bitterness coating her tongue. She vowed to never put her fear of failure over the lives of her people like he had, even if it meant her own life was forfeited to save theirs. *How could a lord follow that moral compass and his king did not?*

"Forget my worries about the orcs," Sarra said, preempting

any word from Ares. She moved toward him with a soft smile, reaching for his hand to hold it tightly with her own. "I trust you. I know you will protect me. I would love nothing more than for you to show me the ocean."

"I know the orc patrols." Ares smiled widely. "They are regular, but they are not without their vulnerabilities, and two people moving quickly can slip through without incident. Well, two people in good health. The crossing could be treacherous for those who are ill and weak. Otherwise, I would have ferried my people out two by two long ago."

His smile faded into a short grimace before he lightened the tone in preparation for their adventure together. "Besides, there is more to combat than swordplay. Often it is far wiser to learn how to avoid the fight entirely, and this will be an excellent lesson for you. Although, we should find you some proper shoes, first. Trekking barefoot through the bogs will not do you well."

CHAPTER 15

ARES TOOK A FEW MOMENTS TO ASSEMBLE A BELTED, leather sheath for Sarra. He assisted her with fastening it loosely around her waist, then he retrieved a steel version of her short sword to pair with her iron dagger. Once the weapons were secure in their sheaths, Ares tightened the belt further, giving her ruined dress a little more structure, and with a proud smile he placed his tattered cloak back onto her shoulders. "I cannot have you distracting me too much when we are outside the wall."

Sarra looked down at the floor quickly, staring at her feet in embarrassment. Neither her nor Ares would ever forget the memory of her coy little tactic.

A quick search through some ragged looking storage crates stashed in a lonely corner produced a pair of lace-up boots that fit her adequately. Boots of just about any form were a rarity in Sarra's world, which Ares seemed to understand, and he helped her by kneeling in front of her to slip them over her dainty feet.

He pulled the stiffened leather snug up her calves and proceeded to lace them tightly for her.

"You will need your boots securely in place as we walk through the mud, or you will lose them in the bog. The forest beyond is full of brush as well, and the sharp edges of the sticks and shrubs will irritate your skin if you do not have it covered."

Sarra nodded with understanding, then inhaled sharply as Ares's cool fingers brushed against her lower leg while he tied her boots. She shivered, aware of how close her body was to Ares and his skilled hands, and, as if sensing her distress, he lifted his head to glance at her, his brow furrowed with concern.

Sarra quickly shook him off, urging him to finish his task. "I am fine. I am not used to the feeling of boots," she fibbed, but Ares seemed to believe the reason for her temporary discomfort. He continued to lace her boots without further incident, his fingers remaining firmly upon the leather instead of wandering along the bare skin of her leg again.

Ares, himself, eventually donned sturdier boots made of much thicker leather that rose to his knees. He collected a bow from a rack, gathered his sword, and retrieved a pack of supplies from one of the crates before he returned to her, holding out his hand for her to grasp. Sarra accepted, her fingers wrapping around his as he led her through the armory entrance and into the halls.

They crept out of the palace together, and into the sleepy, dark village. The sun had fallen during their sparring session, and Sarra questioned her awareness of time. With the palace shrouded in darkness, she still struggled to orient herself. Perhaps she would ask Ares about opening the drapes after sunrise and illuminating the halls with sunlight when they returned after their escape to the ocean. She suspected it would do them both some good.

The village stood in silence after the sun fell, and as Sarra gripped Ares's hand, she felt as if they had to sneak past the slumbering villagers like they were overprotective parents that would punish them for disobeying the rules. Ares slipped his arm around her waist, keeping her steady as they moved on uneven ground along the broken roads. She noticed no fires lit that night, not even in the shanties scattered about, despite the chill in the air that made her shiver under the worn cloak on her shoulders. Sarra looked to Ares for answers as they approached the city wall, her free hand moving to grasp his wrist to halt him for just a moment.

"Where are the fires? Do the greenskins prevent your people from lighting them?" Sarra glanced around at the ruined city, a sadness creeping into her heart as she once again took in the devastation of Ro'al. *What had these people done to deserve such a fate?*

Ares lowered his head, blindfold tilted toward the ground. "There is no oil to spare for lamps, and wood has to be guarded ferociously for the winter nights coming soon. Our resources are quite limited, as I have mentioned." He shook his head twice, lifting his chin. "Push those thoughts in your head aside, Sarra. You are going to see the ocean for the first time shortly. You should be enjoying yourself, not troubling yourself with thoughts of fires."

Ares held his hand out for hers again. Sarra smiled faintly, accepting his gesture without a word. Together, they scaled the steps leading to the top of the stone barrier. Moonlight peeked through the clouds, illuminating the bog below. Ares retrieved a rope from his pack, looping it around a post in the stone. He tugged on the end, testing its sturdiness, before he turned to Sarra.

"Are you ready?" he asked with a wide smile. "I will protect you with my life, I swear it. As you may have surmised, I do not fall easily to orcs." He turned his back to her, holding the rope firmly in his hands. "Come here. Put your arms around my neck. I will lower us down."

Sarra glanced out toward the bog, unease gripping her for a split second, but ultimately, she obeyed Ares's request, moving forward until her chest pressed firmly against his back and her arms wrapped around his neck and shoulders.

"I am ready, but please be careful." Sarra pressed her face into the side of his neck and closed her eyes tightly. "I am occasionally fearful of heights, especially those that lead down to a bog full of orcs."

Ares rested his hand over her arms, and Sarra burrowed into him, holding him in a firm embrace. "Do not be frightened," he said softly. "I will keep you safe."

The conviction in Ares's words reassured her, and with the scent of him strong in her nose, Sarra relaxed, just as she had each time she curled in his cloak to sleep. Thoughts of the sea greeted her as she avoided thinking of their descent into the bog. The sight would be wondrous, and Sarra had dreamed of seeing the ocean for as long as she could remember. Lakes and ponds of all shapes and sizes decorated her home province, but the tales of the salty ocean were unlike anything else she had ever heard. Perhaps the waves shimmered like the stars and the sounds of them crashing would become her favorite melody.

Ares moved under her hold in smooth, fluid steps, steady as he turned to the edge of the wall and slightly bent at the hips. He hoisted his leg over the wall, grasping the rope tightly as he began to lower down to the ledge to the soft ground below. He oriented them over a firm patch of earth, and as his feet touched the ground, they did not sink immediately into the soil as the stone orc had when she had watched from the telescope in the library. Ares placed her down gently, removing her from his back, and whipped the rope to unhook the loop at the top of the wall. It dropped to his feet quickly, and Ares wrapped it over his shoulder.

"Perhaps it would be best if you remained on my back until we reach firmer ground," he said as he stepped down into the bog, his feet sinking several inches into the mud. The muck reached near the middle of his calves, and Ares walked back toward the firm patch of earth with some difficulty. He gestured to Sarra, inviting her to him, and leaned forward slightly so she could wrap her arms over his shoulders again.

"Oh, all right," she replied, moving forward, and hoisting herself upon his back. Her legs held tightly against his sides, but her eyes widened, and a warm rush flooded her when his hands wrapped firmly under her bare thighs, lifting her into a more comfortable position to keep her further from the muck. There was an interest, *a need* inside of her that she had never quite felt before, except for in the armory where she had received her first taste of his touch.

Is this want? Is this desire?

"I think the modifications you made to your dress may have been for the best," he said, interrupting her thoughts with a low chuckle as he began to trudge forward. "It would be dragging in the mud had you not shortened the skirts."

"Am I wrong in assuming that you already found my alterations to be for the best prior to our adventure in the bog?" Sarra asked, her smile stretching as her face once more gently pressed into his neck. "I remember you being concerned about my modesty, but I was not the only one with color in my cheeks."

Ares grinned, his answer to her question resting in the squeeze he gave her thighs.

Darkness enveloped the bog the deeper into it they moved,

though Sarra's eyes began to adjust, and in the faint moonlight, she spied the large, stone statues of Ares's green skinned victims. For every human statue living in the palace, Sarra wagered a guess that at least a dozen orc statues sank into the mire as repayment. The large figures stood in various states of disarray, some coated with mud, some eroded from years of merciless sun and rain. As if it had not been clear before, it was obvious that Ares did not fear the orcs. Pride unfurled inside her, impressed by his audacity and cunning, but Sarra's feelings quickly dampened. The numerous statues posed a frightful question that she had not previously considered. *If this many greenskins had already been petrified, how insurmountable was their number that Ro'al remained besieged?*

"Stay quiet," Ares muttered, a warning in his voice. Although the bog lacked most color, a few faint shapes moved far in the distance along the tree line like large, black spots among the gray. Ares seemed to give them a wide berth, avoiding their attention at all costs, but seeing the roaming forms made Sarra anxious. The statues with their ferocious snarls and frozen roars unsettled her, but the thought of encountering an orc, alive and well, in person, made Sarra quiver with fear, even with Ares as her defender. However, they crossed the bog easily and without any troubling events, and when Ares finally found firm footing on solid ground, he lowered her to stand next to him.

Sarra wrinkled her nose once she straightened herself. An unpleasant sludge from the mire covered Ares's boots in a thick, vile coating Sarra knew would be difficult to clean. He did not seem bothered by it, especially not as he held her hand and lowered himself into a crouch. Sarra followed suit, looking on as Ares gestured silently in front of them. The landscape had shifted, and they stood on the edge of a forest whose trees had swayed in the breeze while Sarra had watched them from the parapet during the sunrise. Ares moved forward, tugging her along with him at an intentionally slow pace. The quietness of the trees, the lack of wildlife, and the pale, unhealthy yellow-green colors of the plants alarmed Sarra. The greenskin destroyed the vitality of the land. Ro'al was dying.

"Be mindful of undergrowth and fallen sticks. They are nature's inherent detectability devices. One wrong step, and you will send an entire battalion of orcs down upon us. Stay close to me. I will not lead you astray." Ares squeezed her hand with reassurance, dropping it as he concentrated on brushing aside leaves with his boot to ensure their path remained clear. Easing through the trees became simpler the further inward they walked, but the sight of a fire raging in the distance almost made Sarra ask to turn around and abandon their adventure. Instead, she took a deep breath and pushed onward. Her fear would not best her, not when she had come this far already.

Ares pointed at the flickering flames in the forest, and he placed his arm around her protectively, keeping her tightly by his side. He stopped walking, taking time to whisper instructions to her before they traveled any closer.

"That is one of the greenskin camps. Remember, the orcs have eyes like yours. They struggle to adjust from light to dark rapidly. The safest place to be is just beyond the reach of the firelight before their eyes can adjust to the change in visibility. If one of them approaches, be still. They are unlikely to spot you if you do not move." Ares took her by the hand, gently moving her behind him. "Just in case, though," he whispered, raising a hand up to his blindfold and pushing it above his closed eyes.

Sarra understood. Although he kept a firm grip on her hand, she knew to stay behind him at all times. One stray glimpse of his deadly eyes, and she would become one of the unfortunate souls trapped in Ro'al forever. Sarra lowered her head, staring at her feet until she felt certain she was safely out of his sight.

They moved forward, toward the outer rim of the camp where the fire's light barely reached. A group of orcs sat around the fire, eating something indiscernible. Their large forms hunched as they occupied themselves with their food, grunting and laughing with deep, haunting voices that shook the trees when they gave a particularly deep bellow. They took no notice of Sarra and Ares, though one orc rose to his feet and walked into the darkness ahead of them. Ares moved Sarra beside him, taking a knee in an effort to remain low to the ground. Sarra joined him, and he drew the tattered cloak around her shoulders over her head, pulling it down just over her eyes.

The orc's loud footfalls landed upon the ground just ahead, and Ares took Sarra's hand, placing it over his chest so she could feel his slow heartbeat. He was not afraid of the orc, and Sarra knew she should not be either. She took a deep breath and trusted him to guide her around the beast without detection. The orc passed them by, its proximity close but not too oppressively so, and true to Ares's word, it did not see them, still blinded by the fire it had stared into with its companions for too long. As it moved by to begin its patrol around the camp, Ares gave Sarra's hand a squeeze and stood, trailing slowly behind the orc and away from the camp. The entire interaction with the greenskin lasted only a matter of moments, but Ares drew Sarra under his arm, and with that gesture, Sarra knew for certain they were safe.

As they moved out of earshot of the camp, Ares relaxed and placed more space between them, although Sarra had not minded his close proximity. Light began to filter through the waning branches, and by the time they emerged from the forest, the cloud cover overhead had faded. The ocean lay just ahead.

Shining brilliantly above them, the stars illuminated the black canvas of the clear sky, the moon next to them, large just like the sun. Sarra glanced up from the ground, hearing a faint crash and roar in the distance as the ocean waves pummeled the beach. Ares moved his blindfold back below his eyes, his smile returning as the sight of the endless expanse of water crested wide in front of them. Sarra gasped, taken aback by the pure beauty of the sight before her. She spotted white caps rising and falling with the tide, and the waves did twinkle like the stars. Excitement took her breath away, and she moved faster, Ares walking just as quickly beside her. Her booted feet kicked sand once they hit the beach, and Sarra closed her eyes, breathing the fragrant salt in the air deep into her lungs as they reached the water's edge.

"Worth the walk?" Ares asked, surveying the ocean for a long moment before turning to face her.

"Yes," Sarra replied breathlessly, opening her eyes wide to watch the water. "I would have walked five hundred days for this."

She laughed like a little girl, her smile joyous and bright, and her happiness in the moment rivaled any she had ever experienced in her most favorite memories. "This is the greatest gift I have ever received. Thank you. For everything." Sarra turned to Ares with a swell of emotion in her chest. "For taking me away from my home and for showing me that right is not always right, wrong is not always wrong."

And that love was where you least expect it.

She paused before she spoke her thoughts aloud, reconsidering the desire to mutter what she knew to be truth. *Love.* She did not take that word lightly, and it seemed fast, too quick, almost as if there was no way it could be real. However, Ares made her feel things she had never felt before. *Does he hold me in the same esteem?*

"And that even curses cannot stand in the way of a man that loves his people," Sarra concluded with a sheepish grin before lowering her eyes from his blindfolded gaze and turning away. She vowed then, silently to herself as she listened to the water and experienced the beauty of this distant part of her kingdom, that she would do everything she could to see Ares survive. She would argue with her father, fight him with her bare hands if she had to. She would destroy the entire greenskin battalion herself, and ride through the trees of the forest with a sword in her hand. She would travel to the ends of the realm to find a way to keep him with her, even if it meant sacrificing everything she held dearest to her.

Because if Ares were no longer of this world, Sarra did not know how she would exist in it without him. The thought of losing him forever sliced so deep, it reached her soul, and even just a glimmer of that pain made her yearn for the comfort of his touch.

CHAPTER 16

FOR A LONG WHILE, SARRA LOST HERSELF IN HER THOUGHTS, and she did not register Ares moving beside her until he fell to his knees in front of her. Surprised, she glanced down at him, noting how his hair fell over his brow, when his hands began tugging the ties in her boot laces free. She wiped her cheeks quickly to hide a few stray tears leaking from her eyes, and then she wiggled her toes inside of her boots to steal Ares's attention. He focused on his work though, barely acknowledging her movements.

"What are you doing?" she asked, her smile returning as she watched him.

He ushered her foot from one of the boots and lowered it into the soft, fine silica of the beach. "It is the quintessential experience to feel the sand between your toes, and at this time of year, the water should hold some warmth. Though, I suspect it will still be a little brisk. You would curse me forever if you did not have a chance to feel the waves on your skin."

The sensation of the sand between her toes made them

curl pleasantly into the soft earth. The sun's warmth still radiated just below the top layer of sand, and Sarra closed her eyes briefly with a hum of approval. Content, she grinned at Ares with her eyes half lidded. "Are you certain I would curse you?"

He removed her other boot with a laugh. "I do not know. Perhaps you can tell me."

The easy air continued to play around them as Ares stood and directed her toward the water. Both of her boots sat abandoned on the beach a safe distance away. Ares kept his own upon his feet, not even attempting to remove them while introducing Sarra to the luxuries of the ocean.

"It is a very refreshing sensation, is it not?" he asked once she reached the water's edge and began to wade into the salty waves.

"It is. You should remove your boots and join me." Sarra lifted her hands, stretching her arms wide as if embracing the ocean herself. She twirled slowly in a circle, enjoying the crashing of the water around her ankles. "What kind of memory will this be if I have to experience it alone?"

Ares stood silent, and Sarra dropped her arms to her sides, turning to look at him with a bright smile. Seeing her enjoyment, he appeared to reciprocate, nodding in agreement with his lips turning upward as he began to move to his knees.

"Ares, wait!" Sarra shouted quickly. She stepped forward toward him, falling in front of him to place her own knees in the sand. "Here."

She reached for his boot, hesitating momentarily with uncertainty, but Sarra looked up at Ares's face and became encouraged by the memory of his kindness as his hands had untied her boots earlier. She carried on with her task, moving forward, and her slender fingers tugged at his muck covered laces.

"Sarra," he whispered as she worked the strings, a protest in the tone of his voice that Sarra dismissed.

"These boots need to be cleaned anyway, and when we finally finish doing that, I will demand you give me one final thing." She freed the laces from a knot, pleased with her work, and brushed a rogue hair out of her face with the back of her hand. "You will dance with me. Our toes will dig into the sand while the waves caress our feet and smiles stretch our faces."

Sarra looked at her fingers, wondering if he would deny her demand. *Will he pull away from me and not allow me the glimpse into the life I wish for more than anything?* Meeting and learning about Ares had changed her entire world, and Sarra recognized that he was addicting and fascinating to her, so much so that she desperately wanted more from him.

She needed more. More conversations. More innocent touches. *More time.*

However, her father would arrive one day soon, and dancing on this beach with Ares could very well be the last chance that she had to enjoy his company forever.

"You will pretend I am not a princess, and I will pretend that you did not abduct me. We will be just two people enjoying the company of one another under the stars." Sarra giggled, bringing the back of one of her wrists to cover her mouth. "I would ask if you are agreeable, but I am afraid you have no choice in the matter."

She tugged the boot off his foot and fell back into the sand with the force of the act, landing on her rear with her legs stretched straight in front of her. The awful smelling shoe remained in her hands, and despite her wrinkled nose, Sarra's smile stayed intact. A short laugh bubbled out of Ares, and he stared down at her undignified pose. He placed his other foot on the sand between her legs, moving it close enough she could easily reach the strings keeping it tied. Sarra's fingers moved over his remaining boot, offering this small act of kindness as yet another thank you for the present he had given her. A long, pained sigh drew out of him as she took to it. Ares raised his hand, pressing it gently to the soft skin of her cheek. The cool caress of his fingers burned like a delicious fire, and for a brief moment, Sarra turned her head into his palm, allowing more of his touch to sear her.

"Sarra," Ares whispered, his voice laden with emotion he so obviously tried to conceal. To everyone else, she was their princess, but to him, she was unapologetically Sarra. Nothing about their interaction was proper. Nothing about her was proper. It made Sarra revel in the moment more, because for the first time in her life, she could finally breathe. She yearned to feel the space between them fade away, and her fingers itched to push his blindfold over his eyes. Desperately, she wanted to see him, all of him, but danger dictated otherwise.

Ares rubbed his thumb across her jaw, and Sarra bit down on her bottom lip. His finger traveled to the plump skin she snagged, pressing down so her teeth released it. "I am so fearful of what one dance with you would bring. I am terrified of how it would make me feel, how you would feel, and then losing it."

His hand fell away, but a sadness lingered, holding her heart like a vice grip. However, Sarra quickly moved, capturing his hand with both of hers. His boot laces fell, forgotten in the moment as she returned his palm to her cheek. His touch earned a contented sigh from her lips, and Sarra closed her eyes tightly, soaking up every moment he allowed her to.

"But you have forgotten. We are not those people, Ares. We do not have to worry about what-ifs here." Sarra smiled, eyes tightly shut. "I came to visit with my father. You held a great feast for us in your palace. We laughed all night long, and you promised me a dance that never happened. It was late and everyone else retired for the night, but not us. You stole me away, whisked me off on the back of your horse, and brought me here to show me the ocean and to give me the dance you promised so that there would be no way I could forget you when I left."

Ares inhaled a quick, unsteady breath. His fingers shifted to just below her ear to caress her hair. His free hand took hers, holding her tightly.

"Do you see it, Ares? For tonight, that could be our truth." Sarra opened her eyes, regarding him dreamily. "Please let it be."

Ares pursed his lips, an errant drop of liquid escaping from beneath the blindfold near the corner of his eyes, and he nodded. "I can see it. I can see it, Sarra."

His hand trailed down along her neck, his fingertips less than featherlight touches that shifted down her skin to her shoulder. He traced her arm to take her other hand in his, rising slowly from the sand. Ares assisted Sarra, helping her stand before him and then bringing her close. He kicked free of the boot she had loosened, and sent the muddy thing sprawling into the sand.

Sarra thought she had made just a simple, innocent request of him, but she fought with herself as he drew her to him, bargained relentlessly with logic and convinced her desperation that she could fix it all. As she stepped into Ares's waiting embrace, she wished for a miracle, shooting stars be damned.

Their toes met in the sand, and her stomach fluttered. Words she desperately wanted to say waited on her tongue, but, in an effort to save a little piece of him from the little piece of her that she wanted to give, Sarra refrained. The conviction of the thought that no one else would ever deserve to hear those words except for Ares startled her. *How can I feel so strongly for a man I have just met?*

"Sarra," Ares hummed politely, striving to fall into the role she had assigned him. "May I have this dance?"

He stood close, so close she wondered if he could feel the way he made her heart race with just the low tone of his voice. "You may have this dance and a thousand more if you wish it, Ares."

What a joy to dream he could claim the other thousand. A lifetime's worth of dances, embraces, laughter, and memories waiting to be created. It fueled her passion, but also made her hands tremble. "You make me nervous," she admitted with a little laugh, glancing down at his chest instead of meeting his eyes through his blindfold. "Me, a fearless princess, nervous over a man that makes my mind and my heart war with one another. Do you know the power that you hold within your hands? The spell you weave around me with every step of this dance and every gentle word you have spoken to me? Even your touch has done things to me that I do not quite understand. I want to feel your arms wrap around me tightly, as if you will never let me go. I want to hear your heartbeat, memorize your face, learn as many things about you as I can because I just—"

She could not bear to look at him, could not bring herself to accept embarrassment if her admissions were not received and reciprocated. Rejection from the only man she ever wanted to give a chance would sting worse than any bite she had ever had. "I just wish that morning would never come."

"I do know," Ares responded, moving one of his hands to her hip. "I am hypnotized by you, haunted by you. You are far more than I could have ever imagined, and yet I feel as if I have always known you. As if we were destined to have this moment."

His words crumbled, leaving a final string unspoken.

And lose it.

Sarra understood, her face falling under the weight of the sentiment. Ares stepped to his left, guiding her along. He moved them backward and repeated the motion, pushing them into an easy gait of a simple, unassuming waltz under the moon.

Ares tested her with his words, daring her to embrace

whatever brewed between them. *Does he see just how attached I have grown to him?* He spoke the deepest secrets of her soul, whispering thoughts like he felt he had known her all of his life. It jarred her in a way, because truly, Sarra felt the same. The minute she met him, she had been fascinated by him. A man of morals and sacrifice. Ares was everything she wanted to be, everything she needed him to be.

"I cannot take my eyes off you," he muttered, raising his hand from her hip to her cheek to lift her eyes back to his face. "Can you feel them? Do you know their want, their intent, and how they ache to behold you forever?"

Sarra swore she could see his eyes despite the silk over them. In fact, she knew they memorized her just as she had memorized him back in the palace. She nodded in answer to his question, sheepishly admitting her awareness of him. Her stomach continued to flutter under his gaze, and she felt heat return to her cheeks yet again. *Why does he matter so much?* Knowing he felt the same as she did was the ultimate gift.

Pausing their dance, Ares removed his hands from Sarra. He drew the cloak off her shoulders and tossed it away onto the sand as a mischievous smile grew on his face. One hand quickly returned to her hip, his fingers moving around her waist to her lower back. He drew her in closer to him, pressing her chest to his. With no warning, he stepped into a more daring, sweeping movement, lifting her off her feet as he whirled around. He skipped in the shallows with a short, barrel-chested laugh, twirling her through the water as Sarra giggled along with him. After a few quick repetitions, both of Ares's hands fell to her waist, lifting her gracefully and effortlessly into the air. He brought her down to her feet gently, eyes never leaving her face, placing her feet into the wet sand. Their dance continued, more upbeat and energetic. The sadness disappeared, and as if under a spell, their reality faded away. This moment with Ares would forever haunt her dreams, and as the moonlight shined down upon them, Sarra wondered how this perfect place rested just outside of somewhere so entirely dark.

Can we just disappear together? Tonight?

"You are a good dancer," Sarra said, refusing to ruin the moment with her stray thoughts. "I am quite pleased that I agreed to it."

"That you agreed to it? I remember it a bit differently." Ares chuckled in mock dissatisfaction. He retaliated abruptly to her jest, taking her hand, and twirling her out from his center before wrapping her up in his arms again, even closer than before. They swayed in the clear, white light cascading down from the sky above them, and Sarra wrinkled her nose with a laugh.

"As surprising as it might seem, many men do not ask me to dance with them. I do not even believe I have ever been alone with one as long as I have with you." The heat in her cheeks built into an inferno. "I suppose they find me intimidating. But you do not, do you?"

"Many men are fools," Ares said with a shake of his head, teasing in his tone. "I do not find you intimidating. You were quite easy to abduct."

Many men were fools, but the one she danced with was not. She could not lump Ares in with her other suitors when he so boldly stood out in a sea of vibrant color while the rest were dull and gray at best. Sarra could pick Ares out of a crowd without any hesitation. He was so arresting to her, so exotic, and perfect. *Does he know? Does he understand how deeply I have begun to care for him?* In her eyes, he was the furthest thing from a monster, and it was he she held upon a pedestal.

Sarra's smile faded, a somber look overwhelming the brightness of her joy. "I always thought that perhaps I was not soft enough. Pretty enough. Endearing enough. Princess or pauper, deep down, we all just want to be loved for who we are, not what we are."

With a soft sigh, Ares's hands fell to her hips, moving Sarra slightly away from him so he forced her gaze to his face.

"But you are," he said, and Sarra felt the truth in his words. "You are beautiful, more so than any man could ever ask for."

He raised his hand, drawing the backs of his fingers over her cheek. "And soft, also. Sweet and kind, but strong and resilient. Poised and graceful." Ares twirled her again, her toes lifting off the sand until they splashed into the water as he spun her. "Ever so graceful."

As they settled back into their easy rhythm again, he gave her a quizzical look. "Perhaps they simply know, on some level, that they are unworthy of such a creature as you. Perhaps they are cowed by your beauty and your goodness. Maybe they lose themselves staring at your lips."

The moment was too clean, too perfect. His toes sank into the sand beneath them, just touching hers. Sarra's eyes dipped toward Ares's lips as she wondered what a taste of him would be like.

"Sarra." Her whispered name felt like a fine wine that danced across her tongue, smooth, decadent, and perfect. His voice drew her attention, enticing her back to his eyes. Ares had succeeded. Sarra felt so much her heart physically ached in her chest. "I . . ."

He leaned closer, his breath shaky, and his lips parted. Sarra's eyes grew heavy, her lashes drifting down to touch her cheeks. Ares lifted her to him, his hands wrapping around her waist, as he moved with clear intent.

There was no moment more perfect than the one they were living.

A crashing roar forced Sarra's eyes open with surprise and

diverted Ares's attention. Their dance had seen them stray further down the sandbar, and the waves had drifted lazily back toward the sea. All at once, though, the fury of the ocean returned, and a large, loud wave barreled toward them. Ares grasped Sarra's hips, lifting her high over his head. The tattered ends of her dress fluttered in the ocean breeze, and Sarra gasped at the alarming change in atmosphere. Ares protected her from taking the brunt of most of the wave. Sarra could not help the sob of need that shook her. Anger unfurled inside of her. Fate played a cruel game with her heart, and when she almost tasted ambrosia on her lips, it was ripped away as fast as it had been given to her.

Ares staggered a few steps back, the water of the rough wave reaching up to his neck. Sarra squealed with the cool chill of the water that assaulted her from the knees down. The wave broke on the sand, and Ares lost his grip on her hips, wrapping his arms around her legs as she fell from his grasp. He held her steady and safe above the water with her stomach to his head, his soaked hair rubbing against the bodice of her dress. He turned his head to his side, sputtering droplets from his lips, and carried her to the sandy shore before lowering her down so her feet touched the sand. Then Ares fell to his knees, coughing.

Sarra shook, the cold water chilling her skin, but her concern was for Ares as he crumbled into the sand. Drenched in the cold water, his clothing stuck to him like a second skin. He shivered violently, more so than Sarra did herself, and in moments, he quickly began to strip off superfluous layers of his clothes.

"S-sh-should have w-w-waited until s-s-summer," he stuttered, and Sarra instantly remembered what she had read about basilisks and those cursed like them. Most died of hypothermia within the first year, and cold was perhaps their greatest weakness. She wasted no time, dipping down next to him on her knees, rubbing the warm palm of her hand across his cheek.

"Are you all right?" she asked, concerned. He tried to wave her off, attempting to reassure her that he would be fine, but one look at him and Sarra knew better. She scoured the depths of her mind, searching for information that might be useful. Surely after everything she had read in her life, she knew something that could help him. Noting the path her palm took over his skin, an idea came to her. *Perhaps it could work, but will he be agreeable?* Sarra shook that question away, deciding again that Ares truly had no choice in the matter. "Here, let me help you."

She reached for the hem of his shirt and began to tug the material off him. After she deposited the cloth on the beach, she climbed to her feet and walked behind him. "The sea is in front of you. Stay that way."

She remained calm, even as her fingers trembled along the material of her dress. She reached for the belt securing her weapons, allowing her dress to fall loose around her torso. Her fingers grasped the bottom laces, their tight hold secure but now unwanted. Within moments, Sarra's gown fell into a pile around her feet. Gingerly, she stepped out of the material, wrapping her arms around her torso to cover her breasts, keeping them from the cool air licking her bare skin. Sarra had to wonder what on earth had possessed her to act so unabashedly wanton around Ares like this. Her hands found his shoulders after a moment, putting a gentle weight upon them as she slid her body behind him into the sand. Her chest pressed against his back, and Sarra's hands began to rub along his arms in an attempt to warm him.

"Skin to skin contact," Sarra said quietly. "It is supposed to take the chill right out of someone prone to hypothermia. I will warm you, but I need you to relax."

CHAPTER 17

Ares stiffened under her touch as Sarra watched realization hit him as hard as a second ocean wave. She might have chuckled at his response if circumstances had been different, but given the way he shivered repeatedly, she focused on warming him instead.

"Relax?" he asked incredulously between chattering teeth so loud Sarra could hear them, but at her direction, Ares tried his best, shifting from his knees so that he sat on his rear. He closed his eyes, seeming to focus on slowing his breathing. She had expected some type of response from him, but Sarra wondered if maybe he hated the way she felt pressed up against his back. *Do not men enjoy the feeling of a woman's body?* Her lack of experience in intimacy might have made her misstep. Regardless of whether or not this was enjoyable for her companion, Sarra knew it was the only option they had to warm him before he succumbed to hypothermia.

"I am sorry," she said softly. "I know this must be

uncomfortable, but truly, it is for the best. I read it in a book once. Travelers use this tactic when they get stranded outside in the winter. It is supposed to be less jarring to the system than using warm water boiled over a fire." Sarra tried to keep her voice smooth, hoping beyond hope that his body would not be so tense if she were to talk to him and keep him calm.

"L-lucky t-t-travelers," he laughed between chills.

"Shivering like this is good. It is a sign your body is trying to warm itself. I would have been more concerned if you had not noticed the cold."

"Oh, I am aw-w-ware of the c-c-cold, I assure you, but you are h-h-helping me forget it."

Sarra's hands slowed their massage of Ares's arms. She drew back, sliding her arms under his, then returning her body to his back. Her hands pressed palm side down upon his chest, and she moved her cheek to rest against the back of his shoulder.

"I can hear your heartbeat," Sarra said after a long moment of silence. Her eyes drifted closed, and she focused on listening to the soft thrumming sound inside of his chest. "It sounds like a drum playing the most enchanting melody. It is soothing. I could almost fall asleep like this."

Except she was becoming all too aware of the man she held onto. Her body could not deny its attraction to him, not with the way his muscles felt under her fingertips or how her breasts teased against the strong masculine wall in front of her.

"You should feel honored. No other man has gotten me to disrobe and touch him like this." She boldly moved one of her hands, grabbing his arm and maneuvering his hand to press it against one of her thighs. Her voice soft in his ear, she whispered, "I enjoyed the weight of your hand here earlier. Are you uncomfortable with me like this, Ares?"

Daring. That was a word she had never thought to use to describe herself before, but in that moment, with Ares's hand upon her thigh, Sarra felt it resonate deep within her soul. She did not shy away from him, even as his shivering slowed, and his body warmed as best it could. Sarra stayed in place, patiently waiting for his response, and when he finally spoke, the inferno inside of her roared with a renewed source of fuel.

"I am honored," Ares replied, turning his head to glance down at his hand, and the warm, soft flesh his fingers pressed into. His hands caressed her skin, fingers curling against her flesh and giving a soft squeeze. "And less uncomfortable than would be proper."

He leaned back into her, moving his cheek to the top of her head as she leaned into his neck. "But . . ."

Her breath sharpened with a deep inhale, and it shuddered through her until Sarra smiled to herself. She savored the connection between them, not allowing his unfinished sentence to deter her.

But he is a dead man.

The thought nearly forced her to choke on her own air. Sarra pressed into Ares tighter, holding him until the suffocating sadness faded. She steered her thoughts away from his presumed doom, directing it toward something more entertaining to tease him about.

Sarra smiled into his back, her lips grazing his skin in a soft kiss. "But you are too concerned with my virtue, Ares. I am not asking you for anything except to enjoy the moment and what I offer to you."

"And what of *my* virtue, Sarra?" Ares asked with a short

laugh. "You do not seem to be the least concerned about that."

His words were true. She was not concerned about his virtue, but that was because she did not anticipate that she would take it from him. He was reserved, not nearly as willing to embrace the ideas she had painted, and because of that, Sarra understood there would always be something holding him back from expressing his true interests in her if those interests even existed. With his words, admissions, and the things mostly left unsaid, her heart sang with the feeling of reciprocity.

Sarra moved her hand over his that covered her thigh. Her voice was a gentle tone, serene and at ease as she continued, "If your fingers wander, I will not fault you, but we can stay here, like this, and just enjoy the remainder of our time together if it pleases you instead. No promises and no conditions. Just two people, watching the stars together upon the beach, curled in the comforts of having one another for even just a fraction of forever."

A cool, smooth exhale escaped him as she laid out her wants, and he nodded. "I would like that."

They sat upon the beach for several minutes in silence, Ares's breath steadying and the last of the shivers leaving his system. Every deep exhale from either of them hummed approval for the situation, and he angled his head against hers. Sarra savored the time they had together.

"I do not want you to get cold either." Ares shifted, raising his hands to his blindfold, and lifting it off his head. He placed the silk cloth in Sarra's hand. She attempted to question him, but he pushed himself to his feet and turned to face her intentionally without the barrier of the silk for the first time. His eyes stayed firmly closed, and Sarra admitted that it was easy to underestimate what a handsome man he was with the small portion covered in cloth. Sarra was not sure she had ever seen a man more deserving of her heart.

His kindness showed itself in the creases at the corners of his eyes, and Sarra could see the worry that had marred his features for years in the tired dark patches under his closed lids. Goodness seeped from every single pore upon his person. She opened her mouth several times to speak, but she could not find the right words to express herself. Instead, Sarra watched as Ares turned and fetched her discarded cloak. The blindfold in her hand was his promise that he would not steal an untoward glance at her.

Ares used his feet to guide him, catching the tattered material with his toes. He reached down to grasp it with his hands, then he moved back toward her, a hand in front of him finding the surface of a large, weathered stone. He pressed his back to it, sliding against it as he sat with a warm smile on his face. He spread his legs apart, patting the sandy spot of the beach between them.

"Your consideration is charming," Sarra said as she stood and walked toward him, bare skin exposed to the elements. Easing herself into position, Ares held the cloak to cover her while Sarra pressed her back to his chest. He covered her expeditiously, bringing the cloak over her to shield her from the cool ocean air and to help her retain her precious body heat, but what she truly desired were the strong arms poised to hold her instead. As if understanding her desires, Ares brought his arms around her, both of his palms settling onto her warm, plush thighs, giving them a soft, reassuring squeeze. He lowered his head, brushing his nose against her hair.

Sarra embraced his hold, allowing herself to be

entangled with him. Her hands played with the material of the cloak, fiddling with the frayed ends as the butterflies in her stomach took flight yet again. "Your cloak has kept me warm since the moment you gave it to me. Where did you find it? Was it a gift?"

"The cloak was my father's once. He gave it to me before he rode out to meet the orcs in battle. To remember him, if the attack failed," Ares explained, and Sarra clutched the cloak closer to her chin. "It gives me great pleasure to see it comfort you so, as it once did for me. I would be honored if you kept it as a way to remember me as well."

He held her, both simply savoring the moment. The crashing of the waves played like a song in the quiet night, one she had never heard before. A shudder of a breath rushed through her, her boldness intensifying as the tease of Ares's fingertips sent a shiver up her spine.

"Ares?" Sarra asked quietly.

"Hmm?"

She moved under the cloak, her fingers sneaking from the material to trail along his arm, wanting to touch him as much as possible. She lifted her hand after a moment, pressing her palm against the side of his face to draw him toward her. "Is it possible to ask you for one favor? Perhaps in return for being so easy to abduct? I know how much of a relief that was for you."

"For you, anything." Ares chuckled, pushing his scruff-covered jaw into her palm, teasing the soft skin with the stubble from his cheek. Sarra dropped her hand and looked down at the cloak, heart beating faster. However, she could not back down now. Morning would eventually come, stealing their moment, and Sarra refused to waste a scarce opportunity such as this.

"I mentioned that other men were intimidated by me, and that no one has ever asked me for a dance. I—" Uncertainty forced her pause. *How will my next words be taken?* "I would like to be kissed, once, by you to know what it feels like so that I might remember it forever."

The request hung in the air for a long moment, leaving Sarra wrestling with her insecurities, a sense of longing for Ares and the fear of his rejection.

He did not reply to her with words, instead moving slowly behind her to extricate himself. The only thing she could hear was the roar of blood in her ears as she fought down the overwhelming anxiety gripping her. Sarra knew that she asked for a hefty favor, one that came with a price just as big as the reward. One kiss from this man and she would be ruined, but her lips ached to taste him, and her body yearned to be touched intimately by the hands on her thighs. She held her breath as Ares settled her against the stone with care, her hands ready to reach for him with an apology on her lips should he dash away. He stayed, pushing himself over her to straddle her legs and place an arm on either side of her torso. Sarra lifted her gaze, eyes watching as an incredible softness shone upon his features.

One by one, he reached for her hands and brought her palms to his lips, giving them both a soft, ineffably sweet kiss on each as if testing the waters. Sarra forgot about the cloak, letting it fall, abandoned, farther down her bare form, exposing her breasts to the cool night air. She did not worry about her modesty. Ares was a gentleman.

He brought each kissed hand to his shoulders, encouraging her to wrap her arms around his neck. His lips parted and he leaned into her. Sarra's eyes drifted closed as he drew closer.

They connected softly at first, a short, simple press of their lips that was as clean and unassuming as they came. It lasted for several moments before he withdrew, and although the kiss was simple and sweet, Sarra had never felt such electricity in a touch. When Ares pulled away, she did not feel content enough with what he had given her, and as he inhaled more sharply than before, she knew he felt the same. In moments, he returned, his lips brushing against hers with a hunger she had not felt in his first taste of her.

His second kiss slammed into her like wildfire, hot and unrestrained. Rough hands clutched her soft cheeks, unwilling to let her go, and his lips moved across hers in coercion. Sarra made a soft sound before her hands gripped him tighter, meeting each of his movements with a complimentary one of her own.

She could not and would not stop kissing him.

Her skin burned for him, and Sarra's body reacted to Ares's kiss so intensely she could have sworn she had done this before with him. Her teeth snagged his bottom lip. She arched into him to bring more of her into contact with his body. Arms coiled around his neck with a need bordering on desperation, Sarra mewled when his tongue parted her lips, delving into her mouth, tasting her. With a soft, playful nudge, Ares invited her tongue out to play in an inviting dance, just a short waltz he punctuated with a soft sound of needy delight.

Heat funneled through her body, pooling between her thighs as Ares rolled his hips into her. An unyielding, insistent firmness made itself known, pressing against her increasingly desperate center, before it withdrew. Sarra whimpered, a gentle hum against his lips. She willingly allowed Ares to explore her, and the taste of him was like a savory wine coaxing her to overindulge.

Her breasts longed for his touch, her skin so fiery that she might have melted if not for the chilliness of him. However, she nearly cried when her back suddenly pressed against the cool stone, bringing the loss of Ares's lips slanting over hers. He quickly corrected his mistake in leaving her, hands slipping under her arms and wrapping under her shoulders. His questing digits traced her neck, his fingers curling into her hair and giving her head a sharp tug away from his. Ares angled her face away, lips never truly leaving her body as they traced over her cheek. He gave her a soft rumble of approval when he reached her earlobe, capturing it with a brief tug before he continued planting innumerable soft kisses down her neck to her collarbone.

Her thighs clenched, and the nibble to her ear made her skin pebble with goosebumps, her nipples tightening into taut buds. A shivering inhale filled his chest, his lips lingering, daring not to travel further. He kissed slowly up her neck on the opposite side, following her jawline back to her mouth, concluding his brief exploration with another crash of his lips to hers. With his grip in her hair, there was no escape from this, his final gift to her.

As he finally disengaged, Ares seemed heartbroken, pain imprinted upon his features as he angled back away from her. Sarra's breath came in harsh gasps, her hands all but digging into his skin. Her want for him made her quake, but Ares attempted to cool the blaze between them, bringing his forehead to rest against hers. "We should be getting back soon. It will be sunrise before long, and we may lose our opportunity to sneak past the orcs undetected."

Sarra's lip trembled, clinging to their passion. "No," she whispered. "I do not want to go back, Ares."

She touched his cheek with one of her hands, begging him with each soft stroke of her fingers. "Let us run away together. My father will still come here searching for me. He will never know that we have gone until he has broken through to your people. We could go anywhere." Her words broke, and a gentle string of tears spilled over the edge of her eyes onto her cheeks.

"I am so very afraid," Sarra admitted, voice trembling. "You have changed my entire life, made me feel in ways that I cannot explain, and the way you kiss me . . ." She paused briefly, her implication weighing heavily between them. "Tell me that you do not feel it. Tell me that I am just imagining it all, that it is impossible for me to love someone so fully in a matter of days, that the idea of souls having mates is nothing but a dream for little girls."

Ares kept still, his eyes remaining clenched shut as she pleaded with him, but as she spoke of love and soul mates, he shifted his head side to side, biting down on his lip.

"Sarra," he whispered back softly. "I feel it, I truly do, but it cannot be like that. When your father arrives, he will be furious. Men will die clearing the way to Ro'al, and if you are not there, if I am not there . . ." His expression turned sad again, pained. "Sarra, I cannot take the chance that he will not rescue my people and leave them with broken walls. They are not the most charming folks, as you well know. If I am there I can at least give him a face for the villain that stole you away from him, and I can keep my people in line long enough to help them escape with the troops."

Her pleas fell upon ears that could not choose to hear them. Her heart, swollen with feelings ripped from her mercilessly, ached inside of her chest until she felt helpless. *How could fate be so cruel? What have I done to deserve a pain like this for a second time?* The death of her mother had shaken her foundation but resigning Ares to face her father made her circle the darkest black pit of despair. Tears dripped along her long lashes, continuing to stream a path down her cheeks. She barely made a sound, words completely escaping her as she listened with anguish.

Ares, a man with every quality she desired, had duties that bound him, just as she did herself. Being alone with him made her feel extraordinary, something different than she had ever experienced within the walls of her court. For her entire life, the only act of rebellion she had committed was chopping her long, thick hair, but Ares showed her a different way. Loving a man that did not ask for it, that did not pay for it, that did not beg her father for it, was more delicious than anything she had ever tasted before.

"I need to do this, Sarra." His thumb brushed her tears away. "It has to mean something. What kind of life could I give you? You would live like a fugitive, rustling through the woods like an animal. Even if we found a way to be together and get you home, you would forever be the brainwashed princess who fell for her captor. All of the good you could do for this world abolished, your every achievement tainted by slander." He shook his head. "I cannot do that to you. I cannot bring you down with me. You are too precious to me."

"I would live in rags and dirt if it meant I could have you forever. I have lived in luxury for all my life, but that is not what I want more than anything else." Sarra's hand gently grasped his wrist. "I want this. To feel your touch and listen to your voice. To have you hold me when I am sad and laugh with me when I am happy. You have changed me, and I am still trying to understand just how you did it."

A soft laugh escaped her, despite her tears. "Loathsome, sturdy, unfortunate, miserable, part troll despite saying otherwise, civil, honorable, and—" Moving the hand attached to the wrist she had grasped, she pressed his palm against the bare skin of her chest, over her beating heart. "The very man who has stolen my heart forever."

They stood quietly together, her name on his lips but unspoken. Sarra closed her eyes, listening to the waves crashing behind them, losing herself in the memory of Ares and his passion. He cleared his throat, reminding them both of the time. "It is not safe here during the day. We need to get you back within the walls of the city."

Sarra dropped her hands, moving away from him. She retrieved his blindfold, returning it to his hand, before seeking her own clothing.

"Yes, you are right. Morning will be here soon." She agreed sadly, and with one last look over the sea, toward the moon hanging above it, Sarra wished upon the twinkling stars, wondering if this time they would hear her plea.

CHAPTER 18

ARES OFFERED HIS HAND TO SARRA, THOUGH SHE did not take it. The hurt of his reluctance and the truth of his words made her ashamed of her actions, and she could not bear the thought of meeting his gaze, let alone touching his hand, as they walked away from the beach and into the thicket of trees and brush. Ares moved ahead of her, his head angled toward the ground to watch his feet, and Sarra's heart sank, knowing she was the cause for the distance placed between them. She ached for Ares, but to save them both some dignity, she did what she felt was right.

The sweet memories stung as she mulled them over while they walked together, and Sarra hurt as if one of the greenskins had beat her mercilessly. Her skin remained pearly and clean of abrasions, but her soul was marked and scarred by the fiery kisses delivered by Ares. *I will never be the same. How can I be?* To love so completely as she did was the most uplifting yet terrifying feeling in the entire world. Not even the power of the gods watching from the cosmos could combat the swell of pure and absolute feeling flowing from her soul. However, Ares's rejection because of their circumstances forced her to take a step back. She scowled at her own feet, each step feeling heavy and labored as if her body were weighed down by some outside force. Her boots crushed a few crisp leaves, and her toes dragged in the dirt.

Avoiding her pain stood as an impossible task. She bargained silently to the gods, offering them anything to give her a chance to keep Ares forever. They could take her own life if that meant she could save him, and Sarra cursed them as loud as she could in her head to draw their attention toward her. The louder her cries, the less they could ignore her, if they existed in the first place. She grieved as she crawled across the forest floor, slinking past the greenskin camp with more ease than it had taken them to reach the ocean before. The large forms of the orcs rested in silence, except for the loud, earth shaking snores ripping from their throats and snouts. Ares ensured she stayed a safe distance away, and, in moments, they cleared the camp to wade into the bog.

She refused his assistance through the muck, and Sarra trudged through the grime with all of her strength. She stumbled once or twice, but she persisted, coating not only her boots in the horrid liquid of the mire, but the ends of her tattered dress as well. Her future loss weighed heavily on her mind, and she grew angry until the sight of the wall came into view. Ro'al stood like a reaper, waiting for them with patience. The city appeared lifeless and forlorn, even as the sky began to lighten, indicating dawn was nearby.

Standing below the crumbling stone structure, Ares uncoiled the rope slung over his shoulder. He whipped the loop on one end upward and it snagged an abutment. Sarra could not refuse his assistance as she had through their return to the city, and Ares pulled her to his chest, bringing her arms up around his neck. He avoided her eyes, looking around her at everything else but the sadness she knew he would see. Out of every step of their adventure outside of Ro'al, the ascent back up the wall was easily the most difficult, despite Ares hardly losing his breath during the process.

Once more atop the stone wall, he placed her on her booted feet, and Sarra felt his touch linger as if he wanted to keep her in his embrace for just a moment longer. She withdrew, perhaps as reluctantly as he was to let her go, and Ares turned away, glancing out over the bog and forest from whence they had come. Sarra turned, facing him as her mouth opened with an apology, but she drew up short, stopping as her gaze crossed the horizon.

Numerous columns of smoke rose in the distance from campfires, only just visible against the colors of the sunrise.

"He is coming," Sarra whispered, fresh fear dripping from her words as she watched the sky. The king was nearly upon them, and the battle for Ro'al's freedom would come today. The end was near, her adventure over, and Sarra looked to Ares for comfort and reassurance. His eyes remained glued upon the billowing pillars of smoke though, seemingly unable to look away. Sarra looked to the smokestacks before she turned, floating toward the stairs leading into the city, and back to the darkened halls of the palace. "I . . . I must bathe. It would not be wise to allow my father to see me in such a dress."

But also, Sarra could not look at him any longer. She could not let him see how she wept for him. She refused to allow him to feel the crazed desperation that made her grasp for whatever insanity she could find that would right this. *Why do I want to live if I cannot live with him? Why would I want to rule my people if they were the ones to cause me so much pain? How can I ever look upon my father with the same love and affection when he would be the one responsible for shoving a sword through my very heart?*

Sarra felt like a shell of a woman. She walked like a thing possessed, driven by something between grievous instinct and perhaps a will to simply be away from him. She felt weak and helpless, neither settling well within her. She wanted to crawl to her knees, beg Ares to run away, but she knew he did not want her to love him. He had made it clear. His people mattered so much to him, and Sarra reflected upon that. Ares held true to his virtues. He was the leader she had always hoped to be, and as respectful as it was, as much as it lured her to him, Sarra knew if she wished him to be otherwise, she would have loved him less than she did.

That did not stop her from wishing that she were nothing but a vagrant, because she would never be in this situation had she not been a princess. Her heart would not feel like a fresh, bleeding wound, and her eyes would not be eternally swollen as she cried with helplessness and misery. She would not feel worn, tired, and exhausted from her grieving, and perhaps, she would not feel empty, as if part of her had been left upon the beach. Sarra firmly decided that she never wanted to love again, especially if it destroyed her soul like this. *Why take the risk if there was not a reward? Why love if it was not able to be enjoyed?*

The tall structure of the palace loomed ahead, sooner than she had hoped. Ares had followed her, and as they reached the doors, he moved in front of her to open the entrance of the foyer. Ares lit a torch for Sarra, using one from a sconce in the wall. Her boots clomped on the floor, their steps echoing as they moved around the stone statues to-gether and into the corridors leading to the bath.

Sarra paused, hands upon her hips, in the doorway of the bath. Her back to Ares, she turned her head toward her shoulder, not daring to look at him while she spoke. "I do not need your help. I am sure you have other things that you would rather occupy your time with than a foolish girl."

She heard him recoil despite being unable to see it. His breath hissed through his teeth, and the shifting of his cloth-ing made her still, especially when he placed a hand against her back.

"Sarra, please," he begged with a cracking voice, making her close her eyes tight to keep herself from crumbling to the floor. "Please do not chastise me so. I cannot bear it."

Ares shuffled around her, squeezing into the chamber, and quickly illuminating the room. "Allow me to warm the water for you," he said, walking into the area with the boil-ers. Sarra had not meant to hurt him with her words, but as he moved in front of her, it seemed every decision she made had been the wrong one. Without another word, Ares began to layer wood, then he added coal and lit a flame. He pumped the bellows, stoking the fires at a breakneck pace. Sarra could not help herself. She wept as steam rose from the water.

Strangled sobs of exertion and misery melded with her own as Ares toiled. They were enough to bring her to her senses, and Sarra recognized her grief had overridden her ra-tionality. She moved into the boiler room, following Ares with her eyes. His clothing nearly blazed from the heat, and he worked harder and faster than he had previously. Sarra did not deserve this. She did not deserve him!

"Stop it!" she shouted, her tear-stricken face heating from the warmth of the room and being that close to the raging fire made her blood boil inside her veins. "Please stop it!"

She had to flee, sweat dripped from every inch of her body as the inferno roared hotter. Steam filled every inch of the baths, the water itself as searing as the flames that warmed it. Outside the room, Sarra finally sank to her knees and covered her face with her hands. Her shoulders shook, and she cared not that there was mud caked under her fingernails or dried in patches upon her legs.

"You are such a stupid man!" Sarra screamed, her voice echoing in the large room. She placed both of her hands upon the stone floor, holding herself up. The tattered ends of her dress spread around her, only a fraction of her bare leg exposed. "I do not want a warm bath. I would rather suffer in the cold because it is what I deserve for forcing you into a corner like a wild animal on that beach. I am so sorry for everything I have done." Her tears dripped onto the floor, her eyes closed as her sobbing ebbed. "You deserve so much better than what you have been given. Please come out of that room."

Ares stepped through the doorway, shedding the jacket that still steamed. He let it fall to the floor as he moved toward her, leaving his shirt in place as he approached. With slow steps he moved closer, dropping to kneel in front of her. He reached and took her hands in his own, pulling her to him.

"I am sorry," he said, slowly beginning to stand. He drew her up with him and brought her into his arms. He felt uncomfortably warm to the touch, but the fabric of his shirt gave away the heat quickly. "I would never give back the memories you have given me. Never in a million years. I will cherish them for a thousand lifetimes."

She could not speak. Her breath came in harsh, shallow

gasps, even as her body began to calm from its desperation. Ares's touch reassured her, the kind squeeze he gave her hands enough to keep her from drowning in a whirlpool of despair.

"Please," he said, turning and backing toward the water, never releasing her, never allowing her to pull away from him. He took the first step down into the large basin collecting water, drawing Sarra slowly down each step with him until the water reached her thighs. He had overheated the furnace with such zealous fervor that the water retained its warmth even now. Releasing her, he once more knelt before her, his hands moving under the now muddy water in the basin, which flowed toward a small circular drain at the far end of the bath. Ares helped remove her boots again, each tug a somber, humble motion that made Sarra's lip tremble. His hands cupped water once her boots were removed, and he began to scrub the mud from her thigh, cleaning her of the muck. Sarra's tears mixed with the water beneath her as she leaned forward to watch Ares. He worked his way upward with his task, cleaning her arms and shoulders as he stood until finally, he wrapped her up in his arms again. With careful steps, they moved together into the falling water, his body breaking the force of its wall so the stream dripped down and over her.

"I could never hate you for the things you've shared with me," Ares whispered, almost inaudible above the crashing water. "Do not punish yourself for it. The woman I love should never shoulder such blame." He rested his chin on her forehead, letting the water continue to cascade over them. "I will always be grateful to you, and it will never, truly, be goodbye. I will find you in another life."

Sarra's heart sang. Once upon a time, she had been just a little girl wishing upon stars, who became jaded after loss and the cruelty of life. She thought her wishes would never come true, and that finding a love resembling those in the fairy tales she enjoyed would forever remain an impossibility. Ares proved all of her doubts wrong. Perhaps the stars did listen.

"I will find you a thousand times in a thousand lives," Sarra swore, a fierce determination in her words. "There is no one and nothing that could keep me from you. They could not in this life, and they shall not in another. I have never wanted to feel another's touch as much as I have wanted to feel yours. I have never wanted to taste another's lips as I have wanted to taste yours. I have never wanted to love someone as much as I love you."

Upon her tiptoes, Sarra stood, her body soaked from the water that flowed over them. Her hands caressed his cheeks, exploring the features of his strong jaw, memorizing every second of their time together as the warmth of the water took away some of the chill from the looming darkness before them. Her face moved toward him, lips still aching and uncertain as they touched his, gentle at first, then more insistent as her passion grew. "Please," she asked of him, drawing back slightly with still parted lips. Her eyes searched his blindfold, yearning for just a simple glance to tell her he understood. A moment passed, and Sarra leaned back in for another taste of him.

Ares did not shy away from her kisses under the cascading waters. He lowered his head, bringing his lips closer to her. His arms held steady around her, bringing her up to meet him, but Sarra felt restraint behind his movements, as if he would not allow himself to fall into the passionate pitfall she knew him capable of. He returned her affections, not with hunger but more with a feeling of longing, his lips moving gently against hers instead of consuming her the way she wanted. They were kisses of chaste promise, of love beyond immediate carnal pleasure, soft and gentle. They demanded nothing of her, and only gave what he had to give. He held her in his arms for several long minutes, unwilling to allow their desire for one another to progress further.

His kisses softened her, melting the hard emotions making her desperate. He tempered her hunger with measured touches—a brush of his finger across her jaw, the push of her hair behind her ear, or his lips trailing over her cheek—but his meaning and intent conveyed fully with each. This was not the heat of the moment, instead it was lasting, a moment of enduring love bound not by the dreadful ones awaiting them. Sarra returned every sweet touch he gave, and she calmed with resignation to what fate had planned.

The only option she had was to try and reason with her father. She had faith the king was a reasonable man, her experience at his side had proven that to her enough, and Sarra felt confident in her abilities to persuade him. If it meant marrying Elias for her father to spare Ares's life, she knew she would play that hand if she had to, as depressing a thought as it was.

As the water began to cool, Ares withdrew and smiled kindly. "We should find you a new dress," he murmured, kissing her cheek sweetly.

"A new dress would be nice. It would not befit a princess to greet her father and his troops in this risqué ensemble, although it would be one they would never forget. The dirt might have added an extra touch. It is a shame it washed away so easily." Sarra brought her hand to her mouth, giggling.

"Well, I shall never forget that ensemble." Ares chuckled warmly, his thumb stroking her cheek and wiping away rogue droplets of water trailing from her hair. "I will miss it dearly, but you are right. I will always cherish the unique perspective you have shared with me and me alone."

He kissed her again, once more softly and slowly. Sarra leaned into it, teasing him with a gentle nip to his bottom lip. She grinned at him when he broke away, and his smile fueled the joy and determination in her heart. She would stop at nothing to right this, to keep him, to love him forever.

Ares brushed her hair behind her ear with his fingers. "And after you have changed, perhaps you would do me the honor of watching the morning sun with me again?"

"The sunrise? From the parapet?" Sarra smiled wider, remembering the beautiful sight he had shown her yesterday morning. "It is my second favorite thing to do with you."

She pressed one last kiss to his lips, quick and simple, only lingering with her touch for just a moment, before she danced out of his reach and away from the water. "The first is listing all of your adjectives as we have already discussed. You have yet to refute the 'part troll' and that is concerning."

His hearty laughter echoed in the bath, his tense shoulders beginning to relax. "If you so wish, you may describe me again in great detail while we watch. I could listen to you do so for all time and be more than content."

Sarra twirled around on her way to the door, walking backward to keep her eyes on Ares the whole way. He started to follow her, exiting the water, and letting it pool at his feet as he observed her from the basin entrance. Sarra paused as she reached the door, easing her back against the frame with her hands tucked behind her.

"I shall find a dress myself." Sarra lifted her chin proudly. "I think I can find my way through the palace alone. I will come back here when I am dressed. We will make the best of the sunrise together."

Ares nodded, gesturing toward the torch near the door. "Do not dash away without a light. If you get lost, shout, and I will find you."

Sarra smiled, lifting her hand in a small wave. She stifled a girlish giggle but did as he recommended and grabbed the torch. Then she slid into the hallway with ease, shutting the door to the bath behind her. Her resolve had firmed, every kiss of Ares's lips had intoxicated her with hope and determination to ensure his fate was one where he survived. *Ares loves me*. Not even the darkness of the palace could take away the bright light inside of her. Sarra would speak with her father, but she would not ask him to spare Ares's life.

No, Sarra thought. *I will demand it.*

CHAPTER 19

NAVIGATING THE HALLS OF THE PALACE CHALLENGED her more than she expected. Although she knew they would not harm her, the statutes still made Sarra nervous. Each outstretched hand, every face twisted in a sob struck her. She wondered about their names, their stories, who their families were, but eventually, she weaved away from her stony companions, finding her path toward the bedroom she had occupied.

She used the room as a starting point, curling around the corner down the hall, and following the route she remembered from her first foray from there days ago. The servant's quarters were not far, if her memories served her correctly. Sarra did her best to recall the various outfits she had seen inside the wardrobe within the room to make her decision simpler when she arrived.

Light shone from under the door, just as it had the first time she visited the room with Ares, and the wooden slab eased open into the corridor with a small creak. Sarra blinked quickly, her eyes adjusting to the change in lighting once she entered. The room remained just as they had left it, with the bed decorated with the prettiest red blanket she had ever seen. Whoever the servant was, if it had been the woman frozen outside the library or not, her personal tastes seemed to reflect Sarra's own. With a small smile, Sarra walked inward, directing herself toward the large wardrobe standing open.

Dresses and gowns of assorted colors peeked from behind the ornate doors, providing her with a plentiful selection. However, as Sarra pushed through them one by one, she grew frustrated with how plain they all looked. Her teeth clenched with irritation, the image of what she searched for burned into the front of her mind. She needed something special, something unforgettable, something that proved just how strong she was. Facing her father would not be an easy feat, and, with a life on the line, Sarra did not wish to make any mistakes. She took every piece of knowledge her father had imparted upon her, and she planned to use it as a weapon, but first, she needed to look the part she would attempt to play.

She nearly gave up when she remembered the chest in the corner. It resembled one in her own castle, although she had not seen the thing in many years. Her mother had used it for storage, and although Sarra had not thought much of it during her first visit to the servant's chambers, it held her interest now.

She bent to her knees, hoisting the top of the chest open with a harsh shove. The hinges creaked as it opened, old and unused for far too long. Sarra caught the glimmer of gold, and pushing some random clothes away, she gasped with surprise.

The material was breathtaking, a sea of shimmering blue as dark as the ocean. Reaching into the chest, she retrieved a gown, holding it to her body once she climbed to her feet. The sheath silhouette suited her, even as it dangled from her hands. A teal skirt sat beneath long arrow-shaped pieces of fabric falling from the hem of the bodice. They reached below her knees, creating a stunning layered effect to the dress, accentuating her natural figure. Embellishments of gold lined the ends of the skirt and danced around her bust. Soft, thin material created capped sleeves, and, although it should have been heavy to hold, the gown itself was lightweight and well crafted. Sarra mused at how perfect it was, lamenting for a fraction of a moment how the only thing missing was her crown.

Sarra was unfamiliar with the style of the gown. Its many accents, flares, and laces were not of any configuration she knew. However, within moments of touching it, she knew she would never see its equal, or forget a single detail of its construction.

She dressed quickly and used the small mirror with the bone comb to tuck her hair into a short, braided chignon. Even with her eyes reddened and slightly swollen from her previous tears, Sarra thought she looked as regal as she had during her father's celebration, except this time, she gladly refused to don the color black.

She exited the room with a whispered thank you to the servant that gave her the gift of her dresses during her stay, and Sarra's feet padded along the hallways back toward the bath with her torch in hand. Once she reached the bath entrance, she teetered on her toes, hesitating for a breath, before she gave the thick wooden door a hefty knock. "Ares? Are you still there? I believe I am more presentable than before."

"You are ravishing." His voice greeted her from behind, startling the unsuspecting Sarra. She quickly pressed a hand to her breastbone and turned to face him with an exasperated laugh.

"You frightened me for a moment. I thought you would be inside."

Ares approached her, his own wardrobe different and clean. Although the material he wore looked simple and almost like a peasant's garb, Ares held himself tall and sure. He appeared more regal than even she. His dark green trousers fit him well, and the white overshirt he had chosen teased at the chiseled chest beneath. Boots and bracers had been cleaned, and their cracked leather did not take away from his handsomeness in Sarra's eyes. He was perfect, and his smile made her heart sing.

He moved with his hands tucked behind his back, charming her just by existing. Sarra batted her lashes, looking down at her feet as she felt his eyes travel over her.

"Never in my life have I witnessed such beauty," he confessed, but a wicked grin replaced his warm smile as Sarra returned her gaze to him, and she giggled with nervousness. "Though, I will say, I do miss certain elements of your old outfit."

Ares made it seem as if she made her ensemble beautiful, not the exotic dress fitting her as it was designed. With a sheepish laugh, Sarra lifted her head proudly. Her bold alterations of her previous dress would be a story told for laughs until the end of time. "My old gown had so much personality. It was a struggle to abandon it. I had grown quite fond of it, but I found this dress in an old trunk and thought to myself 'why not?' "

She grasped the skirt with her free hand, her fingers twirling it back and forth under the light of the torch. It shimmered like a gemstone, and Sarra enjoyed watching it sparkle. Stepping closer, Ares removed the torch from her hand, placing it upon a sconce next to the door. He took her hand with his, bringing the one kept behind his back forward to press a hard object into her palm.

"I would be honored if you would take this with you and keep it safe," he said, and Sarra frowned, confused. She looked away from him to her hand, gasping aloud at the gift he had given her.

A tiara made of gold. Diamonds coated it like frost, the

gems twinkling like the stars in the sky had over the ocean. The metal curled in elaborate waves, holding larger crystals in place. The tiara rose to a point, meeting the largest stone in the center.

"Ares," she said, awestruck. "I do not know what to say."

"Say you will take it." He took the tiara from her hand, placing it upon her head with precision. Sarra had never seen something so beautiful. Her own crown, bulky and plain, glistened dully compared to the elaborate one Ares gave her. "Your gown was customary of the ladies of Ro'al, back when the beauty and craftsmanship of our artisans were renown. I am surprised you found one. I thought the last of them had been bartered off to the mercenaries who braved the orc line to sell us their subpar goods. You likely wear the last surviving one, the only evidence of the prosperity my people once experienced."

His hands fell from her head, reaching for her own. "Ro'al never had a queen, as lord has always been our highest honor and your province has always held that title close to its heart. However, the lady of the land was always honored with a finely crafted, gold tiara. It is small, but it is exquisite." He paused, lifting his hand to tilt her chin up with his finger. His thumb stroked her jaw, and Sarra pressed herself into his palm in a sweet gesture. "My own mother wore this, as did several ladies before her."

Wearing the tiara and the shimmering dress felt right to Sarra, as if destiny screamed at her, as if she were meant to wear them both in this exact moment while she clutched Ares's arm. "I will keep this safe. I will treasure it always. You have given me so many gifts. I am afraid I do not have much to give you in return."

He shook his head as she thanked him. "The way it looks on you—it is as if it has always belonged to you. I was merely holding it until we met. You have given me far more than I could have ever dared to ask for, Sarra. Far, far more." His arm looped around her waist, and he tugged her forward, placing a kiss on her forehead.

"I have decided to talk with my father. Once his men breach the wall and enter Ro'al, I will greet them myself. We will greet them together." Her throat thickened, and her words flew from her lips increasingly fast, as if she tried to explain herself before Ares could stop her. "He has never denied me anything that I have wished before, and after spending time here with you . . ." Her arms wrapped around Ares, hugging him to her. "I will do anything in my power to ensure your people and you can live better lives. I am sorry I did not know before now."

"I know you will, Sarra," Ares replied. He pulled back, directing her away from the bath and toward her bedroom. "But let us retrieve the moonstone and head to the parapet. The sunrise awaits us."

Sarra nodded in agreement, pleased he had not fought her in protesting the actions they both knew her father would want to take. However, something sat uneasy in her stomach, and although she attempted to push the feeling aside, it bothered her even as they collected the glowing orb and its cloth pouch. Together, they walked in the warm light of the moonstone, and it bathed the dark stairwell to the parapet when they approached. Sarra remained silent through most of their journey through the palace, lost in her thoughts as she devised a plan to bargain with her father. The more she pondered, the more power she realized she held, and Sarra felt like the queen she knew she was destined to be. Rising above the challenges before her, she would confront her father and she would save the people of Ro'al. Ares would live, and she would not be forced to exist in a land where her love had faded in death.

Still, there were creeping doubts. *Could her father be so forgiving as to suffer the man who had dragged his daughter into danger? Could he be understanding of the plight of a lord protecting his people? Could he justify the numerous losses his army would see to save the poor, debilitated people of Ro'al?* Her father would be livid when he arrived, Sarra knew without a doubt. Even though she had been well cared for, Ares had wronged the king. The odds were still stacked against him, and Sarra would have to tread carefully, but not even her father could refute the power of love. *He had loved my mother, had he not? He had said so himself many moons ago, despite seeming uninterested during the celebration days ago.*

Ares helped her up the stairs, step by step, and when they reached the entrance to the tower, he paused at the door to give her a long, lingering kiss. His lips slanted over hers with a hunger that still lurked under the surface, parting her lips with his tongue until he groaned with the taste of her. Sarra did not expect such a display of passion, but she encouraged Ares by digging her fingers into the firm muscles of his back. Their mouths warred with each other, desperate to curb their intense desire for one another until the earth nearly smoldered under their feet.

In a way, the kiss tasted bittersweet. Again, an uneasy feeling assaulted her once the kiss broke, and as she pulled back to look at Ares, questioning him with her eyes, she wondered why something felt wrong. However, she refused to allow her worries to override her heart. It was content for the first time in her life, Sarra finally finding her soul mate. Ares was the other half that made her whole, and, while she refused to believe in magic and fate, he had been the one to prove all of her doubts incorrect. With his curse and the moonstone, he had shown her magic was more than a story. With his touch and his delightful kisses, he had proven love was hardly imaginary.

In earnest, Sarra tugged him through the door, leading him into the tower. The door at the entrance slammed shut behind him, leaving the two of them truly alone to observe the sunrise. No petrified people watched with their stony gazes, no immoral mercenaries schemed for gold. No orcs rampaged the city, and no kings interrupted with demands.

As they approached the edge of the parapet, Ares wrapped Sarra up in his arms, and she pressed her back against his chest to enjoy the feeling of being loved by someone else.

How many more sunrises will we have with each other? How many times will I look over the land with him just like this? She could wake up before dawn every day with the promise that he would be there to enjoy the sun rising with her. She thought of what their life would be like, and how they would grow old to-gether. *Will we have children of our own? Would he rule with me when I one day become queen?* Ares would love her, cherish her, adore her every day for the rest of her life. No longer would she be forced to fight off the men of the court or listen to their lack of principles. He saw her for who she was, wanted her for who she would always be, and Sarra wished to be with him until her very last breath.

How was it possible to love someone this much in such a short amount of time?

The sun rose just above the horizon, and the columns of campfire smoke had slowed to narrow tufts. Her father and his troops must have moved in the time since their return to the palace, and Sarra took a deep breath, settling her unease. The impending conflict must have been the source of her nerves, be-cause the thought of her father's soldiers battling the greenskins poisoned her with guilt. There was nothing she could do to stop the soldiers from their duties, so Sarra turned toward the ocean, facing the water with Ares's breath against her ear. His chin rested beside her temple, and his embrace remained inviting, though Sarra knew he saw what she had. Their silence stretched for long moments, and as the sun took away every last bit of the night, Sarra knew her dream was ending.

"What a beautiful night we had together," Ares mused, his lips pressing into her hair.

Sarra closed her eyes, inhaling the delightful hint of sandalwood from his skin. "What a beautiful adventure you have given me," she replied with a smile. "What did I ever do to deserve any of this? One moment, I swore to not even speak to you and now, here we are, days later, and I cannot imagine not telling you all of my secrets."

Sarra opened her eyes, tilting her head back to glance at him. She reached up to brush her fingers across his cheek, sighing with contentment at being in his arms. "I was just thinking how it feels almost like I am living in a dream."

Ares seemed distracted, almost as if he heard something she could not. He angled his head into her touch but eventually shifted in the direction of the smoke. Sarra turned to look herself, watching as birds left the trees of the forest in throngs. In moments, the first of the king's soldiers broke through the edge of the tree line, barely visible to Sarra through the murky bog.

"Sarra," Ares breathed her name in a way she could not quite explain. A shiver ran down her spine as he clutched her to him tighter. He pressed a light kiss to her cheek, moving to bury his face in the crook of her neck. She felt his lips brush against her skin. "I will love you always."

Those words. Those blissful words warmed the chill coursing over her skin. She attempted to turn in his arms, wanting to feel his lips against her own again. Oh, how she loved him, how he loved her. Nothing could take her happiness away.

"Please, forgive me," Ares whispered, withdrawing, and moving away from her with inhuman speed before she could register his words. He stood by the door, retreating through it once she looked at him, and it slammed shut with a heavy thud. The sound of metal screeching behind it hurt her ears, and with a loud *clunk*, the sound of a lock clicking into place sealed Sarra away.

Trapped, inside a prison she never anticipated, she felt herself suffocating with a mixture of overwhelming feelings. Like a swift kick to the gut, she struggled with the urge to double over and curl on the stone floor. Her eyes stared wide, wishing the door would miraculously open again, proving this as nothing but a cruel joke. Her devastated sob lodged into the deepest part of her throat, her lips open in a wordless scream as her vision started to grow cloudy and her lungs ached for a breath. Her hands shook, even as she collected the skirt of her dress in her fingers.

"In another life, Sarra," Ares said from his place behind the door. "We will come together, in another life, and I will find a way to make this up to you. *I swear it.*"

"No!" Sarra screamed, rushing toward the door. Her chest filled with air as she repeated that single word over and over again. Tears streamed down her cheeks, dampening her gown as they flowed in rivers from her eyes. She grabbed the door handle, tugging with all of her might until her fingers burned from the force of her pulls. Footsteps began to fade over the sound of her words, and Sarra used her body to beat against the door, fists and feet flailing with the demand that Ares open it.

"I can save you! I can save you! Ares, please do not leave me!"

But the footsteps fell silent. Sarra melted into a puddle of sorrow, painting every stone with droplets of her grief. Her mindless whispers filled some of the quiet, and she prayed to the gods, asked fate for forgiveness, and hoped that her mother could offer her guidance from the afterlife, because Sarra needed a miracle.

All she felt was emptiness.

CHAPTER 20

I T WAS THE SOUNDS OF WAR THAT SPARKED HER attention, dragging her from her numbed state. Sarra lay on the floor, uncertain for how long, staring at the stone awning overhead. Her tears had dried on her cheeks, her eyes swollen and unable to produce more of them despite her grief. Her sobs had stopped, and her chest ached, although she did not know if it was her heart or the harsh breaths that had ripped through her that caused it.

Sarra picked herself up, stumbling as her limbs shook. The shouts of men echoed around the parapet, roars and blades crashing following behind them. The battle against the greenskins had begun in earnest outside the wall surrounding the city. Sarra struggled with each step, but she found her way to the ledge, and peered down to the ground below, watching Ares and the scene unfolding before her.

Pain sliced through her as Ares moved into her view, and she watched as he weaved through the streets of Ro'al, heading toward the gates sealing it shut. He eyed the barricade in front of him then moved forward, attempting to remove the barrier protecting his people with his bare hands. The citizens of Ro'al watched in horror as their lord tossed away stone and board alike. Sarra could see he tried to reason with them, knowing he promised their safety because the king had arrived, but his people fought him, tossing stones and other objects at him just as they had done when Ares had rescued her from them. They were ruthless, cunning fighters, and although she found it inappropriate that they attacked their lord, an odd sense of pride at their resourcefulness swelled inside her. These were the people of her kingdom, and although their lives had been difficult, they were tough, always questioning, and determined.

In the distance, her father rode upon the back of his magnificent steed, a beautiful roan stallion too temperamental for many to handle. The king led his army, moving his mounted platoon quickly toward Ro'al. He wore shining golden armor, ostentatious and entirely unnecessary, in Sarra's opinion. She was not a tactician by any means, but logic told her it served him no real use in battle, forcing him to stand out in a sea of muted colors so he became an easy target. He never listened to her when she expressed her concerns over the risks he took by wearing it and noting the weathered appearance of the metal as he rode toward the wall, he had taken quite a beating by the orcs himself.

Behind her father's mounted fighters, contingents of soldiers set up a defensive line outside of the city, and waves of green monstrosities crashed against them. The orcs with their crude blades and barbaric strategies plowed through the human forces without much resistance at first, but the numerous soldiers fighting on behalf of her father overpowered them, beating them back with a savage roar of their own. "For the princess," they shouted. "For the king!"

Turning from the falling greenskin, Sarra glanced at her

father once more. There was less hate lurking in her heart, more fear that the course of Ares's fate would take the turn that she had been desperate to prevent. Without Sarra to greet her father at the gates, she could not stop the worst from happening, and deep down, she knew that Ares also knew this. The realization that his plan had been to leave her here, within this tower where there was no chance to compromise her safety or her reputation, from the very beginning dawned upon her.

Seeing Ares fight to remove the barricade reinforced the selflessness he exuded. He thought of everyone but himself. He had no sense of self-preservation, had lost all selfishness in his life of woe. Perhaps he wanted to die. Perhaps he was tired of living. A barbaric roar erupted from him, and Ares tore away his blindfold in a desperate act to push his people away. The citizens cowed, scrambling away from him hastily. No statues formed in their exodus, no people shifted to stone and crumbled before her eyes. Again, Ares practiced restraint, playing their fear against them so he could remove the barrier to save them.

Her father drew closer to the gate, greenskins hot in pursuit and making far faster progress in the mud than the horses. With an impossible feat of strength and a heroic cry of exertion, Sarra watched as Ares lifted a massive iron bar holding the wooden gates secure. He shrugged it off his shoulders, and it clattered to the ground. The split door heaved open wide from the center, and Ares drew his sword. He waved it wildly, directing the horseback soldiers into the relative safety of the stone wall surrounding Ro'al. The horses' hooves found purchase on the firmer soil as they reached the entrance, and they scrambled inside quickly.

Two of the mounted riders in the king's escort fell, beset by the greenskins and quickly crushed under massive clubs or cleaved in half by a brutal, terrible blade. Sarra screamed, her voice raw and broken, as the orcs descended on the open gates. Ares leaped into the fray, killing the stragglers who had chased the horses with rapid dispatch, masterfully bashing their blades away before running them through or sweeping away their limbs with a cruel arc of his sword. Sarra had never seen war before. Watching Ares with the telescope had been a far less personal experience than watching him fight along her father's soldiers, men she knew and adored too. *How many of the dead are people I considered friends? How many are old suitors I turned away?* Her stomach swirled, nausea rising with the threat of overwhelming her. Her hands wrapped around her middle, and she held herself, unable to look away.

The riders dismounted, and the last of the defensive lines were established leading to the gates, protecting them from further interlopers. Ares looked like a beast of a man, a brute covered in the black tar of orc blood and a fair amount of blue seeped from his cuts. The king's men had already surrounded him by the time the melee had settled, and Ares raised his hands, letting his sword fall to his side, sinking to his knees in surrender.

From the middle of his men, her father stepped forward, their conversation far too distant to be audible to her. Still, she strained, trying her damnedest to hear anything she possibly could. Ares lowered his head, his hands clasped in front of him as he seemed to plead with the king. His people watched from a distance, cowering behind their shanties and tarps. Sarra held her breath, waiting to see her father's decision, and the discussion appeared perfectly amicable, much to her relief.

In moments, the king waved at the assembled peasants, all of whom stood stone still for a long breath before returning to their homes and quickly collecting their things. Hope pulsed through Sarra's heart, brightening her disposition, as the citizens of Ro'al began to run out of the gates toward a designated set of soldiers and their freedom. The city had held them hostage far too long. They deserved to breathe with ease.

But Ares did not move. Instead, he slumped, lowering his hands to the ground. The king moved forward, leaning close with a fierce snarl imprinted on his face, and tiredly, Ares raised a hand to point up to the tower. Her father looked over his shoulder, up to the ledge where Sarra stood. He waved two of his men over, and directed them toward the palace with his hands, and then the king returned his sights to Ares.

Her father drew his sword.

"No!" Her scream ripped through the air, fear unlike anything she had ever experienced driving her to lean far over the edge. Sarra flailed her arms, attempting to attract her father's attention, but Ares raised his hands. Her father did not bother looking in her direction, instead his eyes remained on the lord pleading at his feet. Ares gestured toward Sarra, passionately conversing with the king. Her father listened intently, and when Ares was finished with his piece, the king rolled his eyes and pointed at him, commanding two of his guards to wrestle Ares into a standing position.

The men tied his arms behind his back, ensuring he could not escape, but that did not deter her love. Ares continued to speak, and Sarra desperately wished she could hear his words. Something about the way he looked, the way he nodded toward her, confirmed her thoughts. Ares begged for his life, for the privilege of being with her. Sarra, herself, pleaded as she watched, asking whatever or whomever listened to allow her this one miracle.

Her father listened carefully, and his lips curled upward just before he replied to Ares in a short breath of words. The king smugly crossed his arms over his chest, looking up at Sarra in the tower. Her brow furrowed as she met her father's gaze, but her attention was quickly captured by Ares, who began to create a scene. Something changed in him, and he began to fight against the guards. He thrashed against their grips, nearly unseating one of them from his horse. Ares whipped his head back and forth, almost as if he wanted to lose his blindfold. He successfully managed to toss one of the guards aside, quickly freeing a hand from his bindings, and he reached for the cloth before four more guards descended and managed to wrestle him under control.

Her father sauntered closer to him, and Ares bared his teeth like a wild animal. He raged against the guards holding him back, and even more men joined the fray to restrain him. Nearly ten men piled on him in an attempt to try and keep Ares under control, and despite the weight and force of the soldiers, the mass of muscle still shifted and struggled to keep him still.

The king leaned down to Ares, speaking again. He finished with a dark laugh, and Ares returned the favor of his words by savagely pulling back and headbutting the king, sending her father reeling backward. The act was enough to remove Ares's blindfold, and he whirled on the nearest guard. Sarra held her breath, alarmed at the sight of his eyes. They shined a brilliant, shimmering emerald-green.

Green. His eyes are green.

The guard staggered backward, screaming before falling to the ground. He promptly turned to stone, just as the orcs had when Sarra watched through the telescope. Ares wrenched himself free of the guards, and he turned on another, who wailed in horror before falling backward and shattering into pebbles on the ground. Ares then turned his baleful gaze upon the king, who crawled on all fours away from the monster in his midst, until a soldier managed to catch up with Ares and bash the pommel of his sword into the back of his skull. Ares dropped to his hands and knees, his head hanging low from the force of the impact.

The guard ripped a battle standard from the king's horse, and Sarra watched as the colors of her own house wrapped around Ares's head, covering his eyes. Her entire body trembled, unable to watch but unable to look away. Two more men grabbed Ares's arms, lifting him into a standing position again. They tugged the ends tightly around his neck, holding him still. Her father gathered his bearings, standing shakily on his feet, then he turned toward Ares, glaring vengefully upon the lord. The king drew his sword, grasping it with a snarl on his lips, and he took three quick steps toward the man Sarra loved. With a forceful thrust, the blade ran Ares clean through the chest, the silvery blade emerging from his back slick with blue blood.

Her father's sword withdrew, and the guards released Ares. His hands clutched at the chest wound, and he fell to his knees, the banner tangled so tightly that he would never be able to untie it. Sarra could feel his gaze on her, watching her even from so far away. Ares raised a hand toward her, and she knew he longed to feel her touch one last time. She reached toward him, renewed tears burning her eyes as she dangled precariously over the ledge.

She would never forget the slick squelch that reached her as her father's sword bit into Ares's neck, and his head fell to the ground, separated from his shoulders.

She would have lived through a thousand nightmares if it would have changed the course of fate. Anguish, pure devastation devoured her. Her hand, still reaching out to Ares, grasped for something she would never have again.

"Ares, I love you!" She screamed his name, over and over, until a roaring fire engulfed her. It licked up her skin, searing every inch of it as her screams turned to agony. As the heat became too much, her vision clouded, and in moments, Sarra faded, sinking into the stone floor of the tower with one last whisper of Ares's name on her lips.

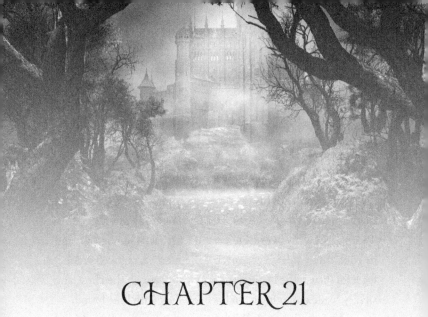

CHAPTER 21

HER BODY SMOLDERED. SWEAT DRENCHED THE SIDES of her face, plastering her hair against her forehead. She lay cocooned, tangled in some constricting softness, inciting panic deep within her gut. Sarra opened her eyes, but everything was far too bright, nearly blinding, and she was forced to close them again. Visions of the greenskins, of Ares, and of the blue blood dripping from her father's sword made her shout in alarm, and she flailed against her bindings, tearing away the silk entombing her limbs. She sat upright with a gasp, pushing her eyes open again, and this time, she kept them wide as she looked around her, startled.

Has my heart been torn from my chest? Has Ares truly died? Have the people been saved from the city surrounded by the crumbling walls? She felt empty, listless, as if there was no point in carrying on, but as the haze clouding her mind faded and the sounds of voices creeped into her consciousness, Sarra blinked. Once, twice, three times.

The bright sun filtered through the glass panes of the

window. Her fingers curled into the blankets she had pushed away. Three maidens stared at her, fear stricken. Two more sobbed in a corner, hugging one another as they stressed over their princess. It was impossible. *How can I be home?*

Sarra shifted, but a sharp pull made her wince. She glanced down to her lap, noting the long strands of blond hair cascading into a pool at her waist. A large lock of it was trapped under her thigh, and she quickly tugged it loose, freeing her movements. Her handmaidens averted their gazes, relief easing the stiffness in their shoulders. Sarra furrowed her brow in confusion, and she could not help but look at all of them as if they were ghosts. *When did I arrive? How long have I been asleep?*

Sarra did not remember her rescue from the tower, but there was no other place that looked like this, no other castle or palace in her kingdom that claimed the luxuries the capital did. Olmalis, the kingdom, was beautiful, but Olmalis, the province, was luxurious and rich beyond imagination. She knew she was home.

Her room remained just as she remembered it. Her crown rested atop the nightstand, a small but sharp letter opener placed beside it. Its handle glinted in the sunlight from beneath a pile of parchment. A quill lay on one of the pieces, a giant black splotch tainting the center. Her family's crest with the large gold griffin stood proudly on a banner over the fireplace, and in the hearth, a fire burned, the cause of the excessive heat. Finally, on the far side of the room, the large armoire with all of her belongings stood open, doors ajar, and the black lace of a gown she remembered so fondly emerged.

But wait, that dress was ruined, was it not?

Sarra's heart thumped hard in her chest. She heard nothing but the rush of blood in her ears, and the scent of sandalwood burned in her nostrils. The youngest maiden, Avella was her name, placed a hand on Sarra's covered leg, and the princess glanced down at the fingers squeezing her kindly.

"Your Grace," the young woman said, her voice soft and reassuring. "You were having a nightmare, milady. Are you all right? You would not stop screaming. You gave all of us quite a fright. We almost called His Majesty."

Avella handed her a damp cloth, then retreated. "For your face, Your Highness."

Sarra's hand touched her cheeks, finding evidence of a stream of tears that dripped down her chin and into the blankets surrounding her. She accepted the rag, pulling it toward her, even as she scooted back in her bed, away from the women watching her with concern. She felt like an animal, trapped and cornered, afraid and untrusting. *Will my father come for me next? Will he drive a sword through my chest and lop my head off without any remorse? Will he laugh cruelly in my face as he watches me slump forward as life leaves my body?*

Everything seemed so different. Gone was the gown of gold embellishments and sparkling blue fabric, instead replaced with a simple nightgown made of cotton that Sarra knew fell short, just below her knees. She no longer wore a tiara of gold and crystal, and her sorrow amplified because she broke the promise she made to Ares to keep it safe. *Did my father confiscate it? Did the soldiers loot and tear it from me when they found me in the tower? Where is the moonstone? Ares's tattered cloak? All of the books inside the library? Had it all been left behind, forgotten in that wretched city called Ro'al?*

Her hand fell from her face, replacing it with the wet cloth, and she looked down at herself as the cool compress worked over one of her eyes. Sarra picked at the long ends of her blond hair, feeling them with her fingertips as she still could not formulate any words to reply to the women that looked at her as if she were possessed. *When did my hair grow so long? Does not the blade I used to cut it not currently sit within hand's reach on the nightstand?*

A wave of nausea gripped her stomach, clenching it hard as if a fist squeezed around the organ relentlessly, and Sarra remembered her final moments with Ares in great detail. The memory of his sweet kisses raised her temperature, made her yearn to feel his touch against her skin again. It was too much for Sarra to handle, and she fell forward, her hands covering her face as the rag dropped, forgotten in her lap.

She missed him. With every fiber of her being, Sarra missed Ares more than her lungs would ever miss her breath. Her shoulders shook hard with a sob, and she heard the hand-maidens whispering among each other.

"Should we tell His Majesty she is ill?"

"No, do not make him fret over nothing. We all have night terrors. She will be all right."

"But those screams. It sounded like someone was murdering her."

"And how would you know what murder sounds like? Do you have something to confess? Leave the poor dear alone."

The back-and-forth continued, but Sarra ignored it. Her mind tried to process the events of the last several days, from the moment she had been stolen from this very room until the second her father killed the man she loved with his sword. Anger unfurled inside of her. Rage unlike any she had ever known boiled her blood. This was her father's fault. It was all her father's fault!

Such a careless man he was, not taking the state of his provinces seriously. He did not deserve to rule as king, and he was such a hypocrite, imparting codes of honor onto Sarra from the time she could talk only to turn around and throw his own people to the orcs like fodder. Her hands balled into fists against her face, pressing into her eyes until she saw stars behind her closed lids. Not even love had deterred his retaliation—not Sarra's love for Ares, not the king's love for his own daughter. *How could he have celebrated on the anniversary of my mother's death after mourning her for years like a lifeless lich? How could he steal my happiness? How could he kill Ares?*

"When did we arrive? How long has it been?" Sarra asked suddenly, her voice soft but clear. Questions streamed endlessly in her thoughts. *How long has Ares been dead? How long has it been since our last conversation? How many days have passed since I traveled to Ro'al?* The handmaidens all paused their bickering, looking at her with confusion and some with added concern.

"Arrive? Your Grace, I am afraid I do not quite understand." Avella stepped close again, patting the edge of the bed. "We spent time together in the library just yesterday, and, as far as I know, you have not ventured out of the palace in quite a few months. The weather has not been the best, and with the failing crops in the east, travel has been more precarious of late. Bandits and mercenaries, everyone scavenging for food and whatnot, and not to mention, the unrest to the north. The king has nearly forbidden you to leave his sight, except within the castle."

"Avella!" One of the older women grasped the young girl by the arm, pressing a finger to her lips to shush her. "You should not speak of such matters to Her Highness. It is not your place. Do you want to find yourself tossed into the dungeons?"

"But she allows me to call her Sarra when no one else is around! I thought she might like to know." Avella turned to Sarra, pleading with her eyes. "Do not toss me into the dungeons, milady. I did not mean any harm."

The older woman's eyes nearly bulged out of her head, and she quickly tried to usher poor Avella away.

"She is fine. I do not intend to toss anyone into any dungeons today," Sarra said, though her face remained expressionless even as she nodded and gestured for Avella to stand closer. "Please sit. The rest of you may leave."

The older ladies shook their heads and clicked their tongues, but they knew better than to dispute Sarra's wishes. As kind and inclusive as she was to her ladies in waiting, she was still their princess, and they understood their place. It did not mean that Sarra treated them poorly in any such way. There was a set of rules between them, and not even her requests could force them all to break them.

"You are certain I have not left the palace?" Sarra asked Avella once they were alone.

"Yes, miss, I am most certain. If you had traveled anywhere, I should suspect I would be with you. The older women grow tired quickly, and they do not enjoy riding in carriages much these days. Makes their bones hurt." Avella chuckled nervously. " 'Tis a shame. Summer is coming to an end and the snow will arrive before too long."

"It is still summer?" Now Sarra sat thoroughly confused. Her fingers grabbed her blanket, drawing it up to her chin as she burrowed under it, considering her time in Ro'al. The sand of the beach had been cooler than usual, Ares had said. Certainly, it had been the end of autumn when she had traveled through the bog? "What day is it?"

The young girl hesitated, nose wrinkling as she considered the question.

"What day is it?" Sarra repeated herself, calming the sudden return of rushing blood in her ears.

"I am not good with dates, Your Grace. I can tell you that His Majesty is expecting visitors from across the kingdom soon. You told me he intends to host a gathering, and you were quite displeased. Something about your late mother, may she rest in peace. I am sorry for your loss, by the way. I know it has been many years but losing one's mother must be difficult. I know how hard it was leaving mine alone in Dovia. You know, the province just north of us? Of course, you know. What am I talking about? You are the princess, after all."

Avella prattled, occupying the silence as Sarra mulled over bits and pieces of the information she gathered. *Could it be? Is it even possible?*

"In fact, he has requested that you join him in the library as soon as you are ready this morn.'" Avella gave her a smile.

"Excuse me, who?"

"Your father. The king? His Majesty? He requests that you join him in the library as soon as you are able. I believe he would like to discuss something with you." Avella pulled her hands to her chest, clasping them together as she swooned in front of Sarra. "I wonder if he will have news of Lord Elias. He would be the perfect consort, would he not?"

Bile burned in the back of her throat at the name of the suitor her father favored. Sarra pressed a hand to her stomach, taking several deep breaths to calm her response to the idea of being with someone that was not Ares. Avella ignored it, carrying on as if living in her own fantasy of Lord Elias and his unending love.

"Do not worry, Your Grace. No one will tell His Majesty about your episode this morning. We all have night terrors sometimes, as the others said. I hope that it has not ruined your rest and you are somewhat refreshed. As a note of positivity, the gowns that you were fitted for arrived. I took the liberty of placing them in your wardrobe."

Sarra followed Avella's gaze as the young woman turned toward the armoire. "The colors are most brilliant, and the laces make them more elaborate than anything else in your collection. You will most certainly enjoy them, although I am quite fond of the black one myself."

Sarra swallowed hard. Her voice cracked before she cleared it, repeating herself. "I apologize, Avella, but the dresses I was fitted for?"

"Do you not remember? His Majesty demanded it. He said it was time for you to impress the men of the court. He wants you to marry, so you must look your best! Although, I must admit, selecting a black gown did not seem like a wise choice at the time, but once it returned, I must say—you should wear it when your father's guests arrive."

"And this black dress," Sarra started, eyes shifting back to the young woman's face. "It has laces in the back?"

"Yes, miss. There are laces in the back. I know how much you hate them, but they tend to be—"

"Flattering toward one's figure. Yes, I know." Sarra pressed a hand to her forehead and ran her fingers through her hair. A feeling of déjà vu astounded her. *How is this possible?*

It feels almost like I am living in a dream.

"I will dress alone this morning." Sarra straightened, dismissing Avella with a flick of her wrist. "Stand outside just in case. I may need assistance with the laces. I have never understood why we are made to wear such silly things. Remember, Avella, substance over shapeliness is what should be valued."

Although, some ladies possess both.

Could it have been a dream? Could he have been just a figment of my imagination?

"As you wish, milady." Avella stood, dipping into a short curtsy. "I shall wait outside."

Sarra watched the young woman exit, waiting until the doors to her chamber clicked shut. When she was alone, the heavy weight roared with a vengeance, forcing Sarra's head back into her hands. She wept until she could weep no longer, and as her tears dried, she raised her head high. If Ro'al and its lord were nothing but dreams, she could not, would not cry over them. She was the future queen of Olmalis, not a child who believed in fairy tales and magic. However, she looked at the black lace peeking from her armoire, her briefly haughty attitude falling. The dress was too coincidental. *Ares had proven to me that magic was real, had he not?*

Sarra slid out of bed, her bare feet padding along the stone floor of her bedroom as she approached the wardrobe. Her hands trembled as she observed the open doors from a distance, not daring to touch the gown out of fear. Fear of what, though, Sarra did not know, but as she worked up the courage to take a piece of the lace between her fingers, something clicked inside of her.

If Ro'al did not exist, if Ares was not the lord of a fallen city, if she had not been abducted and taken away from her castle, if she had not loved and lost, if all of it happened to truly be just a nightmare . . .

Her father would not know a thing about it. He would tell her she was a stupid girl and send her away, laughing as she turned her back to him. There would be no records in the library, and she knew there were none in the shelves she had memories of already. Other records existed, though in the archives deep within the underground halls running beneath the castle.

Sarra pulled the black gown free, holding it to her waist with her hands. Today, she mourned for the only man worthy of her heart.

CHAPTER 22

I T WAS NEARLY MIDDAY WHEN SHE MADE HER appearance, weaving through the halls like a ghost. Her dress earned her a number of odd looks as she made her way toward the library, intending to meet with her father. Poised and elegant, Sarra held her head high with her small golden crown gleaming atop her head and the lace skirt of her dress brushing along with her feet. Black was a nontraditional color, only worn as an accent or for mourning by the ladies of the court. Sarra broke societal norms by parading around in her new gown, but she did not care about the opinions of others. She had not before Ro'al, and she would not after.

Servants bustled to and fro, cleaning and gathering for the celebration her father intended to host. Guests would begin to arrive within days, or so she had heard, and as she descended the large white marble staircase outside the great hall, she eavesdropped on two soldiers sent as emissaries from their provinces.

A large collective of people had traveled from the northern provinces down through Dovia. Anagast and Valenar warred

with one another, despite threats and fines from the crown itself. The lords were petty, selfish, always wanting more and more
land, even with the lack of resources available to give it. The two
emissaries spoke pleasantly with one another, but an ingrained
hatred lurked in their words. She caught it in their tones, their
stares, the way they shifted from foot to foot uneasily. A truce
had not been met. *What does the king intend to do about it?*

"If he were smart, he would just give more land to
Anagast," the large, bulky man boomed, chin raised proudly.
His name was Sir Markus, and he was known across the kingdom for his mustache. It sat full and thick above his upper lip,
and he stroked it with a finger as he smirked down at his companion, a shorter, stocky man by the name of Teleran. They
stood in front of the open door to the great hall, loitering and
seemingly up to no good. "But only time will tell what he
decides."

A man of few words, or so Sarra had been told, Teleran
glared at Markus with his arms crossed over his chest.

"What?" Markus asked, noting the look on the other
man's face. "Do not stare at me like that, Teleran. You and I
both know dissolving Valenar is the only solution to this
problem. Your lordship is pompous, arrogant, completely
moronic—"

"Fools," Sarra said, appearing from behind a suit of armor. The two men turned to her with alarm, mouths open
and gaping like fish. "Both provinces are led by fools. Neither
is exempt from that designation. Do you even know why you
despise one another?"

Teleran furrowed his brow, and scratched the side of his
head, rustling his brown hair. Markus straightened himself,
once more holding his chin high, but even he did not reply
to her inquiry. They stood there, the three of them, in silence,

until both men avoided her gaze, looking about the room sheepishly.

Sarra rolled her eyes. "Precisely what I suspected. People have died because of the trivialities of Anagast and Valenar. I have half a mind to speak to your lords directly myself. My father should shove them into a room and force them to fight about it until they come to an agreement. Needless bloodshed should not distract from more serious matters, and it is not your lords that are suffering because of it." She tapped her foot, the sound echoing into the corridor. "Have they considered you and your people? The rest of the kingdom? The crops will not thrive in Starid this season. We shall rely heavily upon you and Dovia to provide sustenance for all, and here the two of you stand, hissing at each other like mad cats."

Turning her back on them, she walked down the hall, venturing toward the library. "There are people *starving*, and all I hear is, 'More land. More, more, more, more.'" Sarra threw her hands up as she stewed about the conflict, circling around to thoughts of Ro'al and its devastation. "It is no wonder Ares and his father received little help from any of you. Selfish and narcissistic. I finally understand what he meant."

One of the men cleared their throat behind her. "Your Grace, I apologize for interrupting your tirade, but might I inquire as to who Ares is and what help he required? If a request went ignored, perhaps I can mention it to my lord. He is a fairly understanding and generous—"

Sarra stilled, flicking her hand at Markus to silence him. "Ares is the only man in the entire kingdom worthy of the title 'lord.' Feel free to relay the message that Her Highness, Princess Sarra is rather displeased and hopes that your lords all rot in—"

"Sarra! Princess Sarra!" Avella darted in front of her,

sliding across the floor as her foot caught the end of her dress. The young woman flailed, a frightened squeal escaping her lips as she nearly crashed into a short column holding a glass vase full of flowers. Sarra's fingers snatched her by the collar, holding onto her by the fabric of her dress.

"I thought I was done for," Avella exclaimed. "I apologize, Sarra. I mean, Your Highness."

Teleran and Markus narrowed their eyes at the handmaiden, clearing their throats so she did not miss that they both had heard her formalities slip. "But your father, His Majesty. He requires your presence in the library. He said, and I quote, 'that if you do not escort her yourself, you will go without vittles for the next fortnight,' and miss, that is a rather long time to go without food." Avella righted herself, grasping Sarra's hand and tugging it encouragingly. "*Please*, let us go to the library. Quickly."

Dragged forward, Sarra looked over her shoulder and pointed at Teleran and Markus. "I have not finished with you. It is me that will rule this kingdom one day, and you would be wise to remember that!"

Avella escorted Sarra through the halls of the castle in a nervous dance. The young woman stood up to Sarra's shoulders, and her petite form made her seem younger than she truly was. Sarra learned much about Avella in the short time they trekked together through the castle, and by the time they reached the library, Sarra felt exhausted from the conversation.

"And my brother, Fen, always said my red hair was a sign I was possessed by a demon, but ma always smacked him upside the head and said I was kissed by fairies instead! She always tells stories of elves and witches living in the forests. Dovia has many of those, you know. Old forests that legends say were magical once. I do not know if I believe them, but I suppose it could be possible." Avella placed a hand on the double door leading into the library. "Here you are, miss. I will rest nearby in case you need any assistance."

"Thank you," Sarra replied with a chuckle. Her smile faded as the heavy oak doors opened and creaked, and her stomach dropped as she entered the book filled room. There, in the center, in a space clear of shelves and bookcases, her father stood, bent over a large wooden table, his eyes staring down at a colorful map.

"Good day, Father," she said coolly. The temporary joy she had found with Avella and her stories disappeared, and with a little bow of her own, Sarra approached the king.

"Ah, Sarra, my dear!" Her father, a stately man, whose very countenance identified him as a king, stood tall, greeting her with a small wave of his hand. He looked healthy and well, free of injuries and orc blood that might have damned him in her eyes. Despite his advancing age, her father retained a full head of dark hair, tinted with streaks of gray at his temples and in his well-groomed beard. Charisma and intelligence exuded from him as he smiled at her, and each word he spoke came in a warm staccato underlying immense wit and wile. His deep blue robe with golden accents was as crisp and sharp as his mind.

His brow furrowed slightly when he noticed her appearance, and his lower lip protruded before he expressed his concern. "You look terribly forlorn this morning."

Sarra looked to the floor, and as she approached, a guardsman withdrew a chair from the table for her to use. She sat quietly, arms folding into her lap. Her anger reignited, and the cruel smirk her father had worn as he beheaded her love visited her thoughts. Sarra's teeth clenched, but with a deep breath, she relaxed as she released it.

"The servants said you wished for me to join you today. What do we have to discuss? Perhaps the matters of your guests?" Sarra reached for a book on the table in front of her and flipped through the pages to see if it earned her interest. "I believe you mentioned they were coming from all across the kingdom. Which lords and ladies should I be expecting?"

The king arched a brow, but his thoughts drifted by the way his eyes roamed back toward the map in front of him. "Ah, yes, some of the high court will be joining us this evening for consultations on local district disputes. I trust you will find the strength to present yourself appropriately for such an audience." He lifted his eyes briefly, delivering a hard look to Sarra as she replaced the book on the table. She did not miss the meaning behind his glance, knowing the edge of sternness in his gaze better than most.

However, she appeared forlorn because of him, and for a brief moment, Sarra pondered holding that fact against her father. He had been the one to kill Ares, but it was unfair to make such claims. Her dream had felt so real, so tangible, but it had still been just a dream. As far as Sarra knew, Ro'al did not exist, not on any map she had ever seen, and her father had not killed anyone in as long as she had been alive. She mourned the imaginary man, just a figment her mind had conjured, that had made her feel to the deepest depths of her soul.

Yet, even as her father spoke to her, Sarra could not help how much she hated him, how betrayed she felt by him.

"Yes, I shall be able to pull myself together for the high court." She placed a hand atop the hardcover of the book in front of her, tilting her head to look at her father curiously.

"Do you not appreciate the dark dress, Father? Black is so versatile. Really anyone can wear it well, even a princess. Although, truth be told, I am quite partial to the color green. A deep green. Like the color of the leaves upon the trees in the warmer months. I just did not have anything to wear of that color and this seemed comfortable enough." A smile stretched her lips, but she lacked feeling to put behind it. "I will change into something else if it pleases you. I would not want anyone getting the wrong impression of you or me during our conversations with them."

Her father wrinkled his nose and narrowed his eyes, questioning her. "Green? Leaves?" His loud laugh nearly shook the table, and Sarra waited for him to dismiss her for foolishness. "My dear, you know that your color is blue and lavender. It complements the gold on the banners and reflects the standards of our people. The tailors work even now on a new dress for you. It will be blue."

Her father grated on her nerves. The longer she sat in his presence, the more she thought about what cruelty he was capable of. He mocked her over the mention of her enjoyment of the color green, as if it were blasphemous that she did not enjoy blue or purple as much as he wanted. In fact, those very colors made her feel nauseated, because it reminded her of the banner that had restrained Ares when he had been beheaded before her very eyes.

"Blue? Well, then, I apologize for the misunderstanding, sir. I thought you might agree with the color green, but I see that I have miscalculated my interest in other colors." She gave him a swift nod of mock approval. "I cannot wait to see how flattering the blue dress will be. I trust your judgment, and I do believe our guests will enjoy the play upon our love and loyalty for Olmalis."

But Sarra knew she wore her future dress at that very moment. Black would stain the laughter of the king's party. Everyone would whisper about how horrible she was for selecting such a rotten gown. If she remembered correctly, the wheels moving her toward those moments had already begun to turn, even though time and events passed differently in her current reality than they had in her dreams. Despite the differences, Sarra sat, determined to see everything through anyway, even if her memories were nothing but tricks her mind had played upon her.

"It is time we begin to broaden your horizons a bit, my jewel," her father said grandly, quickly changing the topic of their conversation. "Two of our allied provinces, both of whom owe our family fealty, have mutually accommodated land disputes of increasing complexity, and as you may be aware, violence for the first time has broken out. Olmalis is in a state of civil unrest, and we cannot tolerate destabilization of the borders within the kingdom. Our messengers were sent with orders to desist, and leaders from both of their regions will be coming here for a summit. We expect them to come with their entourages and cohorts in just under one month, at which time we will attempt to negotiate peace." He gestured to the two nations, Anagast and Valenar, on the map. One resided against the endless mountains surrounding the kingdom, the other sat mostly against a large river to the east. Across it was Starid, a province full of farmland, and north of that was Vrevia, the home of Elias, Lord Berley's son.

Beyond the borders, to the south of Starid, were the Wildlands, home of the orc horde.

"War—hell, even bickering between these two nations weakens the barrier protecting us from the anarchy of the Wildlands. We will work to establish peace, but both of their leaders are iron willed and stubborn." Her father placed both of his palms firmly on the table, eyeing the map tactically. "You must learn how to make them see that their cooperation supports the greater good, and if we cannot assure them that the greater good is worth maintaining, we will ensure their personal investment in peace the only way such men can be made to see reason: by threatening their sovereignty if they do not fall in line."

He looked up at Sarra. "I would ask that you be with me during those negotiations. I have asked that the scholars spend some time with you to ensure you are ready to stand among these men. Please avail yourself of their knowledge, and when the time comes, you will be better prepared to stand beside me against this lunacy." He straightened, clasping his hands behind his back with a genuine smile. "That is all I had hoped to discuss, my dove. I do hope you find your good spirits again in short order."

Sarra looked down at the map, eyes searching every corner for a hint of Ro'al, for a sign that Ares had existed. *How could he not after an adventure like the one he had given me?* She could still taste his lips, could still feel the love in her heart. Quickly, she rubbed at her eye as if it irritated her, hissing so her father would stand none the wiser. She wiped the moisture on the edge of her finger on the material of her dress as she leaned forward to glance closer at the Wildlands. *Perhaps Ro'al waited there?*

Impossible. No one has stepped foot inside of the Wildlands and survived before.

" 'Tis not about standing against them, Father," Sarra said sharply, reaching her finger out to trace a line along the large river dividing Olmalis in half on the map. "It is merely about having a conversation with them and discovering what the true issue is. If it is the division of land that they do not agree with, then perhaps we split what they are attempting to claim in half. If it is something more than that, we should keep an open mind."

She pulled back, standing to smooth her dress. The memories of her father's celebration from her dream triggered a thought. Perhaps his solution then still held true now, even if it was not real? "Do any of them have children? Older children, about my age?"

A small knowing smile lifted her lips. "A son and a daughter each, maybe? Perhaps the answer is not about splitting land, but more so about love instead. When they arrive, I would implore you to ask about the relationship between the two lordships. It is not lunacy to fight when a father is only trying to protect his daughter, and if the wrong boy is attempting to woo her . . ."

Sarra knew there were more ways than violence to solve a problem and forcing out potentially great leaders because they did not agree with one another was the beginnings of a coup Sarra wanted nothing to do with. While she might disagree with the two lordships of Anagast and Valenar, and she may have called them moronic before, they remained in power and higher social status for a reason. They were two of the most resource rich provinces in the kingdom, and the prominent families had driven their economies without folly.

The king's eyes darted to her. With a shake of his head, he moved to stand beside her, putting an arm behind her waist and gracing her with a kiss to her forehead. "You are wise beyond your years, my daughter."

Sarra smiled, genuinely pleased her father seemed to listen to her ideas. However, her pride fell short only breaths later, the king ruining what ground she thought she had gained with him.

"We must exhaust our other options first, however. If you are to rule one day, your people will rely on you to know when to extend the hand of friendship, and when to clench the fist of rule." He smiled warmly, though she knew from his tone, he was correcting her. "You have done well with every test of diplomacy put before you, but you may someday stand among rough men, at least until I can find a suitable husband to care for you. You must be prepared for this, to show them that the fist will tighten."

Before her dream, Sarra thought her father to be the most honest and respected man in the entire realm. Now, she questioned his judgment, reading more between the intricate lies he told. Her teeth ground against each other as he pressed his lips to her forehead, and Sarra nearly recoiled from the unwanted touch. She refrained, holding still until he pulled back, stepping away from her as they both regarded the map in silence.

She hated that he thought her incapable of understanding her people. She loathed his plan to marry her off to a man just so someone would take care of the duties he did not think her capable of handling alone. He infuriated her, implying she was not fit to rule the kingdom when she knew she could do so better than even he!

As much as Sarra wanted to bark back at him, she held her tongue, just as a good, complacent daughter would. Little did her father know, there was only one man she would ever allow to rule at her side. It was a shame the king had been the one to kill him. *How could Ares be just a dream? He felt so real.*

A spot caught her attention in the Wildlands, and Sarra leaned closer to get a better look. Her father yawned, undoubtedly bored of his peace-creating duties already, and he shuffled around the table to take a seat in a chair himself. Once seated, he picked up a goblet as Sarra tugged the map toward her, a finger circling the spot. It looked like a watermark, although too faint to really tell.

"And what of the lord from Ro'al, Father?" Sarra asked, eyeing the line of the ocean, searching for a beach hidden behind tall mountains. "I know most of the lords and ladies within our kingdom, but I do wonder why you have kept the ones from there hidden." Innocently, she batted her lashes, her smile warmer than before. "Would it not be beneficial for me to meet them also?"

The king's eyes narrowed as he finished his drink, and when he placed the goblet on the table in front of him, the smile on his face grew empty. "Ro'al?" he repeated, tilting his head as his eyes followed her fingers on the map. He glanced back to her, his lip twitching nervously while he regarded her. His grip on the goblet's stem tightened as her finger drew through the Wildlands, his eyes watching her hand out of the corner of his eye.

"Is this another of your games, my pet?" Her father nodded toward her fingers. "Those lands are beyond the safe borders of our kingdom. They crawl with the greenskin menace and have for longer than you have been alive."

"Ro'al," he scoffed, disappointment in his voice. "What kind of a name is that anyway? Honestly, Sarra, I thought you had left these games and stories in your childhood. You know how they upset your mother; may she rest with the gods above."

"I do not understand what you are talking about, Father," Sarra said, giving a narrow eyed glance at him in return. "I have never played games, sir. Not even when I was a child. Mother enjoyed telling me stories. In fact, I thought she told me of a place called Ro'al once, but perhaps I misunderstood."

That feeling, the one screaming at her incessantly, roared inside of her, adamant that Ro'al was not just a fairy tale and Ares had not only existed in her mind. Had her mother been alive, she might have had more answers. The queen had been a dreamer, full of stories about adventure and romance. She created magic with her words, and there was not a storyteller more gifted than Sarra's mother had been. "Mother. Thinking of her stories does make me miss her. Why did you love her, Father? Why was mother so precious to you?"

The king watched her in bemused silence, a faint smirk turning up his lips. Sarra saw a shimmer in his eyes, perhaps one of longing, sad and distant as though he was somewhere else far, far away. "Your mother was a very singular woman. She was kind and good, and cared strongly for her people, and for you as well, my darling."

Sarra lowered her eyes, staring at the map but not truly seeing it. Instead, she listened to her father, remembering the image of her mother as he spoke of her.

"And she was radiantly beautiful, far beyond compare, something that lives on in you." The king smiled fully, almost misty-eyed with his words. "You were her pride and joy. You meant everything to her. She always loved you and cared for you the most."

He raised his hand, swiping his brow as he took a deep breath and exhaled. "Why do you torment me so with memories of your mother, dear Sarra?" he asked, turning away from her, his fingers falling to his lap in loosely balled fists. "If I could only speak with her once more . . ."

Sarra nodded, understanding her father's words more

than she suspected he even knew. He had been absent most of her young life, and although he had eventually taught her many things, she wondered if her father had only done so out of necessity. His pet names for her—dove, jewel, and many others like them—even made her wonder if he sometimes forgot her name. At first, he might have thought her a competent choice of an heir, but over the last several years, something in their relationship had shifted. He grew annoyed easily, hated entertaining her questions about the kingdom, and focused solely upon the fact that she had not married as soon as she turned eligible. Times were changing, the kingdom was different. Olmalis was not the same as it had been during the beginning of his rule as a young man. Sarra would never be his mirror.

Perhaps he intended to marry her to the one who was.

The king cleared his throat, straightening himself upright. "I apologize, my dear," he said quietly. "Some wounds remain tender for the duration of our lives. If you will excuse me, I must go collect myself before we meet with the high court."

"I understand. It has been quite a day already, Father." Sarra stood with respect, and the king nodded, giving her a short bow. He turned, moving to the door, and exited, leaving her alone in the library with the guards and the librarians keeping watch. Once her father left her sight, her eyes once more sought the worn spot on the map. *The Wildlands*. What was she missing? No beach broke from the mountainous terrain, no bog stole the color of the forests. Ro'al, the city she would never forget, did not hold a place anywhere on the thick parchment in front of her. Still, her finger traced the spot, over and over, unable to look away from it.

A loud shuffle across the library startled her, and when

Sarra looked up from the map, she saw an older man with a handful of books. Just another one of the servants, she guessed, one she had never met before by the looks of it. He seemed to be occupied, not bothering to pay her any attention as he moved toward her table, collecting books her father had left behind.

" 'Tis a hefty lot of books," Sarra commented loudly. The servant startled with Sarra's voice, though he quickly calmed. She stood, moving around the table to assist in the collection of the misplaced books. "My father must have kept you busy all morning."

She turned a book over to view its cover, arching a brow curiously at the title and design. "Seems he was in the mood for children's stories if you ask me. A book about myths and legends of the realm is not his usual interest."

He gave her an uneasy smile as he took the book from her, adding it to the growing pile in his hands. Sarra collected a few more tomes, assisting with his task.

"Thank ye, lass. It will save me a few trips," he said. He wore clean, elegant blue robes, and the wrinkles on his face and the calluses on his hands were the evidence of a life spent in service. "Though, His Majesty would have my hide should he see you helping with my task."

Sarra shook her head. "I shall not allow him to punish you for something so meaningless. You are but one person and truly, it would be I that suffered his wrath. Apparently there are some that think royals are above cleaning their own messes."

The servant laughed, mimicking her head shake with one of his own. Sarra gave him space, allowing him to place the books in his hands on a small cart nearby. She went to work rolling the map. She had nearly finished when she noticed a date written on the edge. *What if the map was too new?*

"Excuse me," Sarra said, addressing the servant. "Are there any other maps? Perhaps ones older than this one?"

The servant frowned, hobbling over to take a closer look at the map in her hands. He squinted at the date scrawled on it. "Hmm. This is not a new map. It was made not long after ye was born. But yes, I think we have older ones. They are dreadfully out of date though, some over two hundred years of age. I doubt you would find anything of significant interest, milady."

He gestured for her to follow. "Come along. We have the archives down the stairs."

"Thank you. I merely have a curiosity to satisfy as we begin to prepare for the arrival of the lords from the north. As I am sure you have heard, there is a disagreement over territories, and I would like to reference the kingdom's territorial history myself as a learning experience, of course."

He grunted in understanding, leading her further into the library.

It was just a curiosity, or so Sarra tried to convince herself. Ro'al could not exist outside of her memories, and it was near insanity to scour the entire castle in search of evidence that made it real. It was too much to dream, too much to wish for, too much to hope for, but Sarra did all of those things as she thought of what proving the city's existence meant. She would save those people, if they truly lived, even if she had to crawl through the bogs herself and slay an entire barricade of greenskins alone. She would make Ares proud.

With no small amount of effort, the servant muscled a large bookshelf out of their path, revealing an alcove, almost like a wine cellar, where cool dry air lingered. He led her down a short staircase by torchlight. The thick smell of old books and ink on parchment wrapped Sarra in a strange nostalgia she had never known. Everything seemed to speak to her, whispers of promises draping her in comfort as her eyes closed in the darkness. She inhaled deeply and her heart fluttered as warmth flowed through her body. If she had not known better, Sarra might have said there was magic about.

It took the servant some time to recollect where exactly the old maps were stored, but he found an old volume of small, tattered parchment scraps, resembling an adventurer's journal or something of the sort used to chart the lands of Olmalis many years past. He flipped through a few pages, revealing crude, quickly drawn images. Each map appeared incomplete, some with proportions were too wild to be wholly accurate, and yet, as Sarra opened her eyes and moved closer to take a look, the pages compelled her. They were far older than any map she had ever seen, and something in those pages called to her.

"Are these them?" she asked, and when she received a nod in answer, Sarra allowed herself to reach out toward the book of maps. "May I?"

Taking the papers in her hands, her breath caught the instant the maps touched her fingertips. "Hold the torch high for me while I take a quick look. I shall only be a minute and then we can return to the library."

The servant did as she asked, and Sarra flipped to the first page, running a finger along the drawings as if she could feel how alive they had once been. The parchment was discolored, but still intact, and her eyes were wide as she took in the drawings and notes that were written in the margins. There was so much history here, but as the pages flipped and the maps continued, Sarra grew disheartened.

She stared at one page for a long moment, wondering if she had awoken in the throes of insanity that morning. The vivid scenes in her head, the way that Ares had tasted upon her lips, and the confessions that they had given one another . . . she was crazy for treating the recollections like anything but figments of her imagination. The only logical explanation was that her nerves had gotten the best of her. The idea of meeting Elias made her anxious. The thought had bothered her for a while now. He was talked of like a god, praised more than any other soldier or lord within the kingdom. *If he was not suitable for me to wed, who would be?* The pressure upon her to entice his attention was astronomical. No one would be able to blame her for attempting to find a way to escape from it.

Sarra shook her head, accepting her thoughts as truth, and she laughed darkly at herself as she closed the book. "I apologize. It seems I have gotten carried away in my research. I will just take this with me but rest assured I will return it when I am finished. My father says I should be prepared for what is to come, and between you and me, I am not certain he believes it to be possible." She smiled kindly at the servant. "Thank you for your assistance in this matter. This was all I was looking for."

He gave her another nod. "You are quite welcome, milady. I hope it will assist you with the high court."

The servant escorted her back to the library, closing the hidden door to the archives behind them. Sarra held the distressed book close to her chest the entire way, and when the light of the sun cascaded through the windows upon their return, her father's words came back to haunt her.

Why did I torture him with thoughts of Mother?

It was ironic that her mother was on her mind today,

more so than the days before. She thought of the late queen often, likely more than anyone else in the kingdom, her father included. More than anything, Sarra wished for the guidance that her mother could have offered her. She might have been able to assist Sarra in coping with her heartbreak and reassure her that she would not be used as some pawn for her father's gains. Without her mother keeping watch, Sarra's concern over being traded like property felt more valid than ever before. Sarra knew she would never marry for love. *What if that was what I want now that I have seen what a taste of it can be like? What if I want none of those things, and decide to rule the kingdom alone? What if I see things completely differently from my father? What if I denounce my inheritance and refuse the throne entirely?*

Her hand idly played with her long hair, another reminder of the cage holding her captive. Her father would surely disapprove if she opted to cut her hair, this time in real life instead of in her dreams. Their guests would undeniably judge her for her rebellious actions, and a rogue grin spread across her lips.

No one would want to marry her when her hair was trimmed short like a man's.

CHAPTER 23

W ITH ONE LAST NOD GOODBYE TO THE LIBRARY
servant, Sarra took herself and her new book on a
small journey through the castle. A few people of
the court passed by her, commenting on her radiant appearance
as she weaved around them and dashed through the halls. The
entire time, she thought of how surprised they would be when
she debuted her short hair that night.

She ventured into the southern wing, her onlookers questioning why. Many of the corridors in this particular section of
the castle had remained closed off to most since the queen's
death. Her personal chambers resided within, and the king refused to allow anyone to disturb her things, perhaps as a way
to cope with his loss. Sarra remained the exception to that rule,
and even if that had not been the truth, her father would never
be able to keep her away regardless.

"Your Highness, do you need my assistance?" A familiar
voice accosted Sarra, and she turned to see sweet Avella trailing

behind her. She seemed so eager to help, so excited to be near Sarra, but the princess shook her head despite it.

"Thank you for your kindness today, Avella, but I think I would like to be alone for now. This was my mother's room." Sarra gestured at the dark cherry door behind her. An elaborate design etched into the wood, stretching across its entire width—a unicorn inlaid with gold. "Her things are still inside and sometimes, I come to visit when I am missing her."

She gave the young woman a warm smile. "But please, do fetch me something else to wear. Black is a depressing color as much as it is versatile, and I do not think that I belong in a dress such as this on a day like today. We have visitors coming for court soon, and I believe my father would prefer it if I wore blue or lavender instead."

Avella wrinkled her nose and curled her lip, looking at Sarra with confusion. "Yes, miss. I can certainly prepare another dress for you. I will have it waiting for you in your chambers when you are ready, but for what it is worth, I think you look beautiful in that dress. It is unique, and there is nothing wrong with being a little bit of both."

As Avella left, Sarra stood all alone in the corridor, and instead of feeling warm and welcoming as it always had during her youth, the hall filled with a sad coolness Sarra could not shake. Pushing against the door, it opened into the room with a small creak, a reminder of its prolonged unuse. Once inside, Sarra found it dark, but felt her way across the room toward the windows, and moving aside the curtains, the room was illuminated in bright sunlight.

Everything looked just as it had.

While her parents had been very much in love, her mother had required her own space. She had been an artist, a creator who enjoyed painting and sculpting in addition to telling her stories. Sarra appreciated that her mother had kept some of her things away from her father's touch. Her mother still lived in this room, despite no longer being alive, and although she knew her father had every right to access his late wife's belongings, Sarra remained the only one who visited. As if intentional, illuminating the chamber triggered a memory, reminding Sarra that once upon a time, her father had celebrated his kingdom on the anniversary of her mother's death, and even though it had been nothing but a dream, she still struggled to forget it.

A large bed pressed against the far wall of the room, across from an equally large fireplace. The windows reached to the ceiling, and some of them shimmered with hand painted glass, yet another sign of her mother's artistic abilities. The colors of the glass played upon the floor, shining a rainbow of colors on the stone in a playful manner. Sarra placed an open palm in the light's path, and she felt not only the warmth, but the colors of the glass move across her skin. Again, Sarra felt spoken to, as if magic called to her from every crevice of the room.

Tapestries from all over the kingdom decorated the walls, all of them gifts from the various lords and ladies that had graced her mother's presence over the years. Sarra had always wondered what her mother's life had been like before she had become the queen of the realm, but as she understood, her mother had always claimed that her life had never truly started until she had met the king. Sarra supposed it was a story of love, at least that is what she told herself, and it still warmed her now, despite the wicked dream she had about her father.

He could not be a man that cruel. He had never shown her any reason to believe otherwise, but she remained suspicious, despite his denial of ever hearing the name Ro'al before.

A large fur rug spread before the fireplace and an old, decaying stack of wood remained in the corner. Her mother's wardrobe, which still held her clothing, pushed against the center wall, and an old chest sat hidden in the corner beside it, a sturdy iron lock upon the front of it. Sarra had never been able to find the key for it.

She crossed the room, moving toward the old wardrobe, and when Sarra opened it, a strong whiff of warm spice mixed with vanilla engulfed her. She could still smell her mother's comforting scent upon the clothes inside. She removed an old, cotton gown and brought it to her cheek, rubbing it gently against her skin as her eyes drifted shut. Although the memories faded with every passing year, Sarra could still see her mother's smile in her mind.

I will always be with you, Sarra.

An array of emotion filled her chest, Sarra's grief overwhelming in tumultuous waves, dragging her under. She turned her face fully into the material, her shoulders shaking with hard sobs as she dropped to her knees. *Why was life so cruel to someone who had done nothing wrong?*

"I wish you were here, Mother," Sarra said, moving from the floor to perch upon the bed. She placed the book of maps beside her but kept the material of her mother's dress clenched in her hand, the soft material soothing. "I am so terribly confused. My heart hurts today, as if there is a giant gaping hole inside of it that no one will ever be able to fill again."

She shook her head, looking down into her lap. "That is a lie. I am sorry for that. There is someone that could fill it, but he is just a fairy tale, just a thing my mind created to ebb the caged feelings inside of me. I know you would tell me to smile and reflect upon the happiness that he brought me when I had him, but he was nothing but a dream, Mother. A figment that my mind created to comfort me when I was feeling lost, I suppose. The pressure of our lives is not for the faint of heart, and I have always wondered if I am enough to meet the expectations placed by my father. He says that I was the apple of your eye, your most treasured gift, but what am I to him these days? Just another tool to be used?"

Sarra sighed, dropping the dress into her lap. "Dreams are not meant to feel so real, Mother. You would have laughed when I told you of it. His name was Ares."

With his name, her tale began, and Sarra's smile widened as scenes from her dream passed before her eyes while she lived it all over again. The desire to tell her mother of the man who had stolen her heart grew strong, especially as she thought of how much the late queen would have received him. "Son of Aremar, and lord of the failing city of Ro'al. By birthright, of course. You would have liked him, I think. Strong, stubborn, and a very good man."

Sarra's eyes narrowed, and she fell silent for a long moment. "And ironically, he did not budge for me in nearly anything I asked, which you would have undoubtedly been pleased by. Stubborn as my father, I am, but Ares found a way to soften me. I should have considered that before I fell in love with him."

Her laughter sang around the room, and Sarra fell backward upon the bed, smiling at nothing but the memory of Ares teaching her how to use a sword. Her eyes danced along the ceiling, and she spoke to her mother as if they gossiped together in person. "He was the best kisser. Not that I have any experience that tells me otherwise, but my heart tells me that I am not wrong. He could turn people to stone if they looked him in the eyes, but they were green, Mother. A brilliant green that nearly matched the color of the leaves in the summer."

Her face dropped and the mood grew heavy. "Father killed him at the end. He took him from me, just as he intends to take Olmalis from me too."

Sarra fell silent then, only wiping the tears from her eyes when she felt them spill over her cheeks. "It is quite silly to cry over a dream. Just as it is silly totalk to you too, mother, when you are just as dead as Ares. You, at least, were living and breathing once rather than just a figment of my imagination. I can remember his touch more than I can remember yours though."

Sarra sat upright, lifting herself from her lying position. Her fingers reached for her mother's gown, pulling it close again, hugging it to her chest tightly. "The dream of him is more recent than the memories I have of you, and I suppose you have faded somewhat. Except for when I am here, where you still feel so alive to me. It helps me pull together the memories and assists my fickle mind. It is funny what it remembers and what it forgets."

Sarra took a deep breath, pushing the gown away as she shifted on the bed, inching to the edge to stand on her feet. "That is all we are at the end, is it not? Memories, just small imprints on our loved one's lives, turning and changing them in ways we may never recognize, as though we were merely dreams ourselves."

She moved far less gracefully than she had before, nudging the bed with her hip a small amount, although it creaked under the force anyway as she moved from it. A hard, metallic clatter rang through the room, and with a quick tug to straighten her black gown, Sarra glanced around, alarmed.

"What was that?" she asked aloud, her brow furrowed as she looked about the floor around her. Spotting nothing, she huffed and fell to her knees, lifting the blankets draping over the edge of the bed. There she spotted it, an iron key.

Grabbing it, she pulled herself from beneath the bed to sit upon the floor. Sarra tucked her knees beneath her, holding the key in front of her as if it were a piece to a puzzle she had yet to place. Inquisitively, she turned the metal piece over in her hands, tracing the edges of it with her fingertips. The connection struck when Sarra lifted her eyes, spotting the lonely chest sitting in the corner.

Can it be?

Her heart raced at the thought, a sense of urgency sending her sprawling across the floor. She scrambled on her hands and knees, crawling inelegantly toward the large wooden box. As she reached for the lock keeping it shut tight, her hands trembled, excitement and nervousness both warring inside. She had always wondered what her mother kept inside. *What other secrets will I discover about the woman I have not seen in nearly twenty years? Is it a gift? Something from the cosmos to ease my heartache?*

Sarra placed the key inside the lock, hearing a *click* as it opened. She nearly shouted, and with haste, she removed the lock from the chest, placing it on the floor beside her. Her fingers grasped the edge of the top, still shaking from the feelings wreaking havoc inside her. She held her breath, nearly fainting by the time she shoved the heavy lid up and open. Nothing leaped out at her to take her by surprise, but her eyes caught sight of something glittering, shimmering under the sunlight breaking through the painted glass in the window.

The colors of the glass shifted like waves in the ocean, a sea of color blending together as it brought out the beauty of whatever waited for her inside. Reaching into the chest, Sarra retrieved the softest, finest material she had ever seen.

A dress, but not just an ordinary one. Covered in gold embellishments, the deep blue material sparkled like the ocean reflected the stars, and its teal skirt was made of the finest quality.

Sarra truly forgot to breathe as her fingers touched every inch of material. She gasped aloud, a fresh string of tears dripping down her cheeks. *How can it be? How can a dress like the one I wore in Ro'al exist inside my own castle?* All Sarra heard was the rush of blood in her ears. Her hands shook worse, unable to keep steady enough to hold the dress. She covered her mouth, muffling the strangled sound escaping her.

No map showed Ro'al, yet she wore the very black gown from her dream. In her mother's chest, the dress sparkled like the very one she had found in the servant's room within Ares's cold, silent palace.

Sarra turned her head toward the bed, looking at the tattered journal of maps resting where she had left it. Something urged her forward, luring her toward it, and she scrambled, climbing to her feet with such a force she nearly toppled. Throwing herself onto the bed, she opened the worn pages, flipping through them frantically until she felt certain she had scoured each one.

Still, Ro'al did not appear, and Sarra dropped her head onto the plush bedding, her frustration growing so fast it became hard for her to concentrate. With a loud roar of her own, the princess threw the book against the far wall in anger, and she devolved into a fit of hot, angry cries. Her tears burned down her cheeks, her face heating with her renewed sense of grief as she crumbled. The chest held nothing but a tease, a trick from the gods or fate or even both, for all she knew. The book clapped loudly against the front of the chest, landing facedown and open on the floor. Sarra paid it no mind, too absorbed in her agony to care.

She pushed off the bed to her feet, pacing on the floor until her feet heated like the rest of her. Her mother's dress was a coincidence, yet another item planted in her subconscious to manifest in her dreams. She must have seen it as a child, must have reimagined it as an item of comfort when she truly needed it while locked in that wretched tower in her dream.

Sarra berated herself, called herself a child for mourning over something, *someone*, imaginary.

But the servant in the library did not deserve the wrath of her father should she leave the book behind. Deciding to bid her mother farewell to lick her wounds alone, Sarra walked to the book, kneeling to collect it from in front of the chest. Her hands still trembled as she tucked her hair behind her ears, and even more so as she reached for the map filled journal.

A page fell from the book, falling to the floor in a graceful dance.

"Oh, no," Sarra whispered, reaching for the rogue sheet of parchment. She glanced at the book as she turned it over, pausing as her eyes focused upon the Wildlands. She could not believe what stared back at her.

Ro'al did exist, and when she returned her gaze to the stray page in her hand, she nearly screamed aloud. Etched in beautiful script she knew belonged to one person and one person alone, Sarra read a note addressed directly to her.

My dearest Sarra, he does exist.

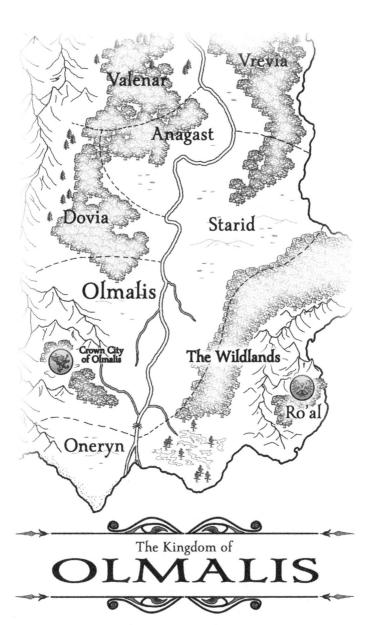

The Kingdom of

OLMALIS

Thanks so much for reading! If you enjoyed *The Serpent Lord* (and #Sarres), please consider leaving me a review! It means the world to me.

Subscribe to my newsletter or join my readers' group, The Bird Nest, on Facebook to stay up to date on future projects and releases.

Up next: *The Seer Princess* (coming early 2022)

ABOUT THE AUTHOR

When Wren was a little girl, she never wanted to be a writer. However, the spark for creating stories lit in the back row of a high school history class, and passing notes to her best friends led her to create her very first character. She has been weaving fantastical tales ever since.

Wren fondly calls the corn fields of north central Indiana home, but currently resides in Western New York with her four children—her daughter, her husband, and her two dogs. Pharmacist by day, author by night, she wears many hats, which also means she takes up most of the closet space. Obsessed with elephants, cute video games, and books, she is also addicted to social media, much to her husband's chagrin

Writer of romance, fantasy, and romantic fantasy, her stories feature strong, relatable heroines, swoon-worthy heroes, and nail biting escapades. Sometimes, if you look close enough, there's even a dragon or two.

For all of your social media needs:

Website: www.wrenmurphy.com
Facebook: www.facebook.com/wrenmurphyauthor
Instagram: www.instagram.com/wrenmurphyauthor
Twitter: www.twitter.com/wren_murphy
TikTok: www.tiktok.com/@wrenmurphyauthor

ACKNOWLEDGEMENTS

I fell in love with *The Serpent Lord* at 2am on a weekday evening in May of 2020. It was the beginning of the COVID-19 pandemic and I had already logged far too many hours on video games after long shifts at the hospital. I can't forget the moment that it happened. It was absolutely *magical*, and #Sarres became my favorite ship name instantly.

I never thought I would be sharing this story with others, and the fact that I have a copy of it sitting on my office bookshelf is an experience I cannot even begin to describe. There are so many people that helped me along the way, encouraging me to keep going when I wanted to give up. If you're one of them, I want you to know that I've accomplished this book writing feat because of your love and support. So here goes my long list of gratitude:

First and foremost, **Jace**, thank you for bringing this story to life with me. If I hadn't come to you complaining about how I would never write the most perfectly angsty story to satisfy my ridiculous need for 'feelings porn', this never would've happened. I am so grateful that I met you, that we continue to write stories together every single day, and I cannot wait to see what insane project I take on next because of an idea you've jokingly suggested in one of our chats. Don't forget—you're my #1!

The tequila to my red wine, **Becky James**, it was pure luck that we found one another, I swear it! Thank you for being my pillar when I need one. Those wobbly days are so much easier to tackle because of you. I adore the heck out of you, and I cannot wait to see where our publishing journeys take us. You are the most amazing person. Thank you for being my friend, and also for not shaking your head at me for being an unorganized disaster most days.

Aria Wyatt & E. R. Donaldson, thank you for your friendship and for being my saving graces as I navigated independent publishing for the first time. It has been the coolest experience meeting and knowing other pharmacists that have authored books in addition to our stressful day jobs. You two are my persons. I cannot thank you both enough for your mentorship.

Holly & Janna, my fearless critique partners, who gave me the good, the bad, and the ugly. Without you, *The Serpent Lord* would be a disaster. Your kindness, support, and honesty have gotten me through a whole lot. I love you both. Thank you for everything.

To my inspiration for Markus, **Reid,** the one who spent many late nights reading passage after passage of this story until he had it memorized like I do. You are one of my favorite people in existence and I cannot wait for you to see more of Markus in the next book. I hope you love him.

The Illiterate Idiot, my bestest friend. Without you, I would have written this entire book in passives. I still cannot believe you turned my story ideas down a thousand times until I finally convinced you to write with me. Your love and friendship mean so much to me, and I hope I can get a signed copy of your future novella too (because you will publish it). One day, I'll write about Damian and Chloe just for you.

To every forum writer & roleplayer, your dreams can become a reality. If you and I have crossed paths once upon a time, I thank you for teaching me how to tell a story and for assisting in the molding of my creativity. From the sites with vampires and werewolves, to the ones with a little more spice in their content, you've all made a huge difference in my life. You are more than friends to me. In fact, you'll always be part of my family.

My awesome beta readers, **Kaylee, Mishayla, Lissa, Hannah, Penelope, Ashley, Katherina, Julie, Cindy, Alishia, Maria, Kari, and Kaila**, you guys got me through the roughest patch of this whole process. Thank you for taking a chance on me, for loving Sarra and Ares as much as I do, for the phone calls and emails to gush over the story, for sharing your thoughts and opinions with me. You all have my eternal gratitude.

A shout-out to my editor, **Eve Arroyo**, for reminding me that a light shade of red is the color pink. I promise to review my colors before I send you book 2—I swear I learned them in elementary school. You are kind, thorough, and so wonderful to work with. I am really happy that you agreed to polish my words. Without you, I would be lost.

Thank you to my proofreader, **Virginia Tesi Carey**, for your fine eye. I would've used too many commas without you, and probably in the wrong spots too.

A virtual hug goes to my formatter, **Stacey Blake of Champagne Book Design,** for making my book baby beautiful. I am in love with your work!

To my cover designer **Miblart**, for bringing Sarra to life in the fantastic cover art you created for me. She is beautiful and I fall more in love with your work every single day.

Thanks to **my husband**, the one who told me to "go for it" when I presented him with this wild idea to write a book. You have given me nothing but encouragement when it comes to reaching for these writing stars, and you make me feel like I can hold the moon in my hands every single day. I love you.

My daughter, who will never remember the days of her momma looking like a hot mess because she was awake until 4am writing her book. I can't wait to tell you all about this experience when you're older. I hope you grow up to be as confident, proud, and kind as Sarra. I love hearing you say "that's mama's book!".

For my mother, who has always been my biggest fan. I remember the day you called me and said "it's a sign! You have to write a book!". Well, I did it. Just like you said I would. You're the best mom, but remember not to judge me too much for the smutty bits in future stories. I know you're going to read them anyway.

To my readers, I appreciate you from the bottom of my heart. I am so thrilled that you took a chance on me and read book one of my debut series. I am so excited to share more with you, so be sure to stay tuned because I have a lot more stories to tell!

And finally, to **Princess Sarra of Olmalis**, for being the character that changed my life. Thank you for trusting me with your story. I cannot wait to share the rest of it with the world.

This is only the beginning.

Wren MURPHY

Made in the USA
Monee, IL
03 April 2024